CW01496621

Spring Green

Elizabeth Cadell

The Friendly Air Publishing

thefriendlyairpublishing.com

Chapter One

This is the story of a girl who took too much for granted.

It tells of her loneliness, her anguish and heartbreak, and it might be expected, therefore, to be grim and harrowing.

I myself—since I am the girl—thought that it would make gloomy reading, but when I came to write it down, I discovered that I was in the predicament of the musician who brought the wrong music to rehearsal and found his mournful solo drowned by the lively airs proceeding from the rest of the orchestra. I had been given a tragic role, but the supporting cast was a light comedy one; all round me were players who behaved in a manner quite unfitted for tragedy. My mournful note can be heard, but it is not loud enough to drown the lively airs. Readers, therefore, who feel that a sombre theme demands sombre treatment, should close this at once and look for something in the Russian style.

Since my descriptive powers are limited, it is as well that the scene is easy to sketch. Except for one or two brief excursions, the background—like the scenery in a play popular with amateurs—remains unchanged. The village of Polden and its off-shoot, Grayleigh, in the county of Buckinghamshire, form the unlikely setting for the drama.

Polden—its full name is Polden St. Peter—lies in a deep hollow between two hills. Those who found it too sheltered, or who wanted a wider view, built their homes about a mile away, on the shoulder of the hill behind the village, and this group— mostly large houses—became known as Grayleigh, and formed at one time the nucleus of what was intended to be a fine residential district. Building was held up, however, while Polden and Grayleigh waited to see how the rapid march of progress was going to affect them.

Progress, instead of marching into Polden, marched past it. Surveyors for the railway extension from the town of Allchester, four miles away, studied the two hills and the uninteresting villages nestling between them, and reported that there was nothing to warrant the expense of two tunnels or the equally costly alternative of going up the hill and, like the Duke of York's men, having to come down again. Horse-drawn coaches had never been able to manage the steep hairpin bend and the narrow drop into Polden; motor-driven vehicles found, in their turn, the same dangers and difficulties. When it became obvious that Polden had been completely passed over, its more ambitious sons and daughters moved into the growing, flourishing town of Allchester and left in the village only those who were not concerned with the passing of the centuries. There was little coming and going; it was difficult to get out of Polden, and unnecessary to get in. The only form of public transport was a small bus that ran twice daily between Polden and Allchester.

Though I had been born nearby, I had not lived at Grayleigh until I was brought there, at the age of eight—fat, and with two pigtails—by my Uncle, to the house which came to be known as the Vicarage. Grayleigh had no church, but my uncle, the Vicar of Polden, believed, quite erroneously, that his chest was weak, and decided that he would feel better in the higher air— two hundred feet higher—of Grayleigh. So strong was this conviction, that he was willing to make the frequent journeys to and from his Church in all weathers, bicycling in summer and trudging through the snow in winter. The Vicarage had been my home until I left it, at twenty-one, to settle in a flat in London. At twenty-four I was back, drawn by the strongest, the most irresistible of magnets.

A short distance from the Vicarage was Grayleigh Farm, which was rented by Stephen Brunswick. His grandmother, Lady Evelyn Brunswick, occupied the little farmhouse, which, like all the houses in Grayleigh, was very ugly. But someone had added green shutters to the windows, so that it was now ugly in a French way. Stephen lived with his grandmother and ran the farm—with my help—and we kept a small herd of Guernseys and supplied the two Allchester hospitals with milk, and kept our heads above water by selling our surplus milk and our eggs, and sometimes our butter and cheese, to anybody who wanted it. We were above the rationing regu- lations—two hundred feet above. Our transactions were open and above-board; any inspector from the Ministry of Food could have seen them for himself, had he cared to come and look. But it would have given him a great deal of trouble: a drive along lanes that hold the world's puncture record, steep climbs that led only to steep drops, bridges with warning but indecipherable notices, and potholes that were brooks in summer and raging torrents in winter. The highways were the concern of the Allchester Rural District Council, who said that the roads would be mended when the Poldenese paid their rates; the Poldenese said the same thing the other way round, and the matter was at a deadlock.

The houses to the east of the farm were unoccupied and were crumbling into decay; to the west, however, was Grayleigh Lodge, and it was at Grayleigh Lodge that my fate was decided.

The story begins and ends there.

The Lodge had once been a beautiful house, but it had fallen into a state of disrepair. It had been patched up and neglected and now looked as ugly as the rest of the Grayleigh houses. It had been occupied throughout her lifetime by Miss Emily Hansard, who had left it on her death some thirty years ago to her niece, Miss Christabel Hansard. She had left no money with it, and Christabel had little of her own—certainly she had not enough to keep up an establishment in the manner in which her aunt had kept it. She had tried to sell it, but there had been no buyers, and at last she had decided to live in it, closing most of the rooms and selling, from time to time, pieces of the beautiful old furniture. Changing times, and Christabel's sour disposition and straitened means had reduced the servants one by one, and when the last one left, a distant relative of Christabel, named Lorna Wells, had come to live at the Lodge, at first as friend and companion, and lately as nurse, for Christabel had become an invalid.

Such was the entire population of Grayleigh: Christabel Hansard and Lorna Wells; my uncle and myself; Stephen Brunswick and his grandmother, Lady Evelyn. There was nobody else. Polden was only a mile away, but the road that led from Polden to Grayleigh ended at the Lodge; anybody walking up from the village had to go back along the road they had come by. There was no through traffic; tradesmen came and went, but that was all. And it was at Grayleigh that I lived in complete happiness—healthy, carefree and even useful, for I was Stephen's sole assistant on the farm. I walked over from the Vicarage in the early dawn, weekdays and Sundays, and milked cows, cleaned out stables and cowsheds, fed cattle and hens and felt my body grow hard and my heart grow tender. I loved the life; I loved Lorna and Lady Evelyn; most of all, I loved Stephen. We worked together, and when we weren't too busy, we rode for miles over the hills; in winter we found time to skate on the shallow pond and in summer we swam in the deep pool in the grounds of the Lodge. It was a perfect existence, and anybody with a less sanguine temperament than mine would have known that it couldn't last.

I had known Stephen all my life. We had a good deal in common; we had both been born at Polden; we lost our parents at an early age; we had met during school holidays, sometimes at Polden, sometimes abroad with Lady Evelyn. We had found ourselves at last, quite independently, in London, where we had both settled down in good jobs. But two years ago, Stephen had been summoned abroad to attend the deathbed of his grandfather, Mr. Brunswick. When he returned, he brought with him his grandmother, Lady Evelyn, who had not lived in England since her marriage, though she had returned from time to time on visits of varying duration, and had never lost her interest in Polden—or allowed Polden to lose interest in her. Stephen brought her back to England after the death of his grandfather, and soon afterwards gave up his job in London, brought Lady Evelyn down to Grayleigh and settled her at the farmhouse. And when he left London, I diagnosed, for the first time, the strange symptoms I had been experiencing for the past few months: I was in love. I was in love with Stephen Brunswick—and when you fall in love at twenty-four, for the first time, you fall a long way and you fall hard.

I came down to Grayleigh on a visit, saw Stephen struggling to keep the farm going, and offered to stay and help him. it took a long time to persuade him; if I hadn't had an income of my own, he would never have agreed to my giving up my job in London—but he had given in at last, and it had worked. Two years; we had had two years together, and for me they had been years of complete happiness. I spent a lot of time dreaming about the day he would realise that he loved me—but for the moment I was content with things as they were. I told myself that it had taken me a long time to get round to the knowledge of my real feelings for him; I was prepared to wait for him to wake up one morning to a similar revelation. It would come; he was twenty-eight and would soon turn his thoughts to marriage; it was merely a matter of being patient. I was as certain as that. And in the meantime, I felt that nothing could happen to disturb the present satisfactory state of affairs.

I can't say much for my psychic reactions. On a clear, invigorating day in March, I got into the little car that Stephen and I ran jointly, and drove the short distance to the Lodge with some eggs and butter. It had been snowing the night before, and although we could do without snow on the farm, up here I had to admit that it looked beautiful. Even the house had a soft, mellow look, and there seemed to be something unusually stately in its lines.

When I think of Grayleigh, I think of it as it was on that morning, and I can feel the sharp, cold air whipping against my cheeks as it did then. I don't suppose I shall ever feel more keenly alive than I did when I left the car and went swinging up the slope to the house and passed Roly, the greyheaded postman, on his way up to the Lodge with a letter. Roly is tiny and skinny and wizened, but he was once a chubby little boy, and the people of Polden have long memories. I offered to take the letter up for him—it was addressed to Miss Christabel Hansard—and he quavered his thanks and handed it to me.

It was—for Grayleigh—an unusual letter; it was in a gaily-bordered airmail envelope, with a line of picturesque stamps. They were American stamps, and I knew that Roly was longing to have them for his collection—and if the letter had been addressed to Lorna, I would have given them to him without hesitation. But nobody would take a liberty of that kind with Christabel.

"I'll see if I can get them for you later, Roly," I promised, and he nodded hopefully and shuffled away. I went up to the house, found my way to the kitchen and put my butter and eggs on the table; then I went to look for Lorna.

The Lodge was a house with large, well-proportioned rooms, but they all needed redecoration; they also needed new curtains, new carpets and new chair covers, for the old ones were so faded as to have lost all their original colours, and now gave an air of dreariness to the house. All the things that make a house alive and cheerful—books, pictures, ornaments— seemed to me to be missing. The place always reminded me of some of the lifeless apartments I had been shown into when I was house-hunting in London: the minimum of furniture, and no attempt at colour or comfort. Only in Lorna's own sitting-room upstairs was there any atmosphere of homeliness.

I was about to go up and look for her there when I heard her coming downstairs. We went into the kitchen and she smiled at me.

"You're looking very pretty," she said.

"Thank you," I replied. "It's my new outfit." I was, as always, in a jacket and jodhpurs, but the jodhpurs were new and the jacket was one I hadn't worn for some time. They wouldn't look so *chic* after a few hours in the cowshed. "How's Christabel?" I asked.

"She's rather better this morning. Someone brought her up some new books, and she's looking through them. Butter and eggs; thank you, Claire. Where are you off to after this?"

"I've got to go into Polden. Want me to do any shopping?"

"Yes, please—but I'll make some coffee first and we'll sit down and enjoy it. It's so cold outside."

It was cold inside, too. The Lodge was never warm. It was arctic in winter and chilly all through the summer.

"I'll make the coffee," I said. "Oh, I forgot. Letter for Christabel."

I held it out to her and glanced at it for a moment as I did so. I can still see it clearly, with its firm address, its gay, red-and-white-striped border and striking-looking stamps, but I looked at it on that March morning with no premonition, no foreboding, no shrinking. It seems incredible to me now, but without fear and without hesitation I put it carelessly into Lorna's hand.

"Save the stamps for Roly, if you can," I said.

"I'll try," said Lorna, which meant that she would try not to show Christabel that she wanted them. "Will you watch that milk on the stove? I'll take the letter up."

"Who's writing to her from America?" I asked, with the freedom of one long familiar with the household.

"I didn't know she knew anyone there," said Lorna, going out.

I watched her go, and I wondered how she could keep so

cheerful in that cheerless house. She was thin and grey-haired and she had the hurried, shambling walk of a woman who is always trying to catch up with the housework. She had beautiful grey eyes, and peered at you when you spoke to her. She had been born at Polden, but had not lived there— except for occasional visits—until Christabel had sent for her about ten years ago. Lorna, though not rich, had enough money to keep herself without working, but she had spent her life answering appeals from people who turned to her in need. She made only two stipulations before answering them: they must be from the poor or from the sick. Christabel had been both when she sent for Lorna, and the latter had lived with her ever since, cooking, nursing and doing all the housework.

She was deeply religious. She had been a member of the Church at Polden, but had left it to search for one more suited to her spiritual needs. She had wavered, at Allchester, between High and Low, and the High had won, for a time. Then there had followed a struggle—brief, but spirited— between England and Rome, and the latter, in the person of Father Ignatius, had emerged victorious. Lorna was now a Catholic, and went to early Mass, summer and winter, sun or sleet, at Allchester, five miles away.

She came down from Christabel's room looking a little drawn; Christabel had opened the letter, she told me, and had been greatly upset by its contents.

"Bad news?" I asked.

"No. Yes—in a way, I suppose. Her cousin, Jeffry Hansard, has died."

I searched my memory and fitted some fragments together. "Jeffry...he lived in this house, didn't he?"

"Yes."

"Isn't that the cousin Christabel was brought up with?"

"Yes. The two of them—Christabel and Jeffry—were brought up by their aunt, Emily. Jeffry was some years younger than Christabel, though."

I did some arithmetic, and decided that his age must have been in the neighbourhood of sixty; further, he had left Grayleigh before I was born, and had never returned. I came to the conclusion that Christabel's distress must have sprung from shock rather than from sorrow.

"Did she know he was in America?"

"No. Nobody knew. Nobody has heard a word from him, or about him, since he left Grayleigh close on thirty years ago."

"What's he done? Left her some money, I hope."

"No—oh, no. Nothing of that kind. But there was some suggestion that the people who wrote the letter should come here to visit her. I didn't think it was at all a sensible idea for Christabel to encourage, in her state of health, and I said so. I'm afraid I upset her—but she gets upset very easily, these days."

"Who wanted to come and see her?"

"Oh—strangers. Complete strangers; people she doesn't know at all, and has never even heard of before. They merely know her as Jeffry Hansard's cousin, that's all, and they wanted to come and meet her."

"But the letter was from America—were they coming over?"

"Oh, no-no-no! They weren't coming over specially to see her. They were going on a tour of some kind—Europe or North Africa, they weren't certain which—and they were going to see Christabel on their way back to America. There was no question of their making a special journey."

"They'd be interesting, perhaps. Wouldn't it do her good?"

"No." Lorna spoke with surprising decision. "No, Claire, it wouldn't. What she needs is rest, and peace—and no excitement. She works herself up dreadfully—really dreadfully. If you'd seen her just now…But I felt I had to advise her, and I think she's thinking over what I've said and feeling that perhaps it would be better for her to refuse to have them."

That's all that was said of the matter for the moment, and though it doesn't seem possible now, I wasn't greatly interested. Nothing told me that there could be any possible connection between Jeffry Hansard's past and my future; nothing warned me that Christabel's scrawny fingers had broken a seal and set some machinery in motion; that when the machinery stopped, my happiness would stop with it. All I felt was sympathy for Lorna, who had obviously had to endure one of the scenes that Christabel made more and more frequently.

I left the house with Lorna's shopping list and went down into Polden to collect the few things she wanted. I also called here and there to leave bills or to collect money—another side of my farm work—so that it was almost lunch-time when I got back to the Lodge with the parcels. Lorna was nowhere to be seen, so I left the things for her and went back to the car. I had climbed in and started the engine when I saw Lady Evelyn coming out of the house, and I leaned across and threw open the car door for her.

"Get in," I invited.

She got in; it was a lengthy business, as she had a string bag, a large umbrella, a massive handbag and two enormous dogs. She was never seen without any of these—except in church, when the dogs stayed in the porch and the umbrella was handed to the verger, whose duty it was to see that the owner never went away without it.

It is difficult to describe Lady Evelyn, because the phrases when written down appear misleading. She was always dressed in flowing black, and her garments were of the straight, loose, shapeless, fashion-defying pattern worn by hundreds of old English ladies at home and abroad, giving them a look of dignified dowdiness; but Lady Evelyn wasn't dowdy. She was tall and thin and angular, and her movements, at times, had an almost coltish awkwardness—but she wasn't awkward. Her blue eyes were faded, but they were lit by her constant and undying interest in everything that was going on round her. Her cheeks, when I kissed them, had a petal softness, and her mouth was often pursed as if she was struggling to keep incautious words from bursting from it. She had an eagerness, an impulsiveness extraordinary in a woman nearing seventy—and, as if she were aware of this, she seemed to keep a firm hold on her voice and actions, and spoke, when she was excited, in a low, deep voice, leaning towards her listener in a manner half confidential, half shy. I never met anyone like her, and I found her company immensely stimulating. At no time did I ever see her bored, listless or subdued. She was unquenchable, unpredictable, a great trouble to everybody—and the pride of Stephen's heart.

I drove back to the farmhouse and unshipped my passenger and the string bag and the umbrella and the handbag and the dogs. Lady Evelyn however, was in no hurry to go indoors. She came round to my side of the little open two-seater— the makers had sent it out with a hood, but this had disintegrated at some period before the car had come into our possession.

"Did you know that Christabel had had news of her cousin, Claire?" she asked.

"Yes. He's gone and died."

"He couldn't have been much over sixty," said Lady Evelyn with an air of vague resentment. "You don't remember him, of course."

"No."

"Of course you wouldn't—you weren't even born. He left here, you know, all those years ago—just after his aunt died—and she must have been dead nearly thirty years, and nobody has heard a word from him since."

"Did he go to America?"

"Well, he must have done, mustn't he, Claire, if he died there? I wonder if poor old George knew?"

Lady Evelyn always referred to her brother-in-law, Mr. Petrie, as poor old George, and it must be admitted that he looked the kind of person that anybody, seeing for the first time, would instinctively call poor old George. He was old and thin and stooping and had a sad and brooding air. Some people said that the shock of his wife's death had nearly killed him; others—who knew him better—went so far as to say that it had quite done so. He had married Lady Evelyn's sister, Lady Alison; on her death, he had retired from the firm of solicitors which bore his name, and he now lived in a small house at Allchester.

"Did Mr. Petrie know him well?" I asked.

"Know who well, Claire dear?"

"Did Mr. Petrie know Jeffry Hansard?"

"Oh, goodness me, yes! Jeffry was a junior partner in the firm—didn't you know that?"

"No."

"Well, you wouldn't. I keep forgetting you weren't born. Yes, he was a junior partner. It was going to be Petrie and Hansard, but before that happened, Jeffry left, and that's all that anybody ever heard of him—-until now. What I can't understand is why they're so grateful to him."

"Who, darling?"

"To Jeffry."

"Yes, I know—but who's grateful?"

"These people, my dear—or rather, this person. The man who wrote the letter that came this morning from America. Now, what on earth would anybody be grateful to Jeffry for? He used to spend his time borrowing vast sums from me whenever I came over to England on a visit, and I always suspected that he borrowed money from everybody else, too. I don't see how he could have had anything to leave to anybody, do you?"

"Did he leave somebody something?"

"So they say in that letter. I think there must be some mistake. Jeffry didn't have anything to leave."

"Not when he was here, perhaps—but that's all those years ago. He could have amassed several fortunes in—what is it?— twenty-five, thirty years. Darling, go on in—you'll catch cold."

"I'm not at all cold, thank you. But I don't see how they can find out anything about him by coming to see Christabel, do you?"

"*Who's* coming, darling?"

"Nobody's coming. But the man who wrote the letter wanted to come—so Lorna says. Lorna didn't think it was at all a good idea. She thought it would be too much for Christabel, and she told Christabel so, and there was quite a scene. Didn't Lorna tell you about it?"

"Not very much. But I thought she looked rather upset."

"Lorna said—and I quite agree with her—that it was quite unreasonable to tell those people they could come all the way from America to talk about Jeffry Hansard, but she had her work cut out to dissuade Christabel from inviting them."

We were interrupted by a puzzled voice.

"What *do* you women find to gossip about?"

Stephen was leaning against the front door, watching us with an air of tolerant amusement. Lady Evelyn and 1 looked at him, and I suppose our expressions must have looked very much alike, because we both had—more or less—the same feelings about him.

He was tall and broad and slow-moving, with large hands and feet; he had cool grey eyes, and there was a solid look about him. He walked down to the car with leisurely steps, and the dogs rushed to greet him. He relieved his grandmother of some of her encumbrances, and repeated his question.

"What're you gossiping about, you two?"

"We're not gossiping," said Lady Evelyn.

"We are, Stephen," I said. "And she'll get pneumonia."

"I'll take her in. Don't go," he said.

He put the parcels and his grandmother impartially into the hall and shut the door on them. Then he came back and stood leaning against the car.

"Did you know Christabel had a cousin?" I asked.

"No. Oh, yes. Godfrey."

"Jeffry. He's dead."

"Murdered?"

"Nobody said so."

"Then why all the excitement?"

"Oh…no excitement. Did you know anything about him?"

"Nothing interesting. I wish you hadn't gone off this morning."

I looked at him and saw that both hands were deep in his pockets—a sign, with him, that he was annoyed about something.

"Anything wrong?" I asked.

He made no reply until he had picked a thread off my jacket and flicked it off his finger.

"Nothing particularly wrong," he answered. "Just that the whole place seemed to be falling to pieces this morning." He jerked his head towards the farm. "That woman came about the pup."

"But she wasn't coming until to-morrow. I've got her letter with the date on it."

"Oh, she's not the type that would worry about a little thing like sticking to a date. She thinks a farm's just a place you can walk into and out of whenever you feel like it. But the point is that she didn't walk in; she drove in and she went smack against that gatepost and knocked the ruddy thing down flat."

It was rather a poor gatepost, and we were always knocking it flat ourselves, but that was no reason why any stray visitor should be allowed to do it.

"Did she buy the pup?" I asked.

"She did not. I didn't give her the chance."

"But Stephen—you said she could have it."

"That was before I saw her. She turned up with a poodle; nice little poodle, too. I've nothing against poodles, but a woman who keeps a poodle doesn't want a socking great retriever lolloping round the place too. The poodle was Tittybit or something that sounded like it. That kind of woman."

"She could keep Tittybit inside and Bruno outside—no?"

"No. Not this Bruno, anyway; I want a good home for him, where he'll get enough exercise and the right amount of feeding and no more. That woman would stuff him—she's that kind."

"If she starved him, he'd eat Tittybit. Did you really let a silly woman rile you so much?"

He smiled—a slow, attractive smile.

"No, not really. She was irritating, but that wasn't what got me down—altogether. You haven't heard the whole story."

"Well—tell me."

"She knocked the gatepost over for a start, and the first thing she did when she got out of the car was to brush against the wood that was holding that door open—the door I mended. Of course, the whole thing went crash, and the blasted door fell down, and, greatly against my better judgment I put a hand out and yanked her out of the way just in time. You know, Claire, she was about fifty, and frail-looking, and not much higher than five foot two, but you should have seen what she did to the place!"

"More?"

"She knocked over a bucket of milk that I was going to give the calves—she said I shouldn't have buckets where people could walk into them. She wouldn't wait for me to open the shed door—she shoved it open herself, and it swung back and hit poor old Regina, who was feeding Bruno and so wasn't feeling like being disturbed—so naturally, she said she didn't like it, and she said it to Tittybit, and the small feeding trough went over in the middle of the row, and now there's about a ton of cow cake all over the place. It was worse than a hurricane."

"Did you get her off the place?"

"After a hard try. She started asking a lot of silly questions about the animals, but I was like the nasty old man of Bermuda, whose answers got ruder and ruder."

"Well, anyhow," I said with relief, "she's gone."

"Yes—but my God, this has been a morning! I put the hayfork through a pane of glass and I cut my leg on a piece of wire. Come back, for the love of Moses, as soon as you've had lunch. And make a note of the date, Claire, will you? It's my unlucky day."

I laughed at him and drove away, and when I look back, I can never understand why all that had to happen to him on that morning. Because it wasn't his unlucky day. It was mine.

Chapter Two

Stephen and I rode up, a week or two later, to take the puppy to a home which Stephen considered more suitable for him. It was a wonderful afternoon. There was some mist in Polden, but we rode through the woods along a path that took us almost sheer up the side of the hill, and then came out on to open ground and saw Polden and Grayleigh spread out at our feet. They looked, from here, completely inaccessible, and it was easy to see why the place had become a backwater; few except those who, like my parents, liked a quiet and secluded life, would ever seek it out.

We dismounted to give the puppy a run, and found him looking as though he had enjoyed the journey in his improvised howdah. He tried to roll himself over the hillside once or twice, and Stephen did some magnificent sprints to cut him off. The horses looked on mildly, the sun shone with a warmth that reminded me that winter was over, and I felt a surge of delight at the perfection of the day, at the gambolling puppy and the shouts of laughter that came from Stephen as he chased it to and fro. I had a feeling that I was experiencing a perfect moment—and that, I suppose, in its way, could be taken as a kind of premonition. But if I could feel so keenly the beauty of the moment, I should have been able to go a step farther and realise that happiness of that kind wasn't to be taken for granted. It was something to be held as one holds a fragile and priceless piece of china— a thing to be cherished with the knowledge that careless handling could shatter it into a thousand pieces. But I accepted it as a spoilt child takes a gift—with a careless certainty of more to come.

We delivered the puppy, and Stephen noted with satisfaction that its future companions were great, husky, masculine creatures, with not a Tittybit among them. We drank milk and ate oven-warm rock cakes, and then came back the long way round and explored grass-grown paths that I hadn't been over since childhood days.

When we got to the outskirts of Allchester, I sent Stephen on ahead.

"I'm not coming yet," I said. "I've got to go in and see poor old George."

"What for?"

"I've got some eggs for him."

Stephen looked for signs of an egg basket, and I pointed to my bulging pockets.

"In there," I said. "Why did you think I stood about up there on the hill, instead of chasing the puppy?"

"Old age," said Stephen unhesitatingly.

"I can still run," I informed him coldly, "but not with eight eggs nestling in various parts of me."

"Fun if they've bust," commented Stephen, turning his horse homeward.

They hadn't. I dismounted carefully in Mr. Petrie's short drive, and tied my horse to a tree. Then I went up and knocked on the door of the little house.

It was opened by Mr. Petrie's unlovely housekeeper, between whom and myself no love was lost. She knew that she was a lazy, sluttish creature, taking advantage of the fact that Mr. Petrie was too inert to notice any faults in the service meted out to him—and she knew that I knew. She admitted me reluctantly, and said she thought that Mr. Petrie was resting, so I went into the drawing-room and said that I would wait until he had had his rest. I unshipped the eggs one by one, countering her look of contempt by carefully blowing the dust off the table before I placed the eggs on it.

"Eight," I said at last. "Now if you'll tell Mr. Petrie that I'm here…"

She marched out, and I looked after her with strong dislike. She was not a native of Polden; she came from Tooting, and was thought little of by the local people until there happened to be a Royal christening, funeral, Coronation or proclamation, when she became almost respected, owing to her knowledge of every aspect of pageantry. She knew all the best vantage-points in London for watching processions, and she could unveil mysteries hidden from most of the rest of us: Garter King of Arms, Portcullis Pursuivant of Arms, Gold Stick

27

in Waiting, Silver Stick in Waiting and Clarenceux King of Arms. She could explain who they were and what they did and when they were called upon to do it. Between processions, she reverted to her position as Polden's worst cook.

The door opened and Mr. Petrie came in with his tall, thin frame stooped and sagging in a way which always made me feel that someone had hung him up on a hook. He took my hand in both his own and pressed it affectionately. Then began the opening chorus which was always played whenever he met anybody, and to which I was now resigned.

"My dear Claire—how are you?"

"I'm very well, thank you."

"And Lady Evelyn?"

"Oh—she's very well, thank you."

"Splendid. How is Stephen?"

"Oh, he's…he's very well, thank you.

"And how is your uncle?"

He saw my uncle in church every Sunday, and often lunched with him, but I droned on:

"He's very well, thank you."

"And how is Lorna?"

"She's very well, thank you."

That was over. He never mentioned Christabel; he had never mentioned her to me since I had known him, and—it was one of those unspoken things that children fall in with instinctively—I had never spoken of her to him. The preliminary

28

exchange being over, I could give him the eggs and go.

"But I must pay you for them, my dear!" he protested.

"No. Present from the farm."

"No, no, no—I won't hear of it. The last ones were a present and the ones before. This time...I insist..."

He was too frail and shaky to be argued with; I let him go to fetch the money, and I stood in the depressing little room —he had come to this house after the death of his wife— and studied the large portrait of her that hung above the mantelpiece.

It was difficult, at any time, to imagine Mr. Petrie married, but it was almost impossible to imagine him the husband of the lovely young woman whose delicate colouring and shy charm had been so well captured by the painter of the portrait at which I was gazing. I had a dim memory of Lady Alison from my childhood days, but there seemed no remote connection between the frail, colourless woman I remembered and the fresh young beauty whose likeness hung in the dark room. Mr. Petrie never brought the portrait to my notice, and I was grateful. I suppose everybody feels the same acute embarrassment that I do when trying to reconcile the wrinkled present with the smooth-cheeked past. Mr. Petrie had never subjected me to this ordeal, but now that I was alone, I could stare at the portrait and trace the likeness between this young Lady Alison and her elder sister, Lady Evelyn. There had been fifteen years' difference in their ages, but I saw now that there must have been as wide a difference in their nature; the face in the portrait was that of Lady Evelyn with all the strength and character left out.

Staring at the long-dead Lady Alison, I found myself wanting very much to ask her what had made her marry a man so much older than herself; a man, moreover, who even in his youth must have been very sober and dull. It might, I thought, have been her way of escape from the great, empty mansion in which she had been brought up. It had been cheerful enough when Lady Evelyn was young, but times changed when she left, and her going would leave a gap anywhere. This sister, fifteen years younger, and born into a harsher world, must have found life dreary enough to have made Mr. Petrie—gentle, courteous Mr. Petrie—an acceptable husband.

There was a sound behind me, and I turned to find Mr. Petrie counting change. I took the money, thanked him and said goodbye.

"Don't come out," I said. "I'll find my own way."

He smiled at me, and stopped me at the door to ask a question.

"I suppose Lorna didn't give you any message for me this morning? I had asked her to lunch with me to-morrow."

"I didn't see her," I said, and added, before I could stop myself: "I haven't seen her since the day she got the letter about Jeffry Hansard. She—Oh, take care, Mr. Petrie!"

He had stumbled against a low chair, and I caught him just in time to save him from falling. I put him gently into it, and stood over him anxiously, looking at the ghastly pallor that had spread over his face. He looked pinched and spent, and I looked round for a cupboard in which some form of restorative might be found. He spoke, however, in a calm enough voice:

"It's…I'm quite all right, Claire."

"Did you hurt yourself?"

"No, no—it was just a—"

"The chair was just behind you," I said in self-reproach. "I should have warned you. Can I bring you anything?"

"No—thank you, no. I'm perfectly all right."

I stayed until he had got back some of his colour and was looking stronger, and then I left him. I had some other calls to make in Allchester, and they kept me longer than I had expected. By the time I had got the horse to the farm and stabled him and was on my way to the Vicarage, I knew I would be late for dinner.

I went into the house and was on my way upstairs when I heard a low growling, and turned to see a cadaverous countenance glaring at me round the door leading to the kitchen.

"Ye're late again, ye are that. Ye canna expec' gude fude to wait aboot for ye. The Reverend's halfway through his soup."

"All right, Cluny. I'll be down when I've had a bath."

"Ye're no' needin' a bath; yon's all healthy dirt."

"Healthy or not, I'm going to get it off," I told him, and went upstairs, followed by his comments on my habits and character.

31

There is no need to describe Cluny in detail. He was the embodiment of the popular illustrations of Don Quixote— dejected look, gaunt, haggard face, reddish beard and extraordinary moustache and all. He had come into the family long, long ago when he acted as boatman to my father, who was on a fishing trip in Scotland. The trip over, Cluny offered his services to my father as—in turn—valet, butler, footman, boot boy, gardener and man-of-all-work. These offers my father firmly refused, and returned to his home in Polden. Here Cluny followed him, saying that he would serve him in any reasonable capacity. My father received him without enthusiasm, told him to return to his wife and home, and paid his fare. A month later, Cluny was back. He had left his wife, he said; he was tired of her bletherin'. Retreating in the face of my father's wrath, he went back to his native land; when next he appeared, he informed my father that he had brought with him proof— irrefutable proof; five closely-written pages of it on the back of an old household account book—showing the deep indebtedness owed by my father's family to his own. Opening the book, glancing at it from time to time to refresh his memory, he began his story— which I repeat briefly and without any of the dramatic emphasis with which Cluny is said to have delivered it.

Macduff, from whom my father traced direct descent, had fled, long, long ago, as all historians state, from the wrath of Macbeth. In flight, he came to the River Tay and there halted. Why, enquired Cluny, did he halt? My father didn't know, and so Cluny told him; he halted, he said, because Macduff had no money with which to pay the ferrymen. There were two ferrymen, said Cluny, glancing at his notes. One of them demanded the fare. The name of this churl is forgotten, lost, and happily lost, in the fog of the centuries. But the other ferryman... the *other* ferryman, explained Cluny, knew just when to exact payment and when to waive it. With King Macbeth's men in thunderous pursuit, with the breath of the foremost horses visible in the distance in the chilly air, the second ferryman acted swiftly. "Pay me," he said, "in bread. Give me the bread you carry"—for it appeared that the knell of danger had sounded in the middle of Macduff's dinner. The bread from the King's table was handed over and the good ferryman rowed Madcuff over to safety. To every descendant of the ferryman there was owed, therefore, by the descendants of Macduff, an incalculable debt. Cluny was a descendant of the ferryman. The proof was there, irrefutable, plain for everybody to read, under the headings, Food, Wages and Laundry.

Cluny stayed; in time, he outstayed every other servant. When the era of lady helps arrived, Cluny watched their labours with savage contempt until at last, driving them out, he himself took over their duties and donned the badge of female usefulness—an apron of the skirt-and-bib pattern, without which nobody now ever saw him. He performed faithfully all the household tasks, and informed everybody that any virtues I had were due solely to his training throughout my childhood.

His visits to Polden were made once a week—on Saturday evenings, when he walked to the inn and drank two glasses of beer. He acted in the high-handed manner of one who could claim a descent longer than any of the other customers and he had, until lately, been accorded the respect he demanded. But there had arisen a man named Butcherd, who said that his name originated at the time that his family suffered almost complete extermination at the hands of Caesar's army. Cluny was still investigating this claim.

Cluny liked Lady Evelyn, and called Stephen a braw-lookin' lad, but he had a shrewd idea of the state of my feelings and viewed the situation with a little alarm. It was obvious that he was doubtful about allowing me to throw myself away on someone whose family had never been heard of until well into the fifteenth century, and which had done nothing of note until sixteen-forty-two.

He was waiting for the sound of my footsteps as I went downstairs after my bath, and came into the hall to give me a gloomy piece of news.

"Yon Christabel" he began.

"Miss Hansard," I said automatically, but uselessly.

Cluny had his own ideas about those to whom he owed respect, and Christabel was not among them. Lorna was Miss Lorna, but Christabel was invariably yon Christabel.

"Yon Christabel's worse."

"Worse?"

"I doot she'll no' last long. Ye mark my words, the next

snaw'll see the last o' her."

"How do you know she's worse?"

"I ken; that's a'. I ken; it's in ma bones. I jes' ken. But Miss Lorna was up this afternoon lookin' for ye, an' you no' here, and no' at the farm, but skytin' awa' there."

"What did she want me for?"

"She wanted to tell ye that yon Christabel wasna feelin' sae gude. I said to her, I doot she'll no last long."

"I'm sure you did."

"Well, awa' wi' ye and hae yer dinner. It's a' cauld. Ye canna keep gude fude waitin' an'..."

I left him and went into dinner, and my uncle raised his head, began to fumble his way to his feet, gave his sweet, absent smile and sat down again. I sat opposite, and we ate in silence, sometimes broken by his automatic "Well, my dear?"—a vague query to which he expected no reply. I looked at his handsome old head and his silvery hair shining under the lights, and thought that he looked far more like my grandfather than Lady Evelyn looked like Stephen's grandmother.

He had been a brilliant scholar and a fine musician, but he had never at any time been fully aware of what went on in his immediate surroundings. Cluny asserted that my uncle had never quite realised that he had a wife, and points to his child-less state as proof. Certainly he hardly knew that I was there. At one extreme of his consciousness was the Church, and at the other his collection of gramophone records of sacred music—which he played constantly—and his chest, which had always interested him greatly. Somewhere between these points, deep down, hidden and shadowed, lay his other concerns. He was gentle, and had beautiful, old-world manners, and he was well liked by his parishioners. The Church was always full. It was small, and was built in the exact centre of the village, so that nobody could complain of having to come farther than anybody else. My uncle copied out his sermons faithfully every Saturday night from those he had preached years earlier; there was no need to copy them, for the originals—if they were originals—were already written out in his own handwriting on loose sheets ready for use—but my uncle wrote them out once more, and the sheets were then given into the care of Cluny, who saw that they were handed to him at the beginnings of the services. He told me that he had once handed him the sheets of the week before, but nobody had noticed—and I'm not surprised, for the opening sentences of the long-drawn-out text, delivered in my uncle's beautiful, mellow tones, lulled the congregation into a state of holy calm from which they awoke only when the number of the hymn was given out.

An unusual feature of Polden Church was its disproportionate number of working members. There were two people at the east door to hand out hymn-books, and two at the west door for the same purpose; one person played the organ and two worked the bellows. Four people went round to take the collection; twelve people sang in the Choir. As there was an unspoken agreement that nobody giving their services should be expected to give money too, the amount of the weekly collections was not impressive.

I think that my uncle would have been a great clergyman if he had been more orthodox, but in his early years in the Church, he had wanted to introduce sweeping changes, not into the forms of the services, but into what went by the name of music in country churches. He wanted to hold the services to the accompaniment of the greatest and best in organ works, heard through recordings. The people would come in, he pointed out, not to the sound of a few wheezy notes played by an earnest amateur, but to the glorious and uplifting strains of the finest organ music in the world. The hymns would be accompanied, the prayers supplemented, by the deep throb and pulse of the music and the sweet tones of boy sopranos soaring effortlessly to the topmost notes. There would be anthems and descants; the assembled heads would bow to a Blessing sung with grace and purity; hearts would be lifted up by the glorious sound into a realm far above that in which they moved for the other six days of the week. They would go out exalted, refreshed. Empty churches would be filled by those who came to hear, and remained to pray.

I think so too—and that makes two of us: my uncle and myself. Nobody else was in agreement or even in sympathy— least of all the Polden Church Choir. Nobody, said Mrs. Welsh, who led the altos on adventurous and inharmonious excursions, wanted canned music. They would praise God out of their own mouths and not out of a gramophone. And so they did, and do. But if Mrs. Welsh is leading the seconds in the Heavenly Choir when I get there, I shall go elsewhere.

We went on with our dinner in silence, my uncle waiting politely until I caught up with him. When we had finished, we rose, and I went into the drawing-room and got a book and my uncle went into his study. Presently the sound of sacred music—which would go on until we all went to bed— came from the study. To-night, I noted, we were to have an oratorio.

When I hear people complaining that the modern child can do nothing without a background of noise, I think of my uncle, whose life was passed to the throb and pulse of organ music. I know every major organ work ever written; more, I know the history of the organ. In my uncle's more active days, I was taken to see every church organ of any size or merit in the county. I can talk with ease and fluency on the subjects of wind regulators, swell keys, great keys, unenclosed bass, main wind trunk, flues and reeds. I read for examinations accompanied by Bach's *Passion* music, and cut out dresses or wrote letters or washed my hair to Handel's *Messiah* and Haydn's *Creation*. For me, the music was merely a part of life at the Vicarage, and I accepted it without question and even—at times—with enjoyment, but to Cluny it had been always what he called a turrible howlin', and he went about, whenever it was howling, with wads of cottonwool hanging out of his ears.

Stephen came in after dinner and we talked, at ease and relaxed, in front of a leaping fire. Holding a drink, his legs stretched out comfortably, he sat until it was time for him to leave, and then answered a question I put to him about Christabel.

"Christabel? She's not so well." he said.

"You mean she's worse?"

He smiled.

"Have it your own way; she's worse. A message came down from Lorna asking Granny to go and sit with Christabel and distract her—the word is Lorna's. Perhaps you'd better go up and see her to-morrow." He rose, drained his drink, stretched luxuriously and said goodnight.

"Enjoyed the ride," he added.

"So did I."

I saw him out and came back into the room and stood staring at the fire—but for once I wasn't thinking of Stephen. I was thinking of Christabel, and of something that had happened that day that was oddly connected with her. My mind went back to something which had impressed itself upon me at the time, but which I had been too busy to analyse. I had pushed it to the back of my consciousness, and it had stayed there, vaguely worrying me, ever since. But now, with leisure to take out the incident and study it, I went over those few moments in Mr. Petrie's room that morning, when I had put an arm round him and lowered him gently into a chair after he had stumbled against it. Something had puzzled me at the time, and now I knew what it was; I had got the details into their right order.

The shock had come first, and the stumble had come afterward. And the shock, and the stumble and the deadly pallor had been caused by my casual mention of the name of Jeffry Hansard.

Chapter Three

I walked up to the Lodge on the following evening, and learned that Christabel was a little better. I went upstairs to see her, and sat with her for some time, reading to her, and talking a little—though we never found much to talk about.

I thought she was looking even more shrunken than usual, sitting up in the big bed with her books and papers lying round her, and felt, as I always did when I was with her, that the drabness of the room went beyond the ordinary bounds of shabbiness or cheerlessness—there seemed to be something almost deliberate in the way in which even the smallest comforts had been excluded from her surroundings. I knew that, from time to time, Lorna brought up flowers, or ornaments, or a bedspread with a touch of pretty colour, only to be met by Christabel's uncompromising refusal to have them in the room. She seemed, in this way, to feed the bitterness she nursed for life in general and for the house in particular.

That was the last time I was to see her, for from that day there seemed to be a slow decline in her condition. Lorna hoped that she might improve a little, and was convinced that if she could hold out through the last cold of winter, she would mend under the influence of the warm spring sunshine. But on a beautiful May morning, when everything in the world seemed to be springing to lovely life, a message came down to my uncle at the Vicarage: Christabel had died, calmly and peacefully, at dawn.

I don't think that there was very much sadness at the news of her death, but it gave us all a feeling of great depression. My uncle went up to the Lodge at once, and took Lady Evelyn with him, and I gathered a huge armful of spring flowers and took them up and left them with Lorna. We were all very subdued; though nobody—except, perhaps, Lorna— had any sense of personal loss, we were all thinking of Christabel's dreary existence and lonely end. I wished I could have liked her more, but she was not a woman who attracted friends; she was cold and selfish and—in her worse moments—she could be mean and vindictive.

It was arranged that Cluny—always borrowed in times of stress—should sleep at the Lodge until after the funeral. I would have liked to have gone up myself, but I knew that Lorna would find it easier to make use of Cluny, and would worry less about his comfort, and so I sent him up instead of going myself. I went up to see Lorna once or twice in the days that followed; she was tired, for there was a great deal to be done, but she was happy in the knowledge that she had done all she could for Christabel. She told me, with tears, that Christabel had left her the house, and when I went to the farm I told this news to Stephen, who felt that it would be almost as useless to her as it had been to Christabel, in spite of the fact that Lorna had a larger income.

"I hope she'll sell it," he commented. "It would be a useful house for anybody that could run it on decent lines. An institution of some kind. It's got all those rooms and the best view round here, and a lot of ground."

"Why don't you talk to her about it?"

"Not yet," he said. "She's got a funeral on her hands." But we were to learn that Lorna had much more than a funeral on her hands. Cluny brought the news to me with a look of unusual excitement on his face—and a look of excitement on Cluny's face gave it an air approaching the diabolical.

"There's the de'il to pay up yon," he said, with a jerk of his head.

"At the Lodge? What's wrong?"

"Would ye believe," asked Cluny, in long-drawn-out amazement, "would ye believe that yon Christabel would do onny sech thing?"

"Any what thing?"

"I kent, in ma bones, that she had it in her. She was a deep one; aye."

"Had *what* in her?"

"This de'ilment. Ye dinna ken what she's been up to."

"No, Cluny, I don't. If you've got any news, then for Heaven's sake"

"She's been sittin' up theer, all these long weeks past,

plottin'.'"

"*Plotting*? What *are* you talking about, Cluny. Plotting what?"

"Aye, wait till I tell ye. Ye remember yon letter she got?"

"Letter?" I repeated uncomprehendingly.

"Och, ye remember, surely? She had a letter. D'ye no' mind? Ye took it up yerself an' put it in Miss Lorna's han'."

"A letter from America—that one?"

"Aye, that one."

"Well, what about it?"

"This aboot it: yon Christabel's been sittin' up there sendin' letters off to them."

"Well, I know she sent one. I posted it—ages ago."

"Aye, but there's been mair since. She's been sittin' up there writin' letters ahint Miss Lorna's back."

"Cluny, that's nonsense."

"It's no' nonsense, and ye'll find oot. Miss Lorna's askin' for ye."

I went up to the Lodge at once, but I felt that Cluny must have got the story a little mangled. It was impossible to imagine Christabel sitting up and plotting. But when I got to the house, I was met by Lady Evelyn, her eyes screwed up with excitement and her voice deeper than ever.

"My dear Claire—have you *heard*?"

"Cluny said something, but it doesn't make sense. He said something about letters. I don't see why Christabel shouldn't write all the letters she wants to. Wanted to, I mean."

"Oh, but it was that American one, don't you see, Claire? The one from those people. The ones who wanted to come here and talk about Jeffry Hansard. They wanted some facts about his early life—don't you remember?"

"Yes, but Christabel put them off. I posted the letter myself."

"Ah, my dear, but she *didn't* put them off. She promised Lorna she would, but she didn't. It's so difficult to talk about it with poor Christabel lying up there in her coffin, but the whole thing has been done in the most dreadful, underhand way. She gave Lorna her word, you know—and then, far from writing to them to say, 'I'm sorry, I don't feel up to having visitors,' she wrote and said, 'Do come by all means.' "

"But—when did Lorna find out?"

"Today. I've been up here every day since poor Christabel died, and I've been helping Lorna to go through all her things, and we've been sorting them out and going over all the papers—you know what a lot there is to do. It was only to-day that we came across the key of Christabel's little writing-case and opened it—and there were all the letters. You can imagine how shocked Lorna is!"

I could; Christabel had given her word, and broken it. It would be a deep shock to the rigidly honest Lorna.

"I'll go up and talk to her," I said. She mustn't upset herself about it. I'm sure Christabel meant to tell her eventually.

Has Lorna written to put them off?"

"That's the quite, quite awful part of it; Lorna can't."

"Can't?"

"You see, Lorna hasn't got anything but their American address and the names of some of the places they've been travelling in. They've been in North Africa. There's nowhere she can get hold of them to put them off."

A realisation of the full extent of the awkwardness of the situation began to dawn on me, and prompted my next question.

"When are they coming?"

"To-morrow!" said Lady Evelyn, in her deepest voice.

"But…but they c-can't! The funeral's to-morrow!"

"That's what I've been trying to tell you, Claire dear. It can't be put off, you know. And we're nearly distracted—we've been searching through everything looking for a letter, a postcard—anything that would help us to get a message to them. It's a husband and wife—their name is Donner."

I felt very sorry for Mr. and Mrs. Donner, and at once joined wholeheartedly in the search for a clue to their whereabouts. I watched Lorna grow pale as we put all the correspondence together and saw the extent and thoroughness of it. It was hard to believe that the peevish and cantankerous invalid could have penned letters of such firmness and clarity.

The first letter from Mr. Donner had been tentative; nothing was known about Jeffry Hansard's early life in England beyond the name of his birthplace and the house in which he had been born. A few notes found among his papers after his death had shown Christabel to be his cousin, but it was not known whether she was alive or whether she still lived in the house. Mr. Donner stated that if she was still living there, he would be grateful to be allowed to visit her, with his wife, to learn something of her cousin's history. He referred to Jeffry Hansard in terms of warmth and friendliness. Christabel's reply to this letter, far from expressing her regret and her inability to offer hospitality, had been, apparently, an acknowledgement of her relationship to the dead man, and an offer of hospitality to Mr. Donner and his wife.

From that point, Mr. Donner's letters became longer. He told Christabel of their projected trip to North Africa, and explained that the visit to England to make enquiries about Jeffry Hansard would be made on their way back to America. His last letter was written in the hope of meeting Christabel very soon, and he told her that he would write or wire if there was any change in their plans—but he had omitted to send an address to which Christabel could write or wire in a like event. There was no way of making contact now; they were on their way, and Lorna could do nothing to stop them. With hope almost gone, we went on with our search for an address, and turned out drawers, shook open books and looked through albums—looked everywhere, in short, where a stray letter might have been placed.

I had known Christabel Hansard only as the peevish old

woman who sat in a chair in the big bedroom, or lay propped against a pillow in the big bed, or who came down, rarely, for an evening or two in summer to walk slowly round the garden. Going through papers, sketch-books, albums, old snapshots that morning with Lady Evelyn, I saw emerge before me a complete picture of an earlier life—the life of the young Christabel. Christabel as a baby, as a child, as a young girl. Lady Evelyn grew as absorbed as I did, and the hunt for Mr. Donner's address was temporarily forgotten. She found me sitting at a table littered with papers, gazing at a photograph of a schoolgirl in a gym tunic, long black stockings, a white blouse and striped tie, and an enormous, stiff straw hat. The hat was the thing.

"You needn't look like that," said Lady Evelyn. "Those were called cartwheels, and if a girl was plain, then they couldn't do anything for her, but I can assure you that some of us looked very charming in them—very charming indeed."

"How did they ever induce girls to put them *on*? Is this Christabel again?"

"Let me see. Yes; that was taken in the garden here—you can see the sundial. She must have been about eleven in that one. She was three or four years younger than I was, but she was a good deal older than my sister Alison. That's Alison with that dreadful governess who pretended to be French—and there's Christabel again."

"Who's that with her—her cousin Jeffry?"

"Oh dear me, no. Jeffry was much more handsome than

48

that. This was a horrid man called Savage—how appropriate!
—who paid Christabel a great deal of attention and then, when
we all thought it a settled thing, went off and married somebody else. He was a scoundrel, and Christabel was well rid
of him. They say he began to suspect that she might not get
old Emily's money, and of course he turned out to be right,
though I can't think where he got his information— nobody
else knew. And here's Christabel again—and who do you
think is standing beside her?"

"*No!!!!!*"

"I don't quite like the way you say that, you know, Claire.
I daresay one changes a great deal, but there must be some sort
of likeness left. *Look* at these sleeves—I remember thinking I
looked terribly dashing in them."

"Is this one Jeffry?"

"That? Good gracious me, no. That's dear old Richard—
my husband. Doesn't he look *leggy!* This is Christabel in her
coming-out dress."

"Those *feathers...*"

"Well, I dare say some people looked uncomfortable in
them, but do you know, Claire, if a girl had any looks at all,
they made her look like a princess. Poor Christabel never had
the right kind of clothes, and that's why they look so odd in the
snapshots. I suppose Emily did her best, but when I compare
our house, with all the young people and all the gaiety, with
this one, even as it used to be, I feel so very, very sorry for
poor Christabel. You see, nowadays a girl can make a circle

for herself, but when Christabel was a girl, it was useless for her to expect to get asked anywhere unless somebody saw to it that she was brought into contact with suitable people, or with eligible young men. Poor Christabel never seemed to have any young men round her, but I think they found her rather difficult—she was very outspoken, even when she was young, and if she didn't like people, she took no trouble. That's this house as it used to be. I suppose you can't see—it's very faded, isn't it? But you can see how trim everything looked. I can't bear to look at the gardens nowadays, all so sad-looking, with all those overgrown paths and bushes and flower beds."

"Who's this?"

"That? That's Christabel, but much later. That was taken just about the time that Emily died, I suppose. She was in her late thirties—she was some years older than her Cousin Jeffry."

"Oh, *do* look at this one. Isn't he *odd!*"

"I don't know about odd, Claire. That's dear old Papa—oh, you needn't worry; everybody used to make the same mistake and think he was odd, but he wasn't odd at all. Those whiskers may have made you think so—they were called Dundreary whiskers, but my mother never liked it— the style, I mean. Do you know, looking at him, I can see quite a look of Stephen."

"Oh—no! I mean...do you really think so?"

"Indeed I do. But you know, this isn't getting us any nearer to finding the Donners' address, is it? But one never knows—somebody might have slipped a little piece of paper with an address on it in between these snapshots. Oh look, Claire— there's Stephen as a baby. Now, isn't it sweet of poor Christabel to have kept that! Dear me, how old that makes one feel—first dear old Papa and then Stephen, and all those years between them. That has kept rather well, hasn't it? You wouldn't think that was twenty-seven years old."

"Twenty-eight."

"Is he twenty-eight? Yes, of course he is. Oh—hello, Lorna, my dear. We're still busy, as you see, but we've found nothing. Nothing at all."

I went downstairs at this point to make some coffee, and Lorna followed me and sat on a chair in the kitchen, looking shaken.

"I don't understand it," she said. "I knew, of course, that she wanted them to come—that was why we had that unpleasantness in the first place. But she seemed to...she promised! I asked her to put it out of her mind, and merely write to put them off, and she...she really gave me her word Claire..."

It was no use telling her not to worry. She was watching Christabel going on her last journey with a lie on her lips and a lot of incriminating letters among her papers, and—being Lorna—she was wondering whether it might have been partly her fault; whether she had failed Christabel in sympathy or understanding. It was no wonder that she looked pale. It was bad enough to have the funeral ahead of her, and the prospect of the Donners walking in in the middle of it, without having to follow Christabel's soul to Purgatory.

I gave her a strong cup of coffee and made her sit still until it was all drunk.

"You're tired, and you've got to rest," I said.

"There's still rather a lot to be done. I think perhaps I would have got on more quickly if…"

She pulled herself up, but I knew what she had been on the point of saying.

"I've got to go now," I said, "but I'll take Lady Evelyn with me."

"Thank you, Claire. If only we could have put the funeral off…"

"What would have been the use of that? Putting it forward might have been more to the point, but it's too late now—and there's a reasonable hope, you know, Lorna, that the Donners will arrive long after everything's over."

"I hope so. But one can't be sure."

"Well anyway, stop worrying, and try to rest."

"I'll just have one last search," she said.

We left her searching, and I took Lady Evelyn home and went on to the farm.

"Nothing," I said, in reply to Stephen's enquiry. "The address in America, which they left weeks ago. Since then they've been on a tour of North Africa."

"Nice," said Stephen. "I wouldn't mind a tour of a lot of places sitting on the edge or a nice, warm desert: Casablanca, Mogador, Marrakesh, Agadir, and all sun-drenched. I feel warmer just by saying the names. Did they say what they're really coming here for?"

"Just to visit the birthplace of Jeffry Hansard and pick up a few facts about him. He left them a lot of money—not them personally, but a hospital they're interested in. It seems odd, doesn't it, Stephen, to think of Christabel actually inviting people to come and stay with her. She hated even the most casual visitors."

"Well, she seemed pretty keen on having this lot. Nobody seems to be looking at their side of it. Speaking for myself, I'd like nothing less than to come away from a nice, comfortable tour of North Africa and find myself in one of those bedrooms at the Lodge. And for Americans, straight from an indoor constant heat of anything from seventy to eighty degrees, according to whether Grandpaw got at the switch and turned it up or not, it'll amount to murder. One night in one of those beds, and we'll have two more funerals to go to. I must look out a couple of Stars-and-Stripes to drape over the coffins."

"There's not much in the way of comfortable hotels round here, you know."

"Oh, I know. And I suppose Lorna can hardly wait at the door and point out the way to one of the Allchester pubs. But all the same, my sympathies are with—what did you say their names were? Donner. Yes, Mr. and Mrs. Donner."

"They're—"

"I'd suggest their being put up at the Vicarage if I didn't

feel that all those 'Alleluia' strains, coming on top of a funeral, wouldn't be even more depressing than life up at the Lodge. I can't help feeling that Christabel must have had quite a lot of fun sitting up there and feeling she was putting something over on Lorna."

"Fun!"

"Excitement. It must have brightened her last days, though I suppose it had a lot to do with finishing her off. I can't imagine how Lorna's feeling. Is she going about suffering agonies of self-reproach?"

"I'm afraid so. Stephen, I feel so sorry for Christabel— she had no friends, and…who'll come to the funeral?"

"Who, indeed…Poor old Christabel. My God, Claire, how I hate funerals! One of the last survivals of barbarism. When I die, I want to be cremated and disposed of at once— and without trappings."

"I'll see to it."

"You'd better. Any of this long, black procession and incantations, and I'll come back and haunt you. Well, I didn't like her—Christabel, I mean—but I'm sorry for her."

"I'm more sorry for the Donners. Incidentally, Mrs. Donner isn't coming."

"Will he be on his own? I thought you spoke of 'they.' "

"His wife was to come, but at the last moment she stayed behind for some reason, and his daughter seems to be with him. At least, all his later letters mentioned her, and said nothing about his wife, so I suppose it'll be the daughter. Anyhow, it's one or the other."

"The daughter, I trust," said Stephen. "Oh God," he prayed, "send me a lovely American girl with a crock of gold!" And that was one prayer that God answered, and fully.

Chapter Four

On the morning of the funeral, I went out into the yard to stop Stephen as he was on his way to the farmhouse. "Don't go for a minute, Stephen," I said.

I wanted to ask him about something that had been at the back of my mind for some time, something that I found vaguely worrying.

"Well?" he asked.

"I wanted to ask you about going over to fetch Mr. Petrie to the funeral."

"That's all fixed," said Stephen. "I'm just going to change, and then I'll drive over and take him up to the Lodge."

"Would you mind if I went instead?"

"What—drive over to Allchester, you mean?"

"Yes."

"Well, you've left it a bit late," he commented. "Is there anything else you want to do while you're there?"

"No, nothing. I just thought I'd like to go and bring him over, that's all. It was…oh, just something silly."

"If you want to talk to him about business matters, to-day

isn't the day, and apart from that, he never discusses business in any form with anybody. He's out of business—for good."

"I know that. I wasn't—it was just an odd idea I had."

"That," said Stephen, "doesn't surprise me. You keep having them. What's this one?"

"It was something I've been worrying about—off and on— but I thought it out in the night."

"I think a lot of things out in the night—and then when I bring them out here at dawn and talk them over with the cows, they don't look so bright. They lose their force, some-how. Well, what's your notion?"

"You'll think it's silly."

"I know, but tell me."

"It was just that when I left those eggs at poor old George's, I happened to mention that Christabel had had a letter about Jeffry Hansard. It was only a casual remark, but it seemed to have a rather shattering effect on him."

"What sort of shattering?"

"Oh—he looked awful, that's all."

"You mean 'with a hoarse cry, he uttered the name fear-fully, his eyes starting; then, with a sickening thud, he fell to the floor in a swoon'—that kind of thing?"

"You put it awfully well, but…no, not quite. He just seemed to stagger, and I put him in a chair and—"

"—patted his hand. I would have enjoyed that, but I think poor old George is past it. Why did it have to be Jeffry Hansard's name? A lot of things can make a frail old man stagger and want to be quiet for a few minutes. He's pretty doddery, you know, Claire."

"I know. But I got the idea, just the same, that it was the mention of Jeffry Hansard's name that did it, and that got connected up in my mind when I thought about the funeral, but I couldn't quite see the connection. Then in the night I realised that nobody had seen poor old George since then, except to let him know about Christabel having died, and so he knows nothing about these American people coming over."

Stephen smiled at me.

"I'm waiting," he said patiently. "Don't hurry this; we've lots of time. The funeral's in an hour; I've got to change and so have you; Granny's got to be rounded up. But I'm certain that we'll soon get the connection between poor old George and the fact that a couple of Americans are coming over to see poor old Christabel."

"I didn't say anything about any connection. I only know that I'm almost sure that—"

"—that you only think that—"

"I'm sorry. I'm not making it very clear. But Jeffry Hansard's name may or may not have upset Mr. Petric; all I want to ensure is that he doesn't arrive at the Lodge and hear—without any warning—that these people are arriving to-day to talk about Jeffry Hansard."

"Couldn't I have told him on the way over?"

"No. You'd forget—or you'd persuade yourself, on the way there, that I'd been letting my imagination run away with me, and that it would be foolish to encourage me. I'll go and fetch him. Stephen, could there be any reason why he doesn't like to hear this Hansard mentioned? Did he dislike him?"

"Nobody's ever said so, as far as I know. Nobody's suggested that he liked him, either. Hansard was a junior partner in the firm, and as far as I can gather, he didn't do a stroke of work and then vanished into the blue. You'll find that the only reason poor old George was upset the other day was because it was the first news he'd had of Hansard since he disappeared."

"Perhaps."

"And, finally, remember that George has had a lot of trouble in his day. Money trouble."

"I know—you told me."

"So he's liable to go off into a fit of the trembles at any moment—when somebody bangs a door, for instance, or when you go at him too suddenly with something. So don't make too much of it."

"I won't."

"And fill up with petrol on your way there. We're low."

"All right."

"Oh—and Claire."

"Well?"

"I'm not going to allow Granny to go to the funeral. I'll take her up to the Lodge beforehand, but she's not going to leave the house. She's not up to it, at her age, but you'll have to help me to make her stay behind."

"Can't you just tell her that Lorna'll need her? Lorna isn't going. She's got to stay at the Lodge in case these people turn up, she said, but I think she's rather relieved to have an excuse not to go to the church."

"Excuse? Oh yes, I see. Father Ignatius. Well, in that case, Claire, you won't go, either."

"Oh, but I—"

"You're a Scot, and the Scots know how to run funerals; they keep all the women out of it, and quite right too. So that's settled; you and Lorna and Granny stay behind. Now for Pete's sake, get a move on and hur-ry!"

I hurried. I changed quickly and drove quickly, and was in good time when I drew up at Mr. Petrie's door. He came out, looking more dreary than ever in his black clothes, and I settled him in the seat beside me. I drove slowly through Allchester and waited until I had negotiated the twists and turns into Polden before I said what I had come to say.

"I suppose you know," I said, "that Lorna won't be going to the funeral?"

"Why not?" he asked. "She needn't have gone to the service, but I would have thought that—"

"Oh, she would have gone, but...she had rather a shock yesterday. She found that Christabel had arranged—without saying anything to her—to have some people from America to come and stay."

"*Christabel* did?" There was surprise in his voice, but there was also something else, and I thought it was distaste at having to mention Christabel's name.

"Yes," I said. "She didn't know them, but they wrote to her and asked if they could come and talk to her about her cousin, Jeffry Hansard."

That was as tactfully as I could put it. There was no reply, and the silence went on for so long that I wondered whether he had heard, or whether he had lost interest. Then I glanced at his knotted hands, clasped on the knob of the stick he had brought with him, and saw that they were so tightly clenched that the knuckles showed white—and I knew that he had heard, and that he hadn't lost interest.

I didn't look at his face, and so I was left guessing as to whether his feelings were those of pain or anger, or whether he was shaken by a swift rush of memories of the days when Christabel and Jeffry and his wife had all been alive. But whatever it was, I found myself feeling better. I like people to know what's ahead of them, if it gives them time to get themselves under control.

We had driven almost to the entrance of the Lodge drive before Mr. Petrie spoke again.

"Do you know why these people are coming?" he asked quietly.

"They want to fill in a few gaps in Mr. Hansard's early

history. He left their local hospital some money—as far as we can make out—and they feel that they ought to know a certain amount about someone they regard as a benefactor. That's as clearly as I can put it for you—but I'm afraid we're all rather in the dark."

He said no more. We were at the house, and the heavy errand upon which we had come was already weighing upon our spirits.

We went into the hall, and I saw that—as I had feared—there were pitifully few mourners. I went over and stood beside Stephen; Lady Evelyn was close to Lorna; besides ourselves, there were Mr. Petrie, the doctor and a small, grim-looking man whose name I never found out, and who had acted as solicitor to Christabel since Mr. Petrie retired.

Cluny had been helping Lorna all the morning; he was to go to the church, but he had expressed his intention of coming straight back to the house after the service. He appeared in a long black coat under which I suspected he still wore his apron, and took his place beside Stephen in the little car.

So the sad little cortege left the house, and we watched it from the window that overlooked the drive. Lorna wept; Lady Evelyn comforted her, but I was thinking, for the first time, that there was something in having a large family and a lot of relations. At least, in the end, they can make some sort of parade and look as though they had cared for you, and they can form a long, companionable line behind the coffin. It was terrible to see Christabel going on that last journey with nobody but the undertakers and a handful of people who were there, for the most part, only in the line of duty.

We sat quietly, saying little or nothing. It was over, in a sense, but our thoughts were with that mournful little procession, and nobody felt like saying anything. It was not until we heard Cluny's footsteps out in the corridor leading to the kitchen that we realised that the first part of the ceremony had ended.

Lady Evelyn roused herself and glanced from Lorna to me, and I read the signal and went into the kitchen and came back with a plateful of sandwiches. She took them from me and went over to Lorna, who was standing staring unhappily out of the window.

"Lorna, my dear," she said, "do come and sit down and put your feet up—you look so tired. Why don't you begin to think of yourself now, for a change? Do come, my dear. Claire has brought these nice sandwiches. Would you mind if I took one? I really didn't feel like eating breakfast this morning."

This roused Lorna's interest effectively.

"My dear Evelyn—of course! How selfish I am! Now look, *you* put your feet up here, and rest. I must find you something to eat."

"No, thank you, Lorna. You're the one we've got to think about. Will you promise me that from now on you'll take care of yourself, and not go rushing into something and getting yourself entangled in nursing somebody."

"We oughtn't to speak of it to-day, with Christabel dead," said Lorna reproachfully.

"We couldn't speak of it before, because she was alive," said Lady Evelyn reasonably. "Do sit down, Lorna, and talk to me."

"I can't, Evelyn dear. I've got to get the place cleared up before those people get here."

Lady Evelyn finished a sandwich and stood up.

"It's really very awkward—both for them and for you," she said. "I suppose we'd better set about helping you to make the room look tidier. I'll take out those small chairs for you. Oh look—somebody's forgotten their Prayer Book!"

"It's yours," I said.

"Mine? So it is. I brought it with me in case I could persuade Stephen to let me go to the service. I do feel that Christabel would have liked someone—some woman—with her. Surely that Father Ignatius of yours wouldn't have minded your going to the church, would he, Lorna?"

Lorna avoided replying to this by picking up one of the extra chairs that had been brought in from another room, and, refusing my offer of help, hurrying away with it.

Lady Evelyn looked at her retreating form with affection that had in it a touch of exasperation.

"It's her own business," she acknowledged, "but I can't help feeling that she chose a very *uncomfortable* religion, Claire. I do think, at her age, she might have been allowed a little more freedom of action. I can't really believe that God requires her to turn out at that heathen hour every Sunday and go all those miles in this ghastly weather we've been having. If you didn't get up and drive her there, like the kind little thing you are, what would she do?"

I am five feet eight and I weigh one hundred and forty pounds.

"She'd—"

"Yes, yes, I know. She'd bicycle. Well, Claire, I've got too high an opinion of God to suppose that He sits up there, Sunday after Sunday, with a clock in His hand, watching a lot of elderly women trooping into church."

"It's a matter of—"

"—self-discipline. I know, darling Claire, but really, you learn all that sort of self-discipline when you're a girl at school. I can remember us all getting up in the dark in those icy cubicles and filing into Chapel and praying on empty stomachs and fainting in droves. Well, God might expect that sort of thing from girls, to build up their characters, but at my age, I'm perfectly certain that He doesn't expect anything of the kind. Certainly He doesn't expect it from me, and I love Him all the more for being so understanding."

"I like going," said Lorna, coming in in the middle of this recital. "No—don't move, Evelyn, I can get round you. Claire, do you think I could ask Cluny to go up and see to the two bedrooms?"

"Two?"

"Yes. I've looked through the letters, and I'm quite certain it's the daughter who's coming."

I hadn't—even then—the smallest feeling of uneasiness. I went without hesitation into the kitchen to find Cluny and give him the message. There were bells—old-fashioned, but in working order—in every room in the house, but Cluny, whose hearing was perfect, affected not to hear them. He wiped his hands on his apron and followed me into the hall.

"Well, Cluny, this is all very sad," said Lady Evelyn.

"I see yoor Leddyship's eatin' the fude," said Cluny severely. "I was intendin' to serve those for lunch—there'll no' be time to cook any."

"The lunch is taken care of, Cluny," said Lorna. "You can leave it all to me. Will you go up and light the gas fires in the two bedrooms? I'm putting Mr. Donner in the blue room and Miss Donner in the lilac room."

"Blue room, lilac room; all yon rooms are the same colour noo," said Cluny. "A fine day for company to arrive, wi' the smell o' death still in the house."

"Cluny!" I said."

"Aye, an' it's true enough," said Cluny. "Yon bedrooms are as big as banquetin' halls, and the gas-fires no bigger than a mon's hand. They'll no' tak' the chill o' death off."

"Never mind about the chill of death, Cluny—go and light them," I said.

"Mr. and Miss Donner will have to stay here to-night," said Lorna. "To-morrow, if they want to, they can go and find more comfortable accommodation elsewhere."

"Hoo old would this Miss Donner be?" enquired Cluny, pausing at the foot of the staircase.

"I've no idea," said Lorna. "And Cluny, would you try to remember to use the other staircase?"

"I'm no' forgetting," said Cluny with dignity. "But I'm an old mon, an' I like to go the short way. Do ye require me to come doon again and go through yon door into the passage, an' through the back landing, and awa' along the red corridor and through the auld schoolroom to the front landin' an' into the bedrooms yon way?"

"No, Cluny, but—"

"Then I'll go this way," said Cluny, and went. We all watched him go with varied feelings.

"What would you do without him, Claire?" asked Lady Evelyn.

"Perhaps I could find somebody who listened to what I said. I tried to persuade him to take his apron off—to-day of all days—but he wouldn't."

"But he's quite right about those rooms," said Lady Evelyn. "You know, Lorna, they *are* as cold as ice. I don't really feel you should let these people stay. You've such a good excuse for not having them! After all, they were coming here to meet Christabel, and to talk about Jeffry—though why anybody should want to talk about Jeffry Hansard is more than I can understand. He never did anything that anybody could talk about."

"Mr. Donner wrote of him in very warm terms," said Lorna.

"Well, I could speak of him in warm terms. Look at all those vast sums he used to borrow from me. I'm quite certain he borrowed large sums from Mr. Donner, too."

I don't think so," said Lorna. "Mr. Donner referred to him as a—a philanthropist."

"Referred to whom?"

"To Jeffry."

"Then I think you'll find that there's been some mistake. Jeffry didn't have anything to be philanthropic *with*. I really wouldn't let the Donners stay long, if I were you, Lorna. You're tired, and besides, they'll be so uncomfortable here. Do send them off as soon as you politely can."

Lorna frowned thoughtfully.

"It isn't as simple as it sounds," she said slowly. "You see, when Christabel first got that letter—the one we argued about—she said that there were three people she'd like to put Mr. Donner in touch with—the three people who knew Jeffry best before he left Polden."

"Who would they be? My brother-in-law, George Petrie, of course—he could speak of him professionally. Who else?"

"Miss Maxwell. Did you ever meet her?"

68

"Maxwell...There was a Maxwell who made a fortune in something, and he had a daughter. Are they the ones you mean?"

"Yes. They weren't in Polden for very long. The father died just after they came here, and the girl stayed on for a little while."

"Who was the third?" asked Lady Evelyn.

"Miss Ferrier."

"Miss Ferrier...Well, she and her sister were wealthy enough; I suppose Jeffry borrowed vast sums from them, too."

"Christabel made a list with those names on it," went on Lorna. "I did my best—in the very first instance—to persuade her to write to Mr. Donner and explain that she was quite unable to meet him, and she seemed to agree with me. I never for a moment imagined that she would say one thing and do another. But she had written the names on a piece of paper and I feel bound to give it to Mr. Donner. If I'd found the list while Christabel was alive, I might have done something to stop her from. . . . But I can't suppress it now that she's dead. When I see Mr. Donner, I must give him the list, and if he feels he wants to stay here long enough to allow him to meet the three people mentioned, I can't see how I can send him away."

"The most sensible course," said Lady Evelyn, "would be to tear the list up. But I know that it's no use asking you to do that."

"In any case," I put in, "wouldn't Christabel have been

sure to send the names to Mr. Donner when she wrote to him?"

"We shall see when he arrives," said Lady Evelyn. "But in that case, he certainly can't be asked to go away."

"Could anything," asked Lorna, "have happened more awkwardly?"

"Of course it could, Lorna dear," said Lady Evelyn comfortingly. "They might have driven in just as poor Christabel was driven out. In that case, tact would have been of no use, but as it appears that they're to stay here, you'll have to be very careful how you break the news to them. You mustn't meet them at the door and just blurt it out. It would be rather unkind, and it would give them a great shock. You must say nothing just at first—let them come in and absorb it gradually."

"But how shall I explain Christabel's absence?"

"Quite, quite, quite easily. You can say that she's been called away, and it will be perfectly true. But you must warn Cluny. Claire, my dear, would you go and ask Cluny to come here?"

I went upstairs and brought him down, and he heard the decision with scorn upon his long face.

"An' what'll ye say ye've done wi' yon Christabel?"

"Just say nothing," commanded Lady Evelyn. "If I'm here when they arrive, you may leave it all to me."

"You'll be here," I said from my position at the window. "They've just driven in."

There was a concerted move to join me, and for a few moments, we stood together at the window in silence, broken only by Lady Evelyn's awed "Good gracious me!" We watched the enormous green car as it came to a stop before the front door, and I wondered how it had negotiated the narrow turns of the road leading into Polden. Cluny seemed to read my thoughts.

"It'll have a hinged tail, I doot," he said. "Shall I go an' let them in?"

"No. I'll go, Cluny," said Lorna. "What a beautiful, beautiful car. What's that figure in front."

"Yon's a silver Red Injun," said Cluny, retreating to the kitchen. "I'm tellin' ye all—they'll feel the chill o' death. They'll rue the day…"

Lorna went through the archway that led to the front door. She was out of sight, but we heard her shy greeting, and the reply in a hearty voice with an unmistakably American accent.

"Miss Hansard, this is a great pleasure. A great, great pleasure. We are both happy to know you. This is my daughter, Miss Hansard. My wife is sorry—very, very sorry—not to be with us to-day, but she was not able to make it. She's hoping to meet you one day. It'll be a great pleasure to her to come over here and get to know you, Miss Hansard."

"Not Miss Hansard," we heard Lorna say. "I'm sorry… my name is Wells. Miss Wells. I…Miss Hansard's oldest friend and companion…"

"I'm glad to know you, Miss Wells."

They had come into view, and Lorna was advancing towards us.

"This is Lady Evelyn Brunswick…this is Claire…"

Mr. Donner was happy to see us. Short, stout, bespectacled, the embodiment of beaming friendliness, he brought his daughter forward and explained, once more, how glad he was to be here. Lorna asked them to sit down, and the daughter tried to do so, but had to stop, first, to pick up a book from the chair she had been offered.

"Oh, my Prayer Book!" said Lady Evelyn. "Thank you!"

Mr. Donner appeared to find nothing extraordinary in anyone's carrying a Prayer Book about on a week-day. His daughter, however, was using her eyes. They were large, and brown, and very intelligent, and they went from the Prayer Book to other signs that the room and its inmates presented of an unusual nature. She saw Mr. Petrie's black gloves left behind on a table, and the empty cups in which Lorna had handed round coffee before the cortege left the house. There were marks of heavy boots on the staircase, and the stair carpet was disarranged as though something heavy had been carried down. The air was heavy with the scent of flowers. Lady Evelyn, Lorna and I were in unrelieved black, and upon Lorna's face were the traces of recent tears.

Miss Donner finished her survey, and turned to me with a cool, friendly smile.

"Coming here," she remarked in a level voice, "we passed a funeral."

I had nothing to say to this, but the remark brought Mr. Donner up short in the middle of an inaugural speech, and made him stare at his daughter in astonishment.

"Why, honey," he began, "I was just telling Miss Wells that we're looking forward to meeting Miss Hansard."

The brown eyes met Lorna's and held them, and the level voice spoke again:

"Yes…but I guess we're too late. We are—aren't we, Miss Wells?"

Lorna could only nod.

Chapter Five

She was twenty-two, and her name was Coolie. When we all heard it first, there was a general attempt to discover whether she had any other designation more suited to conventional English usage, but there was nothing else; she was merely Coolie.

She was small, and slender, and lovely. I shall always think of her as I saw her first, framed in the archway in the hall, with the sunlight from the open front door shining on her hair. I took in everything, I suppose, at that first glance— but even then I had no sense of danger. That she could be formidable, of course, I recognised, but I saw her as a passing stranger; she was here to-day, but to-morrow, or the next day, Mr. Donner's business would be concluded and they would both be gone. So I took in, without uneasiness, every detail of the picture she made—and every detail was perfect.

Money can't do much for some women; it can't give them good features or a good figure, or even a good sense of dress. For others—and Coolie Donner was among them— money can buy a gloss and a finish that places them beyond the reach of competitors. Everything Coolie wore, everything she possessed, was just so much more finished, so much lovelier, than anything I had seen before.

There are women who look their best in a ballroom; others—and I'm one of them—who should be seen in the open, and to whom a bitter January wind brings only a Christmas-card glow. Coolie's perfection never left her. I was to see her indoors and out; I was to see her at every moment of the day, and well into the night. I was to see her in bed in the morning and tired in the evening; I was to see her in tweeds, in taffeta, in pink pyjamas and blue jeans, but I was never to see her looking anything but—no other word will do—perfect. Lovely clothes, of course, had a great deal to do with it, but they weren't the whole story. I think that what lay beneath her unchanging attractiveness was her simple acceptance of the fact that everything she wanted in the world was hers. And always had been. From birth there had lain to her hand everything that she needed to make her physically and mentally outstanding.

She wasn't outstanding mentally—if that is taken to mean that she had attained any great level of scholarship. Her schooling, as such, appeared to have died, unregretted, at a very early age—when I was nine and Coolie fourteen. But she had good sense and a clear outlook and a shrewdness that came, we discovered, from her mother. She had her father's honesty and simplicity and friendly disposition; she had her mother's passion for getting things straight. It was a deadly combination.

She was the neatest person I ever saw. Her luggage— outwardly—was beautiful: matching, expensive, the last word in travel luxury. But the contents, as I saw when I helped Coolie to unpack them—had the same niceness. She had been away from home for nearly two months; she had driven through cities, through the desert; she had unpacked, stayed a day or two, and then packed again. My own luggage, under those conditions, would have shown a disorder bordering on frenzy, but there was nothing frenzied about Coolie's effects. Everything was clean, neat and in order.

She was not, after all, to pass so soon. Mr. Donner was severely shaken by the news of Christabel's death, and made preparations to leave at once, but Lady Evelyn had other ideas. She had looked him over, talked to him and arrived at the conclusion that he was just the kind of person she most liked. It was an opinion which she was never to change, and one which Mr. Donner reciprocated fully. The thought of moving the visitors on, or keeping them for a short time only, gave way to a strong move on Lady Evelyn's part to induce them to settle permanently. It was not her house, but she pressed as warmly as Lorna.

"You mustn't dream of going, Mr. Donner," she said. "And, besides, there's nowhere to go. There's nothing in Grayleigh, and only a quite unsuitable Inn at Polden. You'd have to go to the King's Head at Allchester, and you wouldn't like that at all. Miss Wells has had your fires lit for you, and you'll be very comfortable here. Your rooms are nowhere near Christabel's; she was on the other side of the house, right away by herself—wasn't she, Lorna? Of course you must stay."

It was obvious that they must stay for a night, at least, and Lorna took Mr. Donner up to his room. I was deputed to take Coolie to hers, and I led her upstairs and ushered her into the huge, cheerless chamber and waited until Cluny had brought the luggage in and placed it in a neat row against the wall.

"Is that all ye'll be wantin'?" he enquired.

"Yes, thank you, Cluny."

"The room's no' verra warm; ye'd better keep your coat on," he advised Coolie, who looked as if she had every intention of doing so. "I can turn yon fire up if ye're wantin' it higher, but it burns an awfu' lot of gas."

"That's all right, Cluny," I said.

"There's nobody been in this room since the Jubilee year, and it'll be awfu' damp. Ye'd be better—"

"That's all, Cluny, thank you."

Cluny withdrew reluctantly, and I shut the door and glanced at Coolie. She was looking round the room with the mild, enquiring look one wears when going round a museum. Lorna, fresh from settling Mr. Donner into his quarters, looked in with an enquiry.

"Are you sure you'll be comfortable?"

Coolie was sure.

"You've got your own bathroom," said Lorna, going downstairs.

Coolie advanced hopefully towards a door, and I stopped her.

"No—not there. That leads to the other staircase. It's this way."

I led her out into the corridor and along to a door at one end. I opened this and we went down three steps and along another passage and up two stairs to another door, which I opened.

"This is yours," I said. "Nobody else will use it. Your father has one at his side of the house."

Coolie gazed in simple wonder at the huge bath, which was raised on a platform and looked unpleasantly like a coffin on a bier. Above it was an old-fashioned geyser; beyond was a large wash-basin surmounted by a mirror. Farther on, discreetly placed, was what Lady Evelyn referred to as the So-and-So.

We returned to the bedroom and Coolie picked up a heavier coat and slipped into it.

"Will you be warm?" I asked anxiously. "This house is…"

She gave me a friendly little grin and assured me that she would be very warm. I spent some time upstairs, helping her to unpack—perhaps my helpfulness had as much curiosity in it as good nature—and then we walked downstairs, to find Lorna in the kitchen preparing lunch and Lady Evelyn sitting in the hall with Mr. Donner, deep in conversation.

"Come and sit down." She patted the sofa and indicated a chair; Coolie sat on the sofa, but I remained standing.

"Darling," I said to Lady Evelyn, "it's almost time we went. Stephen will be here to fetch us at any moment."

"Stephen is my grandson," explained Lady Evelyn. "He's taken a farm here, and I'm living with him. You must come and see us, both of you. It's very tumbledown, but I think you'll find it warmer there than you will here. This house, Mr. Donner, should be thoroughly heated—it gets colder year by year. And damper."

"What will happen to it now?" enquired Mr. Donner.

"Goodness knows. It's been left to Miss Wells, but she won't be able to keep it up. Christabel couldn't keep it up. When I left England, long ago, old Miss Emily Hansard was alive and the place was kept beautifully. Beautifully. She had a good deal of money, you know. I don't know how Christabel could bear to watch the place falling into ruin. If I'd been here, I should have insisted on being allowed to do something to keep it up—what is the use of money if you can't use it to help your friends?—but by the time I came back to England, the place was as you see it—a shell. I don't know what Lorna plans to do, but if she wants to stay on here, she'll have to let me do something. This house wants vast sums spent on it, and it'll repay every penny."

"It's a fine building," agreed Mr. Donner.

Lady Evelyn studied him for a few moments and leaned forward. I knew by her carefully controlled eagerness that she had been struck by one of her brighter ideas, and I felt apprehensive on Mr. Donner's account.

"It's obvious, Mr. Donner," she said, "that you must stay among us—for at any rate a little while."

He agreed, cautiously, that he would like to "see this thing through," but added that it ought to take very little time.

"I think it's going to take longer than you imagine," said Lady Evelyn, with some satisfaction. "You see, before Christabel died, she made out a little list of people who—"

She paused; Mr Donner had taken out a bundle of papers from his pocket, and was extracting one of them.

"I have that list here," he said. "Miss Hansard sent me these three names, but I understand they're all local people, and I can get to see them and—"

"They're not as local as you think," said Lady Evelyn. "In fact, one of them isn't here any more. After having come so far, don't you feel that it's a mistake to rush things?"

"I want to do this thing—"

"—thoroughly. I think you're very wise. It's silly to hurry away now that you *have* come. You've got to see my brother-in-law, poor old George Petrie, and you've got to see Miss Ferrier, who's got a charming little cottage that you'll enjoy very much—and you've also got to get hold of somebody called Miss Maxwell, who isn't here any more. So what I've been thinking—and I think you'll agree that it's a splendid idea—is this: why don't you go to Lorna and suggest staying on here for a time as p.g.'s?"

"As—?"

"As paying guests. You and your daughter, as paying guests. Don't you agree that it would be a very sensible plan?

It would help Lorna a great deal, if she'd agree to it, and it would make you feel more comfortable. It would be a thoroughly good move all round. I suggest your asking her if she would put you up for a time, and do it on a business footing. What could be better?"

Mr. Donner felt that a lot of things could be better, but he found it difficult to put them into words without seeming churlish. He was to give Lady Evelyn pleasure and Lorna profit; there was no mention in it of anything for himself. He was to stay on at the Lodge—of which he had had, so far, the merest but most unencouraging glimpse. He was to sleep in the frigid bedroom, and pass his days in this glacial hall. He was to put up with the idiosyncrasies of the geyser and the oddities of the plumbing and…

"You mustn't be hurt," said Lady Evelyn, noting his hesitation, "if Lorna refuses."

"No—oh, no!"

"Then I'll put it to her and tell her that you insist. I'll put it to her very strongly."

"That's…you're very kind," said Mr. Donner dejectedly.

"Not at all. We don't often get charming people like you and your daughter coming to visit us, and I'm going to take care to keep you here as long as possible. I do wish your wife had been able to come with you. You must miss her very much."

"How much," said Mr. Donner sadly, "nobody could realise."

"Then you must cable to her and tell her that you're staying on at this address for a time—then you'll get your letters far more quickly than if they have to be readdressed from somewhere else. Now we'll go and talk to Lorna at once, and get the matter settled."

Thus hedged about, Mr. Donner talked to Lorna, and the matter was settled. Lady Evelyn settled it. He and Coolie were to be p.g.'s, or paying guests. Coolie's only comment was to turn the collar of her coat up more snugly round her neck.

"If you want me at any time," I said to her, under cover of the general conversation, "you'll find me down at the farm. It's not far along the road; come down whenever you want to."

"Your farm?"

"No. I just work there. I help Stephen Brunswick—Lady Evelyn's grandson."

"How old is Stephen Brunswick?"

"He's twenty-eight."

"Is he like his grandmother?"

I glanced across at Lady Evelyn and smiled.

"She's a pet," I said.

"She keeps pets," corrected Coolie. "She's just got herself a new one. Do you live at the farm?"

"No. I live at the Vicarage, with my uncle."

Coolie studied me and then gave me a friendly little smile. "Sounds kind of over-exciting," she said. "Living at the Vicarage and working on the farm, I mean. Where do you go for extra amusement?"

"Oh—I ride a bit, and play tennis in summer, and swim—"

"Is there anybody here," enquired Coolie, "you'd say was young?"

"Well—no. They all go away. There isn't much to keep anybody here, you know. Is this your first visit to England?"

"Yes."

"I hope you'll like it."

"Is it all like this?" enquired Coolie anxiously.

"Like Polden? Good Heavens, no!"

"Then I may get used to it. Up to now, it feels kind of… slow."

"As soon as your father gets through this business of his, you must go up to Scotland and see some real country. You mustn't stay here."

I was to remember the words later, but when I remembered them, it was with the realisation that she had stayed… too long.

I took her into the kitchen, at her request, to talk to Cluny, and watched them get on to friendly terms at once.

"Ye'll no' find anything in this country," he told her. "Ye'll have to get over the Border an' keep on going. Then ye'll see somethin' to feast your eyes on. Aye, ye'll see something. Ye'll find nothing worth looking at this side of the Tweed. Where d'ye come from over there?"

"Prophet, Arizona."

"Arizona. I doot I'll get to see Arizona," said Cluny. "There'll be more room there to drive yon great motor-car ye came here in. Ye won't find room on these roads to go speedin'."

"What'll you bet?" enquired Coolie. 'I'll take you out and show you, any time you say."

Cluny surveyed her from his great height, and she looked up at him with the small, cool smile which I was to get to know so well. But I didn't have time to look at it just then; I had been listening for footsteps, and I heard them now, and went into the hall. Stephen was just coming through the archway, and he smiled at me before his eyes came to rest on Mr. Donner.

Lady Evelyn introduced the two men, and Mr. Donner gazed up at Stephen for a long time without self-consciousness, and with only amazement on his face.

"Why now!" he exclaimed at last. "My, my, but you're a big guy! You must be all of six feet two."

"Three," said Stephen. "That's quite a car you've got out there."

"The girls like it," said Mr. Donner, beaming. "My wife chose it; my daughter wanted another colour, and I let them settle it between them. So they fetched up with this one, and we haven't had any trouble on the road since we got it. Not a mite. Except when we got as far as your roads around here —

84

and then it looked like we'd have to make it more flexible to manage those curves. But we made it—in time. It was kind of slow, though; my daughter's used to keeping the needle up in the nineties, and she couldn't get up above forty the last few miles."

"If she goes past the farm at forty," promised Stephen, "I'll make her pluck all the corpses with her own hands, and cook them."

The word 'corpses' recalled everybody to a sense of the present, and in the somewhat uncomfortable silence that followed Stephen's remark, it seemed to me that weeks, and not hours, had gone by since the sombre events of the morning. Stephen looked at his grandmother and broke the silence.

"We'll have to be getting back," he said. "Claire, are you coming, or can I take the car?"

"I'm coming," I said. "But you'd better meet Coolie first."

"Coolie?"

"Mr. Donner's daughter. She's in the kitchen. I'll go and fetch her."

And I did. It's fantastic, but I did. I went into the kitchen —smiling—and said, "Come and meet Stephen." Four words; a brief prelude. But I didn't know that this was to be a prelude, and if I had known, I don't see what I could have done to prevent what came afterwards. He and she...they had to meet; already Lady Evelyn and Mr. Donner were fast friends, and Coolie was to be here for some time.

But on that morning I thought of nothing but the fact that I wanted to be in the car beside Stephen, driving back to the farm, where I was to work with him to make up for our absence during the morning. I was anxious to get away from the Lodge and change into my working clothes and get on with all that was waiting to be done—but Stephen couldn't go until he had met Coolie, and so I went and brought Coolie in.

It was all over in a moment, and nothing happened. The air didn't vibrate with sinister whispers; my heart gave no warning. My guardian angels appeared to be off duty. Mr. Donner smiled his pride in his lovely daughter; Lady Evelyn said, "She's only half his size. Isn't it absurd?"

I said "Coolie, this is Stephen," and Coolie looked up and smiled and put her hand into his. There was nothing even faintly disturbing in the sight of them standing there together. He said, "Hello, Coolie"—and then we went away and took Lady Evelyn with us. Stephen drove and I sat beside him with Lady Evelyn on the other side of me. The wind blew her scarf across my face and I removed it to ask:

"What did you think of her?"

"She's a sweet little thing," said Lady Evelyn, "but it's Mr. Donner I like. Stephen, isn't he a *nice* man?"

"They both seem pretty decent," said Stephen. "Claire, how did Granny behave."

Chapter Six

Polden had fixed ideas about the American male: he wore a wide-brimmed hat, horn-rimmed glasses and startling ties, and said, "I guess." Mr. Donner did, said and wore exactly what was expected of him, and with this initial advantage was not long in winning Polden over completely. He was a man who loved his fellow men, especially when they would stop doing whatever they were doing and talk to him. He was as free with details of his own life as he was eager for details of other people's. He had no reserves; his origin, his early and recent experiences, his abiding love for his wife, Verna—all these facts he placed freely before the Poldenese, who were gratified but bewildered, since they found themselves deprived of the opportunity to use their well-organised system for extracting information from strangers.

I came to know more about Verna than anybody had ever told me about my own mother—whom I had never known. Verna's looks, her height and weight, where she had first met Mr. Donner and how long it had taken her to return his passion; her business ability, her skill in all the domestic arts and her golf handicap—I learned them all. If Verna ever passed me in the street, I should know her at once, and so would everybody else in Polden.

Some of us thought that Verna Donner sounded an odd combination, but it was agreed that Bella Donner would have been worse. Our only wonder—why Mr. Donner had ever consented to leave her in America—he soon cleared up: Verna had remained at home to nurse her sister, who needed her. Her letters, collected twice weekly by Mr. Donner to save Roly the journey up to the Lodge, kept us all informed of what was going on in Prophet, Arizona, and I cannot describe our feelings towards him better than by saying that we looked forward to her news almost as much as he did. The United States, which—for the majority of those in Polden St. Peter— had been obscured, hitherto, behind a fog of dollar gaps and aid-to-everybody, now emerged, clear and shining and greatly respected, in the portly person of Mr. Donner.

Mr. Donner liked the Poldenese as much as they liked him. Some of his pleasure in their society may have been caused by the fact that nobody wanted to get anything out of him. There was no tourist trade in the village; if it had been marked in any guide-book, Polden would have been described as something it would be as well to avoid—like the gypsies in the wood. Nobody had anything to sell at inflated prices; nobody was contemplating a journey in the course of which dollars might come in useful; nobody had ever heard of Anglo-American get-together. But everybody liked the little man who displayed such unaccountable interest in the school and the church and the Institute and Mrs. Howard's sweet peas; the men enjoyed initiating him into the merits of the various makes of beer; the women liked to hear about Verna's kitchen fitments and her washing- machine, and the children liked the things—usually edible— that he always carried in his pocket.

Polden was not a dull place—or perhaps it was such a dull place that those in it had to find amusement for themselves. To anybody like Mr. Donner, who had time to listen to the local gossip and who had a companion like Lady Evelyn, eager to impart it, there was no lack of interest or even sensation. The young people went out of Polden, but they did amazing things in the world before they returned to grow old in the quietness and seclusion they had once been so eager to leave. We had our characters. There was old Ned Lewis, who had jumped overboard on a dark night only sixty-eight years ago and—he could show you the official notice—"when the ship was under sail, going four and a half knots before the wind, the seas high and dangerous and abounding with sharks"—in went Ned to rescue a comrade, and having rescued him, kept him afloat with one hand, and with the other, began to free himself of his heavy clothing. But the comrade sank once more, taking Ned with him by the trousers, and only the fact that they were half off and "luckily came clear," enabled rescuer and rescued to get to the surface and remain there until a boat picked them up. The grocer's grandfather had been knocked off his horse by a cannon-ball in the Crimea—a forty-two-pound shot. The baker's great-uncle had played billiards with the great John

Roberts, and his grandfather, who was called Sabine Condor, had served in the gunboat *Condor* at the bombardment of Alexandria and received the Admiral's signal, "Well done, Condor," as congratulations of a strictly private and personal nature. Mr. Faudine, the barber, had once been a snake- keeper at the Zoo, and the walls of the Faudine cottage were covered with photographs showing him with boa-constrictors round his neck; his children had kept baby crocodiles in the bathtub. Mr. Donner, who came from a country where, he said, the best reporters rose from a snake story, and who had one or two good ones in his own repertory, ceded the record unhesitatingly to Mr. Faudine after their first meeting.

Mr. Faudine's stories had the unfair advantage of being true, and were backed by a breath-taking range of practical knowledge. It was from him that I first learned that a pig has a hearty contempt for the so-called deadly fascination of snakes. A pig, said Mr. Faudine, will treat a rattlesnake as you would a toothsome morsel. Stephen said that I could get a pig whenever I wanted to, but the rattlesnake was a difficulty, so I have to take this—like all Mr. Faudine's stories—on trust. But if snakes don't fascinate, snake stories do; nobody in Polden felt the lack of a cinema while Mr. Faudine had a tongue and could use it with such artistry.

Then we had old Mrs. Bletchington, who had a strange and wonderful collection of old playing-cards—some of them mere fragments dating from the fifteenth century. There was my uncle's fine collection of organ records, and Colonel

Price's cabinet full of old snuff-boxes. And there was Mr. Mc-
Bride, who had written a history of weathercocks and vanes,
and offered to take Mr. Donner on an all-England tour to point
out the better examples.

On the debit side, there was Wilfred Stone, who now spent
his time taking exquisite Nature photographs, but who was ru-
moured to have grown independent by stationing himself and
his camera at the corner of busy London streets taking imag-
inary photographs of middle-aged ladies as they approached
him, and extracting half crowns from them in exchange for
his promise to send them a postcard-size enlargement. It takes
more than a camera to make a success of a career like that; it
needs Wilfred's look of utter solidity and dependability. There
were the Galbraith brothers, who had made a great deal of
money out of Seasurf Fish Paste before the unduly curious
began to make enquiries about the ingredients that had been
used in its preparation. Seasurf Fish Paste went abruptly out
of production, and the brothers had retired to a little cottage in
Polden and attended church regularly every Sunday.

Mr. Donner got to know them and to like them all. He
came and went among them, and by his side was always Lady
Evelyn. It was plain, from the outset, that they were twin
souls. They were both great talkers, but they were also good
listeners; when she had spoken of Polden, Lady Evelyn liked
to hear some news of Prophet; then it was Mr. Donner's turn
to talk, and she was content to listen. They went into Polden
together every morning, shopping, talking, exchanging views

with the villagers and sometimes taking photographs to send to Verna. Mr. Donner carried the string bag and the umbrella, and taught the dogs to come to heel; he did all Lorna's shopping, called at the farmhouse for Lady Evelyn and brought her back again at the end of the expeditions. He carried packages, ran errands and became a familiar figure in the life of Polden.

It was natural that Coolie should seek young society, and she came to spend more and more time at the farm. She looked at me while I worked, and I looked at her when she wasn't looking at me. She came down in clothes and shoes that looked—as she did—both sensible and pretty. Sometimes she walked into the village with her father and Lady Evelyn; sometimes she walked up to the Vicarage and talked to my uncle about his chest; she was in and out of Cluny's kitchen. She sought out Stephen and, with complete naturalness and her father's brand of simple, inoffensive curiosity, asked him questions which showed almost more interest in the cows than in Stephen himself. She was pleasing to the eye, fresh to the ear; interested, in her calm way, in everything and everybody. It was impossible not to like her.

I found that she was no stranger to country life; Mr. Donner owned a ranch in Arizona, and Coolie had spent a lot of time on it. He also owned a house in Florida, a yacht in Bermuda, a villa in Mexico and an apartment in New York. I was not surprised to learn—by degrees—the extent of his wealth and possessions, but I was puzzled to account for the fact that, in spite of the quiet good taste that characterised everything that Coolie owned, she looked rich. My mother's family once owned a house in London, a castle in Scotland, a chalet in Switzerland and a houseboat in Kashmir, but, judging by the photographs in my uncle's possession, you would never have thought so when you looked at her. Coolie once asked Stephen, when we were idling together, what he had thought of when he first set eyes on her, and Stephen answered, simply: "Money." Most people, answering with equal honesty, would have said the same. I think it was that serene air of hers—her way of carrying her clothes, her accessories, her possessions; her complete lack of self- consciousness. Whatever it was, it impressed the onlooker far more than any display of pride or arrogance would have done.

There was little or no curiosity in Polden with regard to the real object of Mr. Donner's visit. Jeffry Hansard was remembered, if he was remembered at all, as a tall, quiet young man who lived with his aunt and worked for Mr. Petrie at Allchester. He had taken no part in the life of the village, and his frequent coming and going had become so natural, that nobody noticed, at last, that he had gone for good. By the time the fact became known, most people had lost interest in him; Polden had forgotten him. Only in the minds of those most closely associated with him was there anything for Mr. Donner to draw on; to mention Jeffry Hansard to the ordinary people of the village—as Mr. Donner hopefully did—was to be met by blank stares. Mr. Donner's enthusiasm for the task of collecting material about him, so warm on his arrival in Polden, cooled a little in this general lack of interest. He was obviously surprised at finding that so little was known of him—for Jeffry Hansard, whatever he was to Polden, was an object of great admiration in Prophet.

Mr. Donner had met him in Florida; the two had become friendly, and Mr. Donner had spoken a great deal of his own town. It is easy to see how, under his loving hand, the picture of Prophet would emerge for Jeffry Hansard as it had emerged for us. We knew its streets and shops and its leading citizens; we knew the great hospital, built by the citizens of Prophet, but famous throughout the United States. It was to this hospital that Jeffry Hansard came, shortly after Mr. Donner's return to Prophet after meeting him; it was in this hospital that he had died, and it was to this hospital that he had left his entire fortune, amounting to almost half a million dollars. It was the members of the Hospital Board who, learning of Mr. Donner's projected visit to North Africa, had proposed his extending his trip and coming to England to learn something about the man to whom they owed so much.

They had sent Mr. Donner a token of their regard: a small bronze plaque which they wanted placed—if no objection was raised by the owners— on the house in which Jeffry Hansard had been born. Lorna had raised no objection; she had told Mr. Donner that he could put up the plaque wherever he wished, and, after consultation with Lady Evelyn, it had been decided that it should be placed to the right of the heavy oak front door.

This matter being settled, Mr. Donner decided that it was time to pay a visit to the first person mentioned on Christabel's list, and a day or so later, I heard from Coolie that her father was to go over to Allchester to see Mr. Petrie. He asked Lady Evelyn to go with him, and Coolie drove them over in the big green car.

She walked over to the farm on the following morning, and I saw the first crease that I had ever seen on her smooth brow. She pulled out a particularly appetising-looking straw from a stack, and sampled it in silence; after a time she removed it from between her lips and looked at me absently.

"This guy we went to see yesterday," she said, in her leisurely way. "D'you know him?"

"Mr. Petrie? Yes, of course; I've known him since I was so high."

"He's kind of funny, wouldn't you say?" asked Coolie.

"Funny? You mean odd?"

"Yes." She drew out the sound, making it sound more like Yeah. "Yes; that's what I mean. Odd. Wouldn't you say he was odd?"

"Not odd—no," I said. "I think he's…I don't know how to put it, quite. I think there's something *haunted* about him. He gives me a lump in my throat sometimes."

"Oh!" Coolie chewed the other end of the straw. "Well, that isn't what I felt."

"Didn't you like him?"

"I liked him all right. But what I felt was, he wasn't doing any talking."

"Talking?"

"Ye-ah." Issuing from any other pair of lips, it would have been an unmusical sound. Coolie made it sound very soft and attractive. Even her name for her father—which she pronounced "Parp"—had a musical sound.

"I don't understand," I said.

"Me, too," confessed Coolie. "I've been thinking about it, last night and to-day, and I'm kind of at sea."

"Well—why?"

"I'll tell you why. Lady Evelyn and Pop and me—we went over there to Allchester to see this Mr. Petrie and ask him all about Mr. Hansard—right?"

"Quite right."

"Quite right. Well, we get over there, and we talk. I don't talk, but Pop talks, and Lady Evelyn talks. The only one who doesn't do any talking is that Mr. Petrie. Now—why?"

"You mean he didn't say anything at all?" I asked in astonishment.

"He sat there," said Coolie, "and he said plenty. But he didn't talk. I don't know how you say it in good English, but I'm telling it to you in good American—that guy acted like a clam."

We looked at one another, and that was when I first realised how intelligent she was. I'd rather underrated her until that moment; she hadn't any of the qualifications I'd been used to finding in educated people. She knew nothing about pictures, unless they were the moving kind; she knew nothing about music, except of the lightest and latest brand; she used her fingers for adding up, her history was sketchy and she thought that Fiji was one of the Hawaiian Islands. So I'd rather written her off intellectually, and I was surprised to find, in the eyes looking into mine, a cool and calculating look that not only checked up on whether I understood what she was trying to say, but also on how much I was going to be able to enlighten her. Coolie had a brain, and she was using it. Having satisfied herself that my surprise at her remarks was genuine, she went on to state her problem.

"There's something," she said, "that I can't work out. I thought that if I came and asked you about it, you could help me."

"Well, ask me."

"All right." Coolie leaned against a wall and brought her facts out in orderly procession. "First, Pop meets this guy, Jeffry Hansard, and sells him Prophet, Arizona."

"Yes."

"Then Mr. Hansard comes to Prophet, and dies in Prophet. And he gives the hospital all he had."

"All he died possessed of."

"Yes; that. And so we all say, back home, that it isn't right to take all that money from a fellow without doing something to show we're grateful. And so they ask Pop to bring over this tablet thing and put it up so's Grayleigh can see how grateful we are. Are you with me?"

"Yes."

"So we come, and Pop wants to take back all the dope on Jeffry Hansard. And it sounded easy, back home; you come to the guy's birthplace, to the place he lived in—off and on—until he left the country for good. But when we come here, then it doesn't look so easy."

"I can understand that," I said. "I don't want to sound disparaging, but you see, although you thought a good deal of Mr. Hansard over there, nobody here knew very much about him. He didn't have any roots here. For example, take my own experience: I was born here and I spent almost all my holidays here all my life, but though I was in and out of the Lodge, and knew Christabel and Lorna for all those years, I never heard anybody mention Jeffry—or if they did, it wasn't more than a casual reference. He just didn't seem to...well, to be a personality at all. He doesn't seem to have left any impression."

"Christabel is dead, and can't talk," said Coolie. "Lorna is here, but she seems to have been on the way out of Grayleigh every time Jeffry Hansard was on his way in. But this Mr. Petrie—he was the head of that office there in Allchester, where Mr. Hansard worked. Everybody who can scratch up any fact about him says that even out of office hours he spent far more time with the Petries than he did with his own Aunt Emily at the Lodge. So you'd naturally expect Mr. Petrie to be able to say something about what Pop wants to know—wouldn't you?"

"Well, yes."

"But whether he knows it or not," said Coolie, "Mr. Petrie didn't say it."

"You mean he—refused?"

"Refuse nothing. He bowed us in like somebody out of a history book, and we went into a little dark room and sat there while Lady Evelyn told us about how the place next door used to be an old coaching inn, and how it came to be what it is, and etcetera and etcetera. I was glad to hear her voice—the room was kind of creepy, all small and gloomy, with that window looking out on to that tired kind of garden, and Mr. Petrie in dark clothes, and Lady Evelyn in black. Pop and I looked the only living things there—us and the cat, but that was black, too. Then Pop moved the conversation round to Mr. Hansard, and Mr. Petrie said he'd be glad to tell him anything, anything—and then he didn't tell him anything, any<u>thing</u>. And what I'm asking you"—Coolie pointed the straw at me—"is… *why?*"

"That's fairly easy," I said. "He's old and he's tired, and he didn't really grasp what you were there for."

"He grasped all right."

"He remembers Jeffry Hansard simply as a junior partner, and not perhaps a particularly satisfactory one— that seems well established. He can't speak much for a man who was more out of his office than he was in it."

"And what about the other angle—the home-life angle? He didn't even say that Jeffry Hansard had ever been in his house!"

"No—because that would mean bringing in his wife's name, and he'd find that painful. He felt her death very keenly, and he never talks about her. He wasn't exactly a cheerful man when she was alive, but at least he looked less ghost-like than he does now. I honestly think you got out of him all you're going to get, Coolie."

"That's what I think, too. But I'm telling you, and I know I'm right—he wasn't *talking.* Look, Claire, Pop's a great fellow, and there's nobody like him on this side of the Atlantic or on that—but he and Lady Evelyn are both out of the same pod. They both like to know things, and they both go around asking questions, and what they learn is just what anybody likes to tell them. Pop—without Verna—would be anybody's money. Pop thinks that everybody's on the level. Now and then he finds out that somebody isn't, and then it knocks him—for a while. Now you take this Jeffry Hansard. Pop takes a trip to Florida, and meets him; he takes a fancy to him and gives our town such a build-up, that soon we have him coming to live in it. I met him, and so did Verna. We didn't see much of him, because he was a pretty sick man, and he kept to himself. Nobody saw him much— nobody except Pop. And when he died and left all that money, the town was grateful to Pop because he'd been, in a way, the reason it had come to the hospital. But what I'm trying to tell you is that nobody over there knew the first thing about him—about Mr. Hansard. We thought—if we thought at all—that he went over to America a rich man, because nobody ever traced any business connections he might have had. But everybody figured he must have been rich when he was here in England—and the first thing we find when we come over here is that he didn't have anything at all. What's more, he goes round borrowing—"

"Oh, wait a minute," I said. "You mustn't take what Lady Evelyn says—"

"It isn't only her; what little you do get to know about him all proves that he hadn't any money."

"But didn't Mr. Petrie—"

"He's a lawyer, Claire, and they come *smooth.* Pop asked a lot of questions and he answered every one of them. Pop got out the little notebook that he's writing down all the facts in, and he wrote so much, he got cramp. But I wasn't writing—I was listening, and I was watching, and I'm telling you that Mr. Petrie made a detour round every question Pop asked him. Oh—Pop's satisfied! Pop came away with his book half filled. But you can't write and keep your eyes on someone all at the same time, so he didn't see what I saw, and Mr. Petrie isn't the bumbling old fellow you make him out to be. He looked to me like he was on the witness stand, and I could see him counting ten before he answered anything. He knows something, Claire, that he didn't want Pop to know. He wasn't talking!"

That was all she said, and she went away shortly afterwards, but before she went I had made a promise that I would talk to Lorna and ask her what she knew of Jeffry Hansard. And when she left, I thought over what she had told me about Mr. Petrie and laid it in my mind side by side with two other incidents—his shaken appearance on hearing Jeffry Hansard's name in his room on that afternoon after my ride with Stephen, and his silence in the car when I drove him over to Polden on the morning of the funeral and told him that somebody was coming to the Lodge to talk about Jeffry Hansard.

I couldn't imagine Mr. Petrie as a sinister figure in a plot, but I would have liked to know what lay behind his obvious disinclination to discuss the subject. I wasn't interested in Jeffry Hansard, but I would have liked someone to explain why Christabel, who was his cousin, Lorna, who was his contemporary and childhood playmate, and Mr. Petrie, who was his partner, had never, before the advent of Mr. Donner's letter, mentioned his name. When I thought about it for a few moments, I felt that there was a simple explanation: twenty-five or thirty years had gone by since his departure, and he had probably been regarded as long dead; since he appeared to have had little connection with the life of Polden, he had been long forgotten. The instinct which had prevented me from telling Coolie what I had seen when Mr. Petrie heard Jeffry Hansard's name, now persuaded me that there was nothing in his emotion except shock at having the veil between past and present drawn too swiftly aside. I was glad that I had said nothing.

But all the same, I walked up to the Lodge that afternoon

to see what Lorna could tell me about the matter. I found her standing at the front door, talking to a stonemason and pointing out to him the place that the plaque was to occupy, and the man, after taking some measurements, went indoors and left us together. I felt that the plaque gave me something to open with.

"What's going to happen?" I asked. "Is he going to put it up now?"

"Oh dear me, no," said Lorna. 'It won't go up for some days. He only came to take some measurements."

"What's written on it?"

"On the tablet? It's quite a simple inscription—just a few words: *To Jeffry Hansard*, and a line or two about being grateful to him. Mr. Donner would like to show it to you— you must ask him when you see him."

"I will."

"It'll blend in rather well with these stones, and it won't look glaring, as I was rather afraid it might."

"It seems odd to me," I said, "to see a memorial going up to a man who seems to have been completely forgotten by everybody here."

"There's nothing odd about it, Claire dear. People leave their native shores and go away, quite unknown. Then they make a name for themselves in a new place—but the memorial is put up in the place where they were born. You find tablets of this kind on a lot of houses, but the person's fame is very rarely a—if I can use the expression—local fame. It's—"

"Did you know him well, Lorna?" I asked.

"Jeffry? Well—yes and no. I was in and out of Polden and Grayleigh all my life, but I didn't really settle down here until Christabel sent for me—when she became ill. But by that time Jeffry had been gone for years."

"But before that—you must remember quite a lot about him. Was he a *good* man?"

Lorna stooped to pull up a weed that had pushed its way through the gravel at our feet.

"Good...bad. Nobody's entirely one or the other," she said. "A man who leaves all his money to a hospital is, I'd say, a good man."

"But a bad man could do that—on the you-can't-take-it-with-you principle."

It was quite the wrong thing to say to Lorna, and I knew that I had offended her.

"It was a good deed," she said slowly, and with a great deal of emphasis. "It's very easy to take credit away from people, and it's done far too often. I'm sorry to see you belittling the good that someone has done, Claire. Jeffry Hansard's last act was to leave money for a good purpose; you can't wipe out that by—"

"I'm sorry. I wasn't belittling anything," I said. "I only wanted to clear up something."

I waited, half absently, for her to ask me what I wanted

to clear up, but I saw to my astonishment that she had turned and was walking slowly into the house. My surprise made me forget the leading-up phrases I had prepared, and I followed her and spoke bluntly.

"Lorna—*was* there anything about Jeffry Hansard?"

She turned and looked at me with something very like anger.

"Anything?"

"Yes. Was he? I'm only asking because Coolie thought that when they went over to see Mr. Petrie, he was keeping something back."

"Mr. Petrie," said Lorna, "is an entirely trustworthy man in every way."

"I know. Nobody said he wasn't. I'm not particularly interested, but nobody likes to think that there's anything mysterious going on. Mr. Petrie must know more about Jeffry Hansard than anybody else does, but if so, why didn't he talk about him?"

"Mr. Donner filled a great many pages in his notebook. He showed them to me."

Perhaps I shouldn't have done it, but I was getting the feeling that she was trying to mislead me, and so I drove her into a corner by a direct question. Lorna could be evasive, but she couldn't lie.

"Did he tell him any important facts?" I asked.

I saw the colour leave her cheeks, and regretted my question at once. My curiosity had become keener, but it wasn't keen enough to make me hurt Lorna. I said nothing for a few moments, and the silence gave her a chance to recover herself. But a glance at her face, with its set expression, told me that nothing would be gained by even direct questioning; she was on her guard.

"I do hope, Claire," she said presently, "that you won't encourage Coolie to go round building up mysteries out of nothing. It's a silly habit, and it raises absurd ideas in people's minds and makes them gossip—all over nothing. You're such a sensible girl as a rule; do try to influence Coolie not to talk nonsense."

"But—"

"Seriously, Claire, can you imagine George Petrie deliberately deceiving a nice man like Mr. Donner?"

"No, I can't. But—"

"Then we'll say no more about it. Now, there was something I wanted to ask you to do for me. Will you drive me in to Allchester one day soon? I want to see the nuns; I think they're going to make me an offer for the house."

"Oh—are you going to sell it?"

"I think so; I hope so. They plan to use it for a very good purpose—they talk of opening a comfortable sort of home for people who aren't able to look after themselves. It's not more than a suggestion at present, but if it does happen, I shall be able to stay on here and work, and I should like that."

"I'll drive you over whenever you like."

"Thank you, Claire. Now I must go in. This man is waiting to see me about those measurements."

She was gone, and I was left standing on the step. The familiar house looked less familiar than it had done when I saw it ten minutes earlier, and Lorna, after my lifelong acceptance of her as a gentle and kind but completely transparent figure, now appeared as unfamiliar as the house.

I stood there wondering why—if anybody had wanted to hide any facts concerning Jeffry Hansard—Mr. Donner should have been encouraged to come and make enquiries about him. Then I remembered that it was only Christabel who had wanted him to come, and that raised another question in my mind: did Christabel know nothing herself, or had she known something and thought that Mr. Donner ought to know it too?

But it was no use asking Lorna, for Lorna, like Mr. Petrie—had counted ten before answering any questions. She, like Mr. Petrie, had made a detour. She had brushed me aside and had changed the subject.

Lorna was not talking, either.

Chapter Seven

On my way down to the farm the next morning, I thought over my talk with Lorna, and came to the conclusion that it would be sensible to tell Stephen about it and ask him whether he knew anything about Jeffry Hansard. But I decided that I would choose a suitable hour, and that I would wait until I could get him alone. Dawn was not a good time in which to discuss general matters—but, on the other hand, I was finding it more and more difficult, nowadays, to get Stephen to myself to discuss any subject at all. Coolie seemed to be on the farm all day, and she and Mr. Donner came down on most evenings to the farmhouse. At first I had walked over and joined them, but for the past few days I had—for vague reasons which I had not yet begun to analyse—elected to stay at the Vicarage. I think I was beginning to find that I was outside their quartette, and I didn't like breaking it up when I went home and Stephen insisted on walking back to my gate with me.

I found him, during the morning, mending a leaking pipe, and there seemed to be no sign of Coolie anywhere near. I waited until the job was finished—to the accompaniment of Stephen's muttered curses as he attacked the task with more earnestness than skill. When it was done to his satisfaction, I passed him a handy rag and he cleaned himself up.

"Stephen, how much do you know about Jeffry Hansard?" I asked.

His lack of response convinced me that his knowledge of the subject was even less than his interest in it.

"D'you think that damn thing'll work now?" he enquired, staring critically at his handiwork.

"I think it's a nice job. Do you know anything about him, Stephen?"

"Hansard? Not much," he said. "Wonder where he picked up all that money? I think I've fixed it all right, Claire."

"Yes. Was he a *bad* man?"

"Who? Oh—I see. What a remarkable question—from a good girl. No, as far as I know, he wasn't a *bad*"—he imitated my tone, and did it very well—"man. He must have been a fairly tricky one, though."

"Why? Because he was a lawyer?"

Stephen put his head back and gave a shout of laughter.

" '*Oh, Mary was a pretty one*
No lass was ever coyer.
She vowed she'd have a canny man,
And so she wed the lawyer.'

No, not because he was a lawyer. Because he could get what he wanted out of people. I don't suppose it was easy to delude old Emily."

I stared at him with my mouth open.

"D-delude…"

He looked at me with astonishment almost equal to my own.

"Don't gape," he said. "It's ancient history. You've known it all your life."

"I haven't known anything. What did he do to old Emily?"

His voice was bewildered.

"But good Lord, Claire—it's no secret. Everybody's known for the last three decades or so that old Emily succumbed to a dose—a strong dose—of manly charm."

"You mean she—died?"

"Good Heavens, *no!* At least, she did eventually, but then, we all do in time."

"Then what? Oh, Stephen, do wait a minute and tell me. You just can't just walk off in the middle of a remark like that."

"If you don't know, then you must have been sleepwalking all this time. Are you really serious?"

"Dead serious. I've never heard anything about it. Do explain."

"There's not much to explain, and it's all common knowledge. That is, all of us here in Grayleigh know it. There were two of them living with old Emily Hansard— she was aunt to Jeffry and Christabel, who were—"

"—first cousins. I know. Go on."

"Well, it was all fixed up that Jeffry would have the house

110

and Christabel the money. It had always been arranged that way; the house was no use to Christabel, who hadn't a sou of her own, but it would be useful to Jeffry, who had a small income from his mother and a good job in the Petrie firm—in fact, it was old Emily who arranged to buy him the partnership. The idea of leaving him the house was that he'd marry eventually and bring his wife to the Lodge and rear his family there—and perhaps even give Christabel a home with them. But those weren't Jeffry's ideas, apparently, and when he woke up to the fact that Emily was beginning to fail, he gave up his wanderings and stayed home at the Lodge, behaving so nicely that when Emily died, the will was backside foremost; Christabel got the house and Jeffry got the money. Before anybody could be certain whether he'd offer any of it to his Cousin Christabel or not, he'd collected it— and departed. "

"So it was Emily's money that he...that he left to—"

"To the hospital? A good part of it might have been, but he'd have to have added a bit to it to bring it up to half a million dollars. No; Emily's money was a nice fortune for anybody who'd live here quietly, as she did, but as fortunes go, it wasn't too large. I don't say it didn't start him off in America, though, once he got there."

"But but couldn't Christabel have done something? I mean, couldn't Emily have seen how unfair—"

"Nobody's talking about fairness. I thought we were discussing The Cad's Progress, Chapter One. You know, you've always known this, Claire: it just hasn't come up before, that's all."

"I haven't known anything! Nobody's ever said a word!"

"Why on earth should they? The thing's as dead as mutton. Who's going to sit down and rake up stuff that's been forgotten all these years?"

"But—when I told you the other day that Mr. Petrie looked peculiar when I mentioned Jeffry Hansard's name, you didn't say anything!"

"What on earth did you want me to say? You wanted to drive over and tell the old fellow that Hansard's name would be popping up in the conversation from now on. A nice, kind thought—but what connection did it have with what we're talking about?"

"Well, it would have explained why Mr. Petrie got upset at the mention of the name, wouldn't it?"

"Claire, you haven't been reading any of those whodunits, have you? You're not going into business as My dear Watson, or anything of that kind?"

"Don't be silly. I can see now why poor old Mr. Petrie got upset, that's all."

"I'm glad you can see. I can't. I don't see any reason why he should fall down—thirty years later—because his junior partner was a nasty, spiteful cad who bamboozled his aunt and robbed his poor cousin. But if you feel it adds up, and if you're happy, then I'm happy too and we can both get back to work."

"But all the same, nobody has ever mentioned any of this

before."

"Use your sense, and you'll see why. Christabel would hate the very name, as they say—and so Lorna, naturally, would never bring it up. Mr. Petrie has forgotten the whole regrettable business, and only remembers it when some tactless young woman blurts it out in his presence. Granny merely connects his name with vast sums borrowed from her. The subject's dead, and if I were you, I wouldn't let Coolie go about reviving it."

"Why not?"

"Because it isn't worth giving a dog a bad name merely on guesswork. There's no law to prevent an old woman doing just as she likes with her money; there's no direct evidence, as far as I know, for saying that Jeffry poisoned her mind against Christabel. All he did was exert his charm—Granny seems to think he had plenty—and even if it did bring him the money, and even if that was his aim and idea in spending so much time with his old aunt, he must have done a lot to cheer up her last days. Charm's a commodity, in a way, and if you set out to sell it, as Hansard did, you can ask your own price. He got his price—that's all. Now go and work, and don't let Coolie drag up dead and gone matters. I told Lorna I'd see that she didn't."

"When did Lorna ask you that?"

"Last night. And will you kindly remember that this is a farm, and not an investigation bureau. And keep your friend Coolie away from me. She was distracting me yesterday."

"Oh, she…she was?"

"Yes. I wish you wouldn't leave women about the place. I don't mind you—you merge into the scenery, but Coolie... doesn't."

He went away and left me with an odd feeling which I can only diagnose, now, as the first faint stirring of—not jealousy, but wariness. It wasn't like Stephen to show irritation; he had shown it when he mentioned Coolie just now, and the irritation had arisen from his sudden realisation that she disturbed him.

It was by no means the first time she had been with him while he worked; as the days went by, she had been with us more and more—with Stephen and with me, about equally. I saw now, for the first time, that he and I were no longer a pair. With Coolie, we formed a trio; a friendly, easy-going trio, but still...a crowd. I hadn't noticed it before, but it was very clear now. It was easy for Coolie, with her unassuming charm, to slip in anywhere, and—imperceptibly, and so naturally that it was impossible to say when or how—she had become one of us.

I worked that morning in a sort of mental fog. I felt that Mr. Petrie's emotion was now accounted for, but Lorna—the upright, hardworking, earnestly-praying Lorna—was acting with uncharacteristic closeness and evasiveness. Her request to Stephen to head off Coolie's enquiries—for that was what I felt it amounted to—had been made after I had talked to her about Jeffry Hansard. Stephen, with whom I had spent the past two years in unbroken and idyllic companionship, was frowning because Coolie had got between him and his work. And

Coolie, who was to have come and gone swiftly, who was to have brightened our quiet lives for a moment before going out of them for ever—Coolie had become part of our lives...

I walked over to lunch at the Vicarage feeling restless and confused, but my uncle's silence and detachment, Cluny's familiar comments on what my mother would have said if she had lived to see me become a mud-splashed farm-hand; the music, unexpectedly soothing to-day—all these brought me into a steadier frame of mind, and when I went back to the farm for the afternoon's work, I felt much more clear-headed.

Coolie came over in the course of the afternoon, and I found myself dreading her questions about my interview with Lorna, but I found that—with what appeared to be more confidence in her powers of extracting information than in mine—Coolie had spoken to Lorna herself.

"In the kitchen," she explained, "after dinner. She washes, I dry. All I asked her was what kind of a man this Hansard was, but I guess you'd been talking to her, because she was ready for me. She gave me a long, long talk—twenty minutes non-stop, I guess—and all that came out of it was how you'd better leave things as you find them. She says this Hansard is a great guy; he gives all he's got to hospitals. That, she says, is Gen-u-ine Goodness, with two capital g's. It doesn't matter what that guy did before that, she says; that last deed is the deed to end all deeds. It wipes out anything that went before. It's a—wait till I get it straight—it's an Act of Contrition. And when he's done that, and gone where you can't ask him any questions, then you leave him be. You don't go digging round to see what you can fetch up about him. It's against all the laws: the laws of God, of generosity, of forgiveness and even—she dropped this in so neatly, so sweetly—even of hospitality. Did she give you all that?"

"No—not all."

"Well, she hadn't had time to read it up when you talked to her. She's kind of religious, isn't she, Claire?"

"Yes. She's only been a Catholic for a few years, but she's a very devout one."

Coolie was silent for a few moments, and then spoke again: "Lady Evelyn says she wants to spend vast sums on the Lodge—doing it up the way it used to be. Will Lorna let her do that?"

"No."

'Then what'll Lorna do? She can't live up there all by herself in that old—in that house, can she?"

"No. I've got an idea about what she'll do eventually."

"Tell me," said Coolie. "Against all the laws of God and of generosity and forgiveness and hospitality. What'll she do?"

"I think she'll go to the Convent at Allchester and become one of those lay Sisters. The life would suit her very well. I'm not sure that she wasn't meant to be a nun—a real nun, I mean."

"There'd be a lot more nuns," said Coolie thoughtfully, "if they didn't go in for those oversize black outfits. The life's all right—kind of nice and quiet—but look at those costumes…"

"It's easy to imagine Lorna in one of them. But I think there may be a hope of her selling the house and staying on in it—but there's nothing definite yet."

"You know what, Claire?" asked Coolie suddenly, after a pause.

"No. What?"

"Next time Pop goes out on a Did-you-know-Hansard expedition, I'd like to have you around. Then afterwards, we could talk it over and see who was imagining what. Will you come?"

"Yes, I'll come," I said. "But for the moment, you can come with me—I've got to go over to the farmhouse. I've got work to do there."

This was the day on which, the farmhouse's solitary maid being off duty, I went over and prepared an unambitious dinner for Lady Evelyn and Stephen. I am no cook, but if anyone else prepares the food, I'm quite efficient at putting it into the oven and taking it out again when the proper time comes. Coolie walked over to the farmhouse with me and followed me into the large, bare kitchen.

"Do you have to peel anything," she asked with some nervousness.

"No; it's all done."

"That's fine. What do you have to do?"

"Oh—I have to heat this up and lay the table in front of

the fire in the sitting-room, and make some mustard and cut some bread and—oh yes, there's something you can do."

"I didn't say anything!"

"You can put those flowers into that big vase—no, not that one; the white pottery one. Can you arrange flowers?"

"Watch me," invited Coolie.

I watched her, and as I did so, I made up my mind that I must arrange flowers more often. I hadn't realised what a pretty setting they make for the face, for the hands and wrists. The golden blooms against the dark of Coolie's hair made an impressive picture in the white-washed kitchen.

"I look good, hm?" said Coolie.

"Ravishing. You'll find me in the sitting-room."

She wandered in later with the flowers and set them down on a table and walked idly round the room. It was a room full of Lady Evelyn—her knitting, which never grew any longer; her tapestry work, which remained static. All round were lovely pieces—old, valuable furniture and china— converted to new uses. There were curtains and chair covers which had once been used in a far more luxurious setting; there were foot-stools, work-baskets, photographs in silver frames.

"Who's this girl?" enquired Coolie, picking up one of the photographs and examining it.

"That isn't a girl; that's Lady Alison."

"The sister?"

"Yes. I don't like looking at pictures of her. They all make her look as she must have looked then—young and pretty and gay and full of life. When I saw her—it was only once or twice when I was a child—all I can remember is that she looked like a wraith."

"Wraith? Oh, I get it; ghostly. She doesn't look much like Lady Evelyn."

"I think she does—in a weak sort of way. There was about fifteen years' difference in their ages. There were just the two daughters—no son."

"Does that mean that the name doesn't go on, or something?"

"The title went to a nephew—someone who'd settled in Australia and hasn't been back since. Both the girls married local men—Mr. Petrie was one and Mr. Brunswick was the other, but Mr. Brunswick was delicate, and so he and Lady Evelyn always lived abroad. They were brought up—Evelyn and Alison—in a house I'll show you one day, beyond Allchester. It's now a kindergarten for the Allchester Convent."

"Were they rich people?"

"It depends on what you call rich. Both the daughters had what's called a good marriage portion. Alison had no children and Lady Evelyn had one."

"Father of Steve?"

"Yes. Both his parents died when he was young, and so he's always seen a good deal of his grandmother. They've always got on very well."

119

"Got on well!"

"All right. Stephen adores her and she adores him. Is that it?"

"That's a heck of a lot more accurate. He's her favourite pet, and Conrad Donner is her second favourite pet. But I hope Steve's got some money that Grandma can't get her hands on."

"Why?"

"Why? Because why, my gosh, there won't be much of hers by the time she's—"

"—shuffled off this mortal coil?"

"Yes—that. By that time, there won't be any money, because all her Ladyship does is give away var-st sums. I'll say she's generous, but then—I'm not waiting for her money."

"Neither is Stephen."

"My, my, my—don't shoot! Gosh, Claire, I didn't mean that and you know it. But she's getting kind of old, and you'd think someone would keep a watch on all those cheques she keeps on signing. Doesn't Steve ever squirm? Now wait a minute and let me frill that up the way you do: Doesn't Stephen ever exercise any control?"

"Sometimes he does, and sometimes he doesn't."

"Well, I'm glad that sometimes he does, because she sure does run through the money. Why did Stephen bring her down here? Didn't she like London?"

"She...well, this was her home—or pretty near it."

"That's no reason for coming back to it when you're

120

young like Stephen. It's…kind of dead. What're you doing?"

"Trying to do a fancy fold on the napkins."

"Give me them here," said Coolie. *"Now"*—she settled down happily with two table napkins and began to twist them expertly—"now you'll see something. You'll see me go into action. Now, now, Coolie, that's no way to talk, honey. You'll observe where my real talents lie. Gee, Claire, when I get back home, they'll have to carry pocket dictionaries and take them out of their pockets every time I say something. Now, look while I show you. See? *That* round *there,* and then…now watch this; it's going to be good."

"It's lovely!"

"It's nothing; just a gift," said Coolie, brushing her hands together carelessly. "Some can; some can't. I don't say I'm a—what was that you said you weren't in the cooking line?"

"Cordon bleu?"

"That. I'm not one of them, and I don't rope a steer as good's my grandad says he used to, and there's one guy— only one—who can do a better jack-knife off the twenty- metre board than I can, but when it comes to water-lilies for dinner, then just look at those; I'm the girl-wonder."

"You are. Now I'm going to make some mustard."

"Why don't you have it out of a bottle?"

"We don't like that kind. Come on."

She was mixing the mustard when Stephen walked into the kitchen and sniffed the air appreciatively.

"What can I smell?" he enquired.

"You'd be surprised," said Coolie. "Claire got it cornered and put it in the oven and shut the door on it. This is mustard, to kill the taste."

Stephen settled himself on a corner of the kitchen table and helped himself to a handful of small cheese biscuits.

"I suppose," he said in muffled tones to Coolie, "that your kitchen at home—in America—gleams a bit more than this one does?"

"It hasn't got a stone floor like this one, or an old-Oregon- trail oven like that one, if that's what you mean," said Coolie. "If it feels as cold as this in May, what does it feel like in December?"

"About the same," said Stephen. "Ask Claire—she brings across the milk every morning. I'd like to give Granny one of those all-gadget kitchens and watch her pressing knobs— what a time she'd have! Where are the rest of these biscuits, Claire?"

"Out of reach," I said. "Coolie, have you got one of those stoves at home that starts cooking the meal at a prearranged time and then switches itself off when everything's ready?"

"Yes. Don't you have them?"

"I've read about them."

"Then why don't you have one? At home, you could—"

"—telephone and have it sent round," said Stephen. "I know. Do you know why everybody's so rich in America?"

"Everybody isn't," said Coolie.

"I wish you'd let me talk, for a change," said Stephen. "I was going to tell you something that very few people know about your country, and that is, why nobody's poor there— for long. It's because it's the worst country in the world to be poor in. Ever heard of Tantalus?"

"No."

"Well, he was a naughty boy who talked out of turn, and he was tied up with all the nice things he wanted just out of his reach—all hanging round him, on view. That's like the poor man in America; there it all is, just to grab—if he can pay for it. So he works like mad to get rich and get all those glittering prizes—washing-machines and television sets and next year's cars. The carrot in front of the donkey."

"You've got carrots here—and plenty of donkeys," said Coolie.

"You can't be poor in America," said Stephen. "People look down their noses. Now, in Europe, I can show you one or two places where you can be poor very happily and very comfortably. You just eat and grow a bit of stuff, and when your laundry day comes round, you take your clothes off and bash 'em against a stone by the brook and then put 'em on again. Nobody dangles prizes in front of you, and there's not a thing in sight that you want. Sea and sun and sky. Claire, couldn't you just take one or two biscuits out and trust me with them?"

"Don't you, Claire," said Coolie. "Just dangle them. Look—here's Lady Evelyn coming."

I was very glad. I had finished what I came to do, and the kitchen, with three of us in it, seemed to have become too small. I had answered when Stephen or Coolie asked questions, and I had laughed when they laughed, but I was glad when Lady Evelyn came in and I could go away. But even when I went, Stephen and Coolie walked back with me; they left me at my gate, and then Stephen went on with her to the Lodge and I stood and watched them go. He walked with his head bent down to hers, and I suppose I ought to have been racked with jealousy—but it's very hard to be jealous of a girl who shows not the slightest sign of being aware that a man is beginning to look at her with something more than friendliness; a girl, moreover, who had for me a liking that nobody could doubt was genuine. She liked Stephen, but she liked me almost more than she liked him. Later, she began to think of me a little differently—or perhaps she merely began to think; but that evening, and for some time afterwards, I was, to Coolie, just a nice girl placed there by Providence for her to talk to when she had nothing else to do…or when Stephen was too busy to listen.

Chapter Eight

Looking back upon that time, I remember a succession of brilliantly sunny days. People were to talk of "that spring" when it was over, and to mean its freshness and brightness and colour. Everything seemed vivid, but I felt, in some way, that I was standing back and watching events from the shadows. The sun seemed to blaze. We rose in sunshine, worked in sunshine; Mr. Donner, who had brought to England a full complement of mackintoshes, umbrellas and a very un-English pair of goloshes, was convinced that these precautions had ensured bright weather for us all.

I drove over, one lovely afternoon, to see Miss Ferrier, who was next on Mr. Donner's list of those to be interviewed. I was driving—with some trepidation—the big green car, which Stephen and I, in turn, had driven when we took Mr. Donner and Coolie for tours round the countryside. Lady Evelyn was beside me, and Mr. Donner was at the back. Coolie was not with us. She was to have come, but she and Stephen had gone out riding that morning to a farm to look at a calf that we thought of buying; later, they had telephoned to say that they were staying to lunch with its owner. Still later, Coolie telephoned to her father and told him to go without her, and so we had set out.

I wondered what had become of her determination to be present at her father's interviews. I had only promised to go because she had asked me to act as a sort of second observer, and I remembered the keenness and enthusiasm with which she had spoken to me that day at the farm. As I drove, I had two alternatives to offer myself for her failure to come with us: she had found a stronger interest in Stephen's society or—oddest of thoughts—Stephen had kept her away deliberately, to prevent her from probing too deeply. For some reason which I found it difficult to understand, he seemed to be more and more unwilling to discuss any matter connected with Jeffry Hansard.

It was useless to become lost in speculation. I put the matter aside and concentrated on pointing out places of interest to Mr. Donner and supplementing Lady Evelyn's somewhat sketchy history of the locality.

We were to make a detour in order to show Mr. Donner the house which was now the Convent kindergarten, but which had once been owned by Lady Evelyn's father, Lord Gray, and in which she and her sister had been brought up. Skirting All-chester, I drove, presently, past iron gates and up a short, curving drive and came to a stop before the house.

It was a large, spreading building, and, like so many of the houses in Polden and its surroundings, might have had some claim, originally, to some architectural merit; but something had been added here, something there; a wing had been thrown out, a hideous conservatory had been built on, until the whole was an unattractive and uninspiring sight. But Lady Evelyn saw nothing in the place but the figures of those who had peopled it long ago. She led us to the front door and pulled the bell vigorously, and the little nun who came to the door smiled at us with instant comprehension.

"You want to go round? But of course, Lady Evelyn, of course. Please come in."

"We're not going to disturb anybody," said Lady Evelyn in her attempt at a whisper. "We shall *creep*—all of us. I've just brought an American friend who wants to look round. We shan't make any noise, I promise you."

"Just go where you please, Lady Evelyn. I'll leave you to be the guide."

Lady Evelyn led us along corridors and opened doors into classrooms where the nuns, giving her a smile of welcome, went on with the lessons they were giving.

"This is the old drawing-room," she said, leading us into a large, empty room. "They're going to use it as a dining-room for the smallest children. I can remember being brought down here to meet people—imagine a child, nowadays, being out of the way when people call, and not being seen until it's sent for! But I was dressed up and brought down to say 'How d'you do,' and then taken away again, and that went on until I was twelve, and then they used to let me hand things round at tea. I was quite alone; my sister Alison didn't arrive until I was

127

nearly sixteen, and of course by that time it was too late. And this used to be our dining-room. I can remember dinner parties—twelve to twenty-four people, and everybody looking very nice round the candles. At the end of dinner, the women used to troop out—that's how I first noticed my husband, when he opened the door and gave me a very peculiar—what they call a meaning look as I went through. I was at the tail of the procession, so I was able to turn and give him a meaning look back, and that's how it all began. He was very handsome, and he looked quite strong, but England didn't suit him. Bad weather used to give him this and that, and so we had to do all our wooing indoors, which was very difficult in those days, for they didn't like you to be alone with a young man, however delicate. Do you know, I used to come down into this room and wait for him, and he used to come in by that window over there. It was all very risky—not the coming in by the window, but the meetings. That word that nobody understands nowadays—reputation! What would happen if I spoke to little Claire here about her reputation? She'd stare, and quite rightly—they don't have them nowadays. Personally, I think it's a great mistake—men used to be so tender to you if you had one, and so dashing if you didn't! And this used to be the morning-room; they don't have those either, nowadays, but we always used to have breakfast in here, with the sun streaming in. I had plaits—sometimes two, sometimes only one—isn't that *killing?* And this used to be—oh, do forgive me, Sister!"

"Come in, come in, Lady Evelyn. You may sit down, children. Heads this way, please! Now once again: Two and two are…"

"Four," chanted twenty voices.

"Three and three are…"

"Six," squeaked a promising pupil.

"Splendid, Mary. Now, four and four are…"

Dead silence.

"Eight. Now we'll count it with the counters. Now…"

"Aren't they sweet?" said Lady Evelyn, closing the door. "Now we'll go upstairs. This is what used to be used as the ballroom, with those doors at that end opened—that gave us two rooms instead of one. Oh, they're singing—we'll just peep in."

We peeped in, and stayed to listen to a part-song sung by an assembly of little girls and boys. The composer had not written it as a part-song, but only one section of the choir were singing the melody; the others, as Mr. Donner murmured sympathetically, couldn't quite make it. They sang, instead, a one-note obligato not unlike the hum of the bagpipes, but in spite of this reminder of my homeland, I was very glad to get out of the room, and only recovered fully when we had been round the library (now the handwork- room), the eighteen bedrooms (now rest-rooms, assembly rooms, and play-rooms) and went downstairs again and walked out on to the terrace.

"Over there," said Lady Evelyn, pointing with her umbrella, "were two tennis courts and a croquet lawn. You didn't play very serious tennis unless you were one of those strenuous girls. I used to enjoy the teas—enormous teas, and we all ate them and nobody said anything about their diet. It's extraordinary, isn't it, how strong and healthy we all used to grow, eating all those things that they say nowadays are quite unsuitable? Dear old Richard—my husband, though, of course, he wasn't my husband until long afterwards—Papa insisted on a long engagement, because I suppose he thought that it was best to wait and see how delicate Richard turned out to be, but we couldn't wait for ever, as Richard pointed out to him in the end. We used to stay out here in summer, don't you know, sitting under those trees—*you* two can't see anything, of course, but *I* can see, quite plainly, old Jowitt, the butler, dear old fellow, walking out followed by two maids—he never got on with footmen and so we had none, but I think now, looking back, that he…they were always such *pretty* girls, and I used to see a lot that I didn't understand at the time, but that I dare say I'd understand now, if I saw it going on. But there was one thing—we never had any servant troubles, so he must have had some sort of method. The tea was served under that lovely beech tree—it's beautiful, isn't it?—and dear old Richard and I used to walk round the shrubbery looking for tennis balls, and Papa used to come after us—dear Papa, with such a light tread, but he could never disguise his breathing—never. And then old Jowitt used to open these doors down here and you'd know he was going to sound the gong. Poor old George Petrie has that gong to this day, but I think that if he ever sounded it in that little house, the walls would fall down. Such a lovely tone, and how the sound travelled! I don't know whether old Jowitt opened the doors to let the sound out or to save the glass from breaking, but I can hear that *boom!*—always eight booms with about three seconds in between each; and then we'd all come in to dress for dinner, and if dear old Richard was staying in the house, Papa used to be down in the drawing-room earlier than anybody else in case we thought of having ten minutes alone. I suppose girls nowadays find it very much easier to get married, but it can't be as exciting as it once was. Nowadays, girls forage for themselves, but in my day it was the mothers… oh, the mothers!…*Killing!* But if you got hold of anybody like poor old Richard, who wasn't quite what your parents had planned for you, then a girl could really feel that she was living on her wits. Little notes, secret messages, maids who were sympathetic and maids who were watching you—it was really very exciting, though it must bore you tremendously to stand here and listen to it now."

"No—oh, no!" said Mr. Donner, plainly unwilling to leave poor old Richard.

"But all the same, it isn't what we came out for. We must find Mother Superior and say 'Thank you' to her, and then we must be off to see Miss Ferrier."

We got into the car once more and went on our way; nobody spoke, for we were all still intent upon Jowitt and his pretty maids. Then I turned a corner, and we all came back to the present with a jolt.

131

Mr. Donner had never made any comments on the architectural horrors of Grayleigh or Polden or their neighbourhood, but he must have wondered, at times, who touched up the photographs of English villages and represented them as cosy little places with old inns and thatched cottages. I hadn't realised what he was missing until I drove into Rooktree, four miles beyond Allchester, and heard his gasp of surprise and delight. For Rooktree—what there was of it—was pure postcard. Miss Ferrier's cottage, which was called Cherryton, was an artist's dream. Mr. Donner sat in the car and stared at it, bemused, purring, murmuring ecstatic little phrases under his breath and then calling upon us to witness that he would, one day, bring Verna here to feast her eyes. He was so long in disembarking that at last I helped him out and steadied him up the flower-flanked path, giving him time to take off his glasses and polish them. I got him as far as the creeper-hung doorway, and then Lady Evelyn took him in charge.

"It's pretty, isn't it?" she said. "But Lilli-*pu*-tian! Do you know, they used to live in that Gothic horror we passed—oh, I pointed it out. Do you know the one I mean?"

"Yes," said Mr. Donner.

"Well, from that—to this. You'll say at once, of course, that it looks warmer, but these cottages can *whistle*—really *whistle*. Especially when you get those north winds. Claire dear, why don't you knock on the door?"

I had been waiting for Mr. Donner to stop turning round in circles as he took in the windows, the flowers, the dovecote, the bird-bath, the splendid white cat, the lowness of the upper story—a mere arm's length above us—and the feeling of utter peace and stillness.

"Now you must stop looking," said Lady Evelyn firmly. "There's a great deal to look at inside the house. Claire, hurry up and fetch someone."

Miss Ferrier came to the door and gave us a gentle welcome. She led us into the tiny drawing-room, and I remembered—too late—that we had forgotten to explain to Mr. Donner that, although everybody invariably referred to one Miss Ferrier, there were in fact two; a pair of Miss Ferriers, impossible to recognise apart and therefore never thought of separately. Nobody ever knew which was which; Miss Ferrier did for both of them. I explained this now to Mr. Donner, who took one of their hands in each of his and studied them smilingly; if he had never seen Dresden china figures in human form before, he was seeing them now. They were tiny, dainty, fragile creatures, white-haired, and with skins so delicate as to make their cheeks look like pale pink petals.

Having taken in Miss Ferrier. Mr. Donner accepted a seat and began a terrible struggle to keep his eyes away from the furniture. There was general sympathy for him; in coming from their large house to this tiny one, the old ladies had been obliged to abandon all but their choicest treasures. Everything in the house was worth a connoisseur's attention. Sheraton, Hepplewhite and Chippendale were all round us, and even under us. Soon Mr. Donner, giving up all attempt at conversation, delighted his hostesses by begging them to allow him to feast his eyes.

Tea came; a ceremony rather than a meal, and the only part of visiting Miss Ferrier that I dreaded. My hands were too big for the delicate china, and my appetite too healthy for the delicate fare. The bread and butter was paper-thin, the hot scones feathery, the sponge cake a mere breath. One old lady sat behind a silver kettle and spirit lamp; the other handed us our cups and offered us bread and butter.

"Whenever I come here, Mr. Donner," said Lady Evelyn, "I feel just like Alice in Wonderland when she ate that stuff that made her grow smaller. When she'd eaten—"

"Drunk," I said, before I could stop myself.

"Drunk? Oh, I see what you mean! I thought...*killing!* Yes, of course—she drank it, and that's just how I feel. Mr. Donner, don't you like that exquisite table?"

It was plain that Mr. Donner would have given a great deal for the exquisite table, and thrown in his two ears for the chair by the window. He ate his sponge cake absently.

"He's going to give a talk at the Church Hall on Friday," said Lady Evelyn. "You must both be there."

"A talk on America?"

"No; not on America," said Lady Evelyn. "He's going to tell us all about the toys he makes. They're sold all over America and they're called by a special name—a sort of trade mark. What name was it, Mr. Donner?"

"Papoose. My wife should be here to talk to you about them, because she is, always has been, the moving spirit in all our work," said Mr. Donner earnestly.

"But she can't do it, as she isn't here, so Miss Ferrier must come and listen to you instead. Will you come, both of you?" Miss Ferrier—one Miss Ferrier—promised for both of them, and then moved her chair back a little way, to indicate that tea was over and that Mr. Donner might now approach the subject upon which he wanted information. I caught a look of appeal in her eye, and guessed, with dismay, what she was asking me: I was to take Lady Evelyn away, into the garden, and leave Miss Ferrier free to talk to Mr. Donner. Everybody loved Lady Evelyn, but her presence was never conducive to a business-like atmosphere.

I withdrew my gaze and stared steadily at the fireplace, only to hear a gentle voice:

"Claire, my dear…"

"Yes?"

"Do go out with Lady Evelyn and show her those—"

"Now, you're not going to send me outside just because you want to talk to Mr. Donner," protested Lady Evelyn. "He and I have been into this subject together from the very beginning."

But one tiny, fragile creature had risen and was at the door, waiting for us with a pleading expression.

"There's such a lot to see…and nobody ever comes to see

it!"

Lady Evelyn found this impossible to resist, and as I looked at Miss Ferrier's hand, outstretched, waiting for me to put my large one into it, I gave up the struggle and followed her and Lady Evelyn out into the garden. Here Lady Evelyn's attention was held for a time by the lovely spring colours to be seen everywhere, and we paced round the little garden together. Then she stood still and inspected the little cottage critically, her head on one side.

"It's all very picturesque," she said to Miss Ferrier in a doubtful tone, "but sometimes I don't understand how you can be really happy here. After that great place, I mean. You could have divided it up, or made it into flats, or done whatever people do to these over-large houses nowadays. To come from all that space to this…! I wish Claire could have seen your other house, always full of young people. Was it *ever* without them all?"

"Never," said Miss Ferrier.

"They used to come down and spend all their holidays here, Claire," went on Lady Evelyn. "Parties and picnics and balls—and as soon as one lot departed, the next lot appeared—didn't they, Miss Ferrier?"

"Yes; they did."

"Ah well, we're all older now, and so we must be quiet," sighed Lady Evelyn. "Shall we go in now? They've had heaps of time to talk."

"We'll give them a little longer. It's always so much easier to answer questions and give information when there aren't other people there; it's rather distracting if there are," said Miss Ferrier gently.

"Don't you ever find, after that large house, that you're rather on top of one another here?" asked Lady Evelyn.

"Sometimes, perhaps—but we're very contented, on the whole."

"Keeping up those enormous places nowadays, of course, would eat up one's entire income. Money is a great burden, on the whole. I suppose it brings a great deal, but as one grows older it seems to lose most of its value. I often think that the most sensible thing for me to do would be to hand mine over to Stephen now—when he's young enough to enjoy it—instead of waiting until I'm dead. I don't feel at all like dying; in fact, I sometimes wonder if I shall ever die, I feel so strong. And poor Stephen would be so old…And I've no expenses to speak of, nowadays and if he marries, he'll want something to set him up. But when I talk to him about it—not about marrying, but about handing over the money to him now—he gets very cross, and won't hear of it. And he made me promise that I wouldn't talk to poor old George Petrie about it. I couldn't do anything without asking him, of course, because everything has always been in his hands."

"He's a dear old man," said Miss Ferner gently. "He's quite lost, I'm afraid, without Alison."

"He's never been the same man. Did you know that he

travelled all the way over to break the news to us himself? He told my husband first, but I knew something had happened. They were both shut up in the study, and when they came out, my dear old Richard looked deadly white, and I said at once: 'You needn't tell me. I know'—and they both stared at me. They both looked so queer…And I said, 'Alison's dead, isn't she?' I always feel so grateful to him for coming over all that way so kindly.

"He was always kind," said Miss Ferrier. "Shall we go in now?"

We went indoors to find Mr. Donner writing busily in his notebook. He rose to his feet with a smile of satisfaction, and the rest of the visit was merely a series of bows, handshakes, exchanges of goodwill which carried us all through the little passage to the front door. We went up the flagged path, leaving our hostesses—two delicate little figures framed in the doorway. We didn't get into the car, however, at Lady Evelyn's suggestion, we took a short walk up the narrow street so that Mr. Donner could see some of the other cottages. We had only taken a few steps when Lady Evelyn discovered that she had left her scarf at the house, and I went back to fetch it.

The front door was closed, but I expected to find the two old ladies in the drawing-room, and so I stepped over the flower border and went across the grass with the intention of putting my head in at the little open window and saving them the trouble of coming to the door. There was no need to trouble them, however; though they were not in the room, the scarf lay to my hand on the back of a chair just inside the window. I reached for it and picked it up, and I was just about to call a word of explanation and farewell, when I heard something that kept me rigid for a moment and then made me hurry away as swiftly as I could go—and as silently. I didn't follow Lady Evelyn and Mr. Donner; I took my whirling head to the car and sat down in the driving seat and stared through the windscreen at the innocent calm of Cherryton. It looked so tranquil that I felt certain, for a moment or two, that I had let my imagination run away with me. Then my confusion cleared, and I recalled with complete clarity the two sentences I had heard, spoken in the soft, sweet voices of the two sisters:

"…But it might have been better, my dear, to tell him the whole truth."

"No. It was better to say nothing. And besides…he's such a charming man…"

Chapter Nine

With those words ringing in my ears, I was not at all surprised, the next morning, to hear the clatter of hooves in the yard, and to see Stephen's big chestnut standing there with Coolie—as she termed it—aboard.

She was often aboard; Stephen's horse was now at her disposal, as well as a good deal of his time, more than half his interest and...I didn't want to go beyond that.

If I don't sound like a woman whose heart was being slowly torn to shreds, I can only explain the fact by saying that whatever my heart was going through, the rest of me was compelled—by the demands of my job as well as by the promptings of my self-respect—to go on functioning in the normal manner. I was unhappy, because something that was precious to me, something that I had thought of as solid and permanent, was beginning to crumble before my eyes— but I discovered that unhappiness is a lonely state. It seemed to me that there was nothing I could do about mine—except keep it hidden from the eyes of the world, which in my case meant Grayleigh. I had always felt that I had missed the point of the story of the Spartan boy who stood doing nothing while a fox chewed at him; I still thought it a rather pointless thing to do, but I recognised now, for the first time, that I was in a situation very much like his. Chewed or not,I had to go on looking and behaving as I always did; as I did when I was happy; as I had done before Coolie's advent.

My brain went on working very clearly; my eyes were in good order, and my common sense was still functioning. I could see what Stephen could see—her beauty and charm— and my common sense told me that any man who could look at Coolie Donner for long without feeling her fascination, must have something the matter with his hormones. She was lively and sweet; she made no apparent effort to please, but her lack of affectations, her simplicity and natural good manners made it difficult to see what anyone could find in her to dislike. She fitted in everywhere; she was lovely indoors and out of doors; she was exactly right for homely occasions or for grand ones. I could break my heart because Stephen was beginning to love her, might already love her—but at the same time, I didn't see how he could help it.

At times, I still clung to the knowledge that she was, after all, in transit; she had settled, like a lovely butterfly, but she would soon fly away again. And I had another comfort: the feeling that if Stephen, before her arrival, had been hesitating before asking me to marry him and settle down on a small farm in a remote village, then he certainly wouldn't ask Coolie. But what steadied me most of all was my conviction that jealousy, one of the strongest of passions, is also the ugliest. It was impossible to be as I was—young and warm-blooded—without feeling the surge of blind hatred that came in waves every night as I lay in the big bedroom from which I could see the lights of the Lodge. But while its pains racked me, I knew that they could never drive me to any demonstration, to any ghastly scene between Stephen and myself in which, stripped of my last weapon, dignity, I should struggle for something which was no longer his to give. And if it should seem that I sat quietly and took everything that came, I should like to be told what I could have done to prevent it. The only advantage I had over Coolie was in having got there first. If I'd had any foresight, or, better still, if I'd had a mother with the normal tiger instincts Stephen would by this time have been what Coolie called hog-tied. He would, long ago, have been made to declare either his intentions or his lack of them. But he hadn't been asked, because there was nobody to ask him.

Looking back, I don't feel any surprise at the fact that love and marriage had never been mentioned between us. We had taken each other for granted all our lives, and nothing had ever happened, up to now, to jerk us into an assessment of our relationship.

I was to learn, at twenty-six, some new aspects of being alone in the world—a situation I had, so far, enjoyed very much. Lady Evelyn was in the habit of telling people that I had never had any parents, and in a sense she was right; I had cost my mother her life and my father his, I suppose since he found nothing to live for when she was gone. Lady Evelyn had been one of my guardians, but she had always been out of England. The other guardian—my uncle—had provided a home for me; I lived with him until I was old enough to go away to school, and from that time my own inclinations, and an income of my own, had given me a freedom that nobody had ever questioned. If I elected to come home for the holidays, my uncle wrote to say that he was delighted; if I chose to go and stay with friends, my uncle again wrote to say that he was delighted.

Stephen, at fourteen, became—like me—an orphan, and this widened my sphere, for whenever he went to stay with his grandmother, Lady Evelyn, he was instructed to bring me too, and to look after me well. His care began and ended by a warning that I was never to talk to foreigners, and a reminder that it was not he, but the stewardess, who should be approached if I happened to feel seasick. Together we travelled to whatever climate dear old Richard happened to be sampling: France, Italy, Switzerland, and once as far as Alexandria, where we missed the homeward boat and inaugurated a long and inconclusive correspondence between Lady Evelyn and the heads of our respective schools.

Later, Stephen and I had seen less of one another; we had met at intervals and compared notes—but it was not until we were both settled in London that we got back to the easy, friendly terms of our childhood, and it was not until he left London and came down to Grayleigh that I knew that I was in love with him. I had come down and joined him; there was nobody to question or advise. I had been with him for two years, and I had been too happy, and too busy, to notice their passing.

I had never missed my mother, but now, for the first time, I began to feel that if she had been alive and living in Grayleigh just before Coolie came to it, she would at least have done something to define the position; she would have reminded me that I was twenty-six and Stephen twenty- eight. I should probably have resented her interference, but I might have stopped to think. I might.. .. And at all events, a mother would have been aware, now, of what was happening. She would have realised that my happiness was being threatened, and she would have put out a hand—and I might have grasped it. I might… But I had now to realise how completely independent I had become—and how utterly lonely. Nobody saw, and nobody put out a hand. Lorna had her mind full of business connected with the sale of the house; Lady Evelyn had found a new and enchanting friend in Mr. Donner; my uncle wouldn't have noticed if I had gone into a decline.

Cluny saw; but Cluny's concern took the form of administering a stiff dose of the obvious.

"She's bonny, yon wee lass."

"Yes; she's very pretty."

"An' she'll be younger than you, I'm thinkin'."

"A little."

"Three or fower years."

"About that,"

"An' she can ride. Aye, she can that. I was lookin' at her, cornin' up here the other day. She can ride's gude as yersel'."

"I suppose she can."

"Onnyone lookin' at her can see she's bonny."

"Naturally."

"If a mon had een in his heid, he'd see that."

"I suppose he would."

"A laddie wouldna need to look twice. Yon Mr. Stephen thinks she's jest the right kind for himsel'."

"I think you might leave him to decide that."

"Och, I've got ma sight yet. I can see what he's thinkin'. An' so can anybody else. An' so can ye. Ye're no' so green."

"I think you'd—"

"He wad tak' to her naturally; he's big and fair an' she's a wee brown lass. They go together. Ye were always too much like him; ye were big yoursel', and fair yoursel'. I'm no' saying you're no' a bonny girl yoursel', though. But she's the one he's after."

If I could swallow that, and digest it, I suppose it was as good for me as any number of tactful warnings. But there was no comfort in it. The only comfort Cluny offered was of a very practical nature.

"Ye remember yon fellow that used to come doon an' see ye when you came fra' London?"

"Yes."

"Wha' became o' him?"

"I haven't any idea."

"Aye, they don't hang round ye for ever. Then there was yon young laddie wi' the red heid. Wha' happened to him?"

"I couldn't tell you."

"If ye'd no' been sae green, ye'd hae kept one back for fear o' accidents. There's no use in lettin' them all go till ye're properly fixed up wi' one. Ye put all your chicks in one basket an—'"

"Cluny, couldn't you go and find something else to do?"

"Och, I didnae suppose ye'd like to hear it, but it's the truth I'm tellin' ye."

Yes, it was the truth.

And so I stood that morning and watched Coolie dismount from the big chestnut, and I saw that she looked angry. Her small face was sombre and her lips were pressed together and she was frowning—but she still looked lovely. She left the horse at the trough and walked over to talk to me, and I saw that she had a small parcel under her arm. I had a good idea what it was, and I wondered what I was going to tell her. I didn't want to tell her anything. I was full of a rather mean desire to keep away from complications, and to avoid anything that might lead to unpleasantness. She had come to talk about Jeffry Hansard, and I wasn't interested in Jeffry Hansard any more. My interest in the mystery—if there was a mystery— had come to an abrupt end; it wasn't anything to do with me, and I had more important things on my mind.

But Coolie was taking the wrappings from her parcel, and I saw what I had expected to see: Mr. Donner's notebook. The Hansard File. Coolie held it up in front of my eyes and her frown deepened.

"See here, Claire," she began. "I'm mad this morning."

"You're mad angry and not mad crazy—is that it?"

"Like I said. I'm mad. Look, Claire, you went to that house yesterday, didn't you? To the old lady that turned out to be two old ladies?"

"Yes."

"Well, that's what I've come to see you about. Now see here. I've counted the total number of pages that Pop's got written down in this book. Forty-eight pages. Forty-eight pages all on this Hansard."

"Jeffry Hansard, his life and times. Well, forty-eight pages is about all he wanted, isn't it? He said he didn't want an entire history; he just wanted a few facts."

"And he hasn't got them. He's got forty-eight pages of a lot of air that people have been giving him. There aren't four facts—not what you'd call facts—in the whole book. Pop's written down everything just as they said it to him— and there aren't any facts. When Pop gets that book home and hands it over to the guy that's going to do the—"

"—editing."

"—editing, then he's going to find that there's nothing there for him to edit. Pop's talked to these people who were on the list Miss Hansard sent him, and what happens? I'll tell you. They agree to meet him and tell him everything they know about the guy. When Pop gets there, they talk about the weather and the crops. Take this—" she pointed with a small brown forefinger at the book she was holding, but her voice remained quiet—"take this bit and see how it adds up: His age, his looks, his Aunt Emily, his Cousin Christabel, he liked cats but he didn't like dogs, he liked riding but he didn't like walking, he liked theatres, but he didn't like films, he liked this but he preferred that; he went away and he came back. Gosh, Claire, back home they'll want something they can work on to make a paper, a pamphlet, out of. They'll want something that they can tell people about him: his work, what people thought about him, what kind of character, where he got his money, if he had any money when he was here—that kind of thing. You see, Claire, Pop likes to talk to people, and if they're nice people, he believes that they'll tell him what he wants to know. Now, in this Jeffry Hansard business, he's got a lot of information that doesn't add up to a thing—and you know why? Because people aren't talking. Nobody's talking. I tell you, Claire, this man Hansard did something; something nobody likes to tell about. He stole something or he murdered somebody or he ran off with the pay packets. Then why don't they want to say so?"

There was a shadow across the doorway of the shed in which we were standing. Stephen, propping himself against a wall, looked at us with lazy amusement, and I saw that his arm

148

was stretched straight from his shoulder, and that Coolie could have walked under it without stooping. He looked down at her, and his expression was gentle, and faintly amused.

"I heard your voice, and in it angry overtones," he said.

"I'm talking about this Hansard," said Coolie.

"The late Emily? The late Christabel? No. Then it must be the late Jeffry."

"That's who," said Coolie. "I think he was a crooked guy."

"You dug him up," Stephen reminded her. "You mustn't mind if he smells a bit."

Coolie looked at him in anger and disgust.

"You think it's kind of funny, don't you?" she demanded.

"Not particularly—no."

"Well, I'll tell you something," said Coolie. "It's not funny. It's not funny at all. Pop hasn't found out anything from anybody."

"You have to learn patience when you come over here," said Stephen, with exasperating calm. "I've seen it so often before, when I was doing a real man's work in an office in the City. I've seen Americans come in bursting with briskness, with despatch-cases under their arms and blue-prints pinned all over them, and their return passages booked on the next *Queen*. Weeks later, they're still bursting, but not with briskness."

"All right," said Coolie. "We like to go ahead and do things fast."

"More; you like to do them thoroughly," said Stephen. 'You're an example to the world, and we're catching up, slowly-slowly. But very slowly-slowly. You must remember you're not in Prophet, Arizona, now. You're in a slow backwater with simple English types and—"

"What's simple about lying?" asked Coolie.

"*Lying*? Nobody in Grayleigh or Polden could possibly be accused of lying. Nobody has ever—"

"Well, there's got to be a first time," said Coolie. "I'm accusing them."

"Coolie," I put in, "listen to me and learn. You must never, never argue with Stephen about anything. He'll preserve an unshaken calm, and drive you to the verge of murder—all to amuse himself. State all your facts and don't let him get in any interpolations."

"Meet my friend, Polly Syllabic," said Stephen. "You know Polly Syllabic?"

"I know that nobody's going to make a monkey out of Pop," said Coolie firmly.

"Your father," said Stephen, "is the most popular man in the county. Now come and hold that horse while I let the cows out."

They went out together, and soon Coolie, putting her head round the door, told me that she was going back to the Lodge. I heard the clatter of her departure, and then I looked up to find Stephen standing beside me.

"Dreaming?" he asked.

"In a way. I was thinking about Coolie."

Stephen made no reply. He sat on a convenient box and stared into space, and he could have been thinking about anything—Coolie or cattle-food. But I didn't think that he was thinking of cattle-food.

"Coolie's got a bee in her bonnet," he said slowly at last, "about Jeffry Hansard."

"It isn't exactly a bee, Stephen. I know that Miss Ferrier knew more than she told Mr. Donner yesterday. I went back for a scarf of your grandmother's and I heard something they didn't intend me to hear. There's something queer about him, I think."

Stephen stayed browsing for a few moments, and then rose to his feet with an air of weariness.

"Don't let Coolie go too hard at it," he said. "People aren't going to disinter the family skeletons for every tourist who asks to see them. *Requiescat in pace*; it's a pretty good epitaph, and you might recite it to Coolie when she gets on to the subject again."

I looked at him.

"Stephen—*you* don't know anything about him, do you?"

"Specifically, no. But I don't want anything dragged out for anybody else to look at. I don't suppose anybody in Prophet, Arizona, will lose any sleep about the *post mortem* on Hansard —benefactor or no benefactor."

"I don't see how I can stop Coolie from doing anything she wants to do."

"You needn't tell her what you've just told me—about the Ferriers knowing more than they told her father—for a start. And if she brings the subject up, you can talk about something else. Not farming. They know too much about farming."

"What do you mean?"

"Mr. Donner. He hadn't been on this place five minutes before he asked me what I was doing on it. You see, Claire— it sticks out a mile. I'm no farmer."

"What did you tell him?"

"I forget. But his daughter's right about him—he's easy to sidetrack."

He went away, and although that can't be said to have been much of a conversation, it was the last free, natural exchange that Stephen and I were to have. It was the end of a phase for us all; for me, it was the beginning of the end of everything. I'm not good at metaphors, but, looking back, I see us all getting into position at the top of the slope; we were lining up; one of us was looking down with dread, but soon we were all to slide down, steadily and irresistibly, to the end of the run.

When I went home that evening, I found Lady Evelyn and Coolie coming out of the Vicarage gate.

"We've just been in to chat to your uncle, Claire," said Lady Evelyn. "Isn't he charming, Coolie?"

"He's a honey," said Coolie.

"He insists that his chest is weak," said Lady Evelyn, "but he won't take my advice about any remedies. Or at any rate, he won't give them time enough to do any good. If you want a cure to work, then you've got to give it time to work. What I like most about him, Coolie, my dear, is that he never asks me for money. Every time I met his predecessor, dear old Mr. Bligh, it used to cost me vast sums. If it wasn't the organ fund, it was the roof or the heating, or new cushions for the pews. I must have rebuilt that church, one way and another, inside and out, many times over. But Claire's uncle is charming—he doesn't behave as though the mere sight of one put him in mind of crumbling walls. He never speaks of money at all, and when you give him a cheque, he tries to press it back into your hand. I think that's a far more effective way of getting money, or at least of making people anxious to give you money. If you're rushed at, you don't feel you want to be generous, but if you're not, you feel disposed to give whatever you can afford."

She had more to say on the subject, and while she was saying it, Coolie and I strolled down to the farmhouse with her and said goodbye to her at her gate; then we turned and went back to the Vicarage. I asked Coolie to come in, but she said she wanted to get back to the Lodge. She didn't, however, go immediately. I stood inside the gate and she stood outside, and we talked across it.

"You're always busy," she said. "What time do you start in the mornings?"

"Oh...crack of dawn. But I like it. I like it much better

153

than working in London, as I used to."

"And Steve—he used to work in London, too."

"Yes. Until about two years ago. Then his grandfather died, and before he died, he sent for Stephen. Stephen went over, and when he came back, he brought Lady Evelyn back with him, and then he gave up his job in London and brought her down here. She really belongs here, of course."

"But he doesn't," said Coolie.

I said nothing to this, and she looked at me speculatively over the top of the gate.

"What I can't figure out," she said slowly, after a while, "is *why* he stays down here, farming. *Why?*"

"Why?" I echoed a little stupidly.

"Yes, why. He's no farmer. Farming isn't just milking cows and following feeding formulas. Farmers know a lot of things about crops and yields and soil. I know. Verna's people and Pop's people were all farmers. I know what I'm talking about, and I know a farmer when I see one."

"This is only a tiny dairy farm—that's all."

"That's all," agreed Coolie equably. "But he doesn't *like* doing it. So why does he do it?"

"Why don't you ask him?"

"I asked him. He said—you know how he play-acts—he said, 'Coolie, I'm Granny's boy and I like to be with my Granny.' That's all I got. Very funny, but no answer. Claire, what's the *matter* with this place? Nobody tells you the first thing!

You ask, and they hand you out blanks."

"You've never been in England before, have you?" I asked. "You haven't had time to get used to us."

"Yes; I have. There's nothing to get used to, except this way everyone around here has got of talking plenty until you want to know something—and then they won't talk at all. Stephen now—you ask him, and you get a joke, but no answer. When he was in London, what did he do?"

"He was a chartered accountant."

"You have to do a long training for that, don't you?"

"Yes."

"So he does a long training, and he gets a good job, and then he gives up and comes back here and takes up farming, which he doesn't like and which doesn't pay and which he does badly. Now *why?*"

"Don't you rather imagine things?"

"No; I don't imagine things," said Coolie, in her level tones. "I just think things out, and when I get to a knot, I ask somebody a question so's I can get the knot straightened out. I ask a question that you could answer in ten seconds—if you wanted to. But nobody around here answers questions."

"That's what I was trying to begin to say. England's a bit different, and—"

"What's different about English people? If a boy back home goes to the big city and trains himself for a good job, and takes a long time training, and lands himself a good job, we all

155

say he's doing fine. If he kicks it all over and shows up again where he started off and starts serving you milk-shakes behind the counter in the drug-store, then you say, 'Sonny, what brung you home?'—and he tells you. If he doesn't tell you, you're entitled to draw your own conclusions. That goes for America, and it goes for here, too. Where's the difference?"

"Perhaps the difference," I said, after deliberation, "is that over here, we...don't ask."

We looked at one another for a long time, and then Coolie smiled.

"Claire," she said slowly, "you say the cutest things." Then, with a lift of her hand, she was gone, and I walked slowly into the house. The strains of music met me before I could open the door, and went upstairs to its solemn sound. I felt sorry for Coolie, and sorry for Stephen.

But most of all, I felt sorry for myself.

Chapter Ten

I was beginning to know something of Coolie's mild and seemingly effortless direction of her father and his affairs, but I was surprised, nevertheless, at the outcome of the brief struggle that was waged between her and Lady Evelyn a few days later.

We were to call on Miss Maxwell, the last person on Christabel's list of those qualified to give first-hand accounts of her Cousin Jeffry. I say "we" because I was to go and drive the car through London; Miss Maxwell lived at an address in Kensington, and Coolie, whose *forte* was speed rather than navigation, was to drive to the outskirts of Town and then hand the wheel over to me. I had not been anxious to go at first, but I had been pondering over the subject of Jeffry Hansard, and I had reasons of my own for wanting to be present at the interview—and they were not the same as Coolie's reasons.

Mr. Donner was, of course, to be one of the party, since he was—he imagined—to conduct the interview. There was no question in his mind, or in Lady Evelyn's, as to her making the fourth of the party; his devotion to her was now such that he enjoyed nothing unless she was there to tell him how killing it was. As to Lady Evelyn, she felt, when Mr. Donner left her side, the same sense of loss that gripped her when the string-bag, the umbrella, the two dogs or the handbag were mislaid. They were part of her; she put them aside only when she retired for the night, and she looked for them the first thing next morning. The idea of the big green car going off to London and leaving her behind was something she had not thought of.

Coolie not only thought of it, but brought it off with a subtlety and a gentleness that moved me to admiration. I met Lady Evelyn on the morning before we were to go to London, and expected her to continue her description—interrupted the day before—of the coat she intended to wear. But there was no mention of the coat. Instead, she came up to me with her face full of eagerness and spoke in an excited stage whisper.

"Claire, you'll be discreet, won't you?"

"Discreet?"

"Not a word to him, mind. By the time you get back, I shall have got the whole thing settled. But Mr. Donner's not to know beforehand; there may be a hitch of some sort, you know. People might prefer a cocktail party or something of that kind. I'll have to sound them."

"Nobody," I said, "has told me anything. If you want me to be discreet—"

"Coolie hasn't told you?"

"I haven't seen Coolie."

"Well"—Lady Evelyn took a firmer grip of the umbrella— "we've had rather a good idea. I'm not going to take the whole credit for it, but I think Coolie will agree that I said it first. It's this: Mr. Donner has got to go back to America *some* time, hasn't he?"

I supposed so; the thought gave me an unexpected pang. I wouldn't miss Coolie, but the portly form of Mr. Donner, trotting here and there by the side of Lady Evelyn, beaming through his glasses, holding up his hand and waggling a fore-finger to give point to his remarks...I would miss him very much. I agreed, however, that he would have to go.

"Well, then," said Lady Evelyn, "We can't—after all his kindness to us—allow him to go away without a sign, can we?"

I thought it would be better if we didn't. Lady Evelyn had a special warmth in speaking of his kindness, for wherever Mr. Donner halted on his travels, food parcels from Verna found their way to him. He would not, he said firmly, eat our food. Lady Evelyn said that she didn't blame him a bit, and was assured by the horrified Mr. Donner that its quantity, and not its quality, was what he had had in mind. Some of the parcels went, of course, to Lorna, but everybody knew the things that Lady Evelyn liked best, and they usually found their way to her.

"What did you think of doing?" I asked.

"Well, it's very difficult to do anything for people like that, because they've got almost everything that anybody can want. All we can do is to show them how much we've en-joyed having them here. I'd just thought of it, when Coolie met me—and she, oddly enough, was also thinking of something of the kind. *She* wanted to give a farewell party to us, and *I* want to give a farewell party to them, and so this is what I'm going to do: I'm going to take the opportunity of staying behind to-morrow, when you all go off to London, to send out a few invitations to people. Do you think I should sound them about it first?"

"People don't have to be sounded," I said. "All you have to do is invite them. They'll all come."

"I hope so, but my idea—and you mustn't on any account mention this either to Coolie or to her father—is to have the party on the day the memorial tablet is unveiled."

"I didn't know there was any question of—"

"—unveiling it. But why shouldn't we? Mr. Donner would like it, don't you think? He could take photographs of the ceremony to send back to all those people in Prophet, Arizona." She always pronounced it as though it were one word – Prophetarizona - and I think she thought it was. "I can't help feeling a little bit pleased with myself, Claire. Coolie mentioned a party, but an unveiling ceremony is quite my own idea. But you and she are such good friends that you might allow something to pop out, and I'd rather you didn't."

I promised that nothing would pop out, and went to finish some work at the farm. Stephen asked me what was exciting his grandmother, and I told him. I could have told him that the excitement was Coolie's way of providing her with interest and amusement while we went to London without her, but I said nothing. Her father had come a long way to get the information he wanted, and I had to acknowledge that Lady Evelyn's presence at the interviews was enlivening, but scarcely helpful.

"What time do you go off to-morrow?" he asked.

"Middle of the morning. Miss Maxwell has asked us to lunch—that means getting there just before one, I suppose."

"Well, see that Coolie starts in time; you can't do ninety on these roads."

"She can," I said.

"I know." Stephen wore a worried frown that had never been there when he checked my speed. "I know. I suppose you couldn't drive all the way?"

"I don't think she'd let me. She says she likes to move." We stood there for some time without speaking. There was work to be done, but we weren't working—either of us— with the energy that we'd once put into the job. The farm, never Stephen's idea of congenial work, was now doubly irksome because it kept him from spending all his time with Coolie. She spent nearly all her days on it—but there were still moments during which she was out of his reach. I had watched his feelings change from frank relief at her absence to indifference, and from indifference to restlessness. Then he had begun to watch for her; now he only seemed to be thoroughly alive when she was with him.

I still wonder, at times, why nobody round us seemed to

see what was happening. Nobody that should have seen, that is. Coolie knew, at last, but Lorna and Lady Evelyn and my uncle remained oblivious to what was going on so near to them. Only Mr. Donner, to my surprise and everlasting gratitude, began to look at me with something more than friendly interest. In spite of his incessant wanderings in and out of the village shops, in spite of his preoccupation with Lady Evelyn, his sternly-kept hours for writing to his wife and his friends, Mr. Donner began to see that Stephen had ceased to have eyes for anybody but Coolie. Whether he ever said anything to Coolie on the subject, I shall never know, but, being Mr. Donner, I think that he preferred to come down and make his own investigations.

He wandered on to the farm that day, with a rather elaborate excuse of coming to thank me for taking so much time off in order to drive them about in London.

"I'll enjoy it," I told him. "I haven't been to Town since… Oh, I can't even remember."

Mr. Donner found himself a comfortable perch, settled himself on it and prepared for a chat.

"Now you," he said, "you're a good hand at this sort of thing"—he waved a hand towards some calves scampering round the yard. "You look to me as if you knew what you were doing. Now Steve there, he looks as though he's holding the book in one hand and doing what it says with the other. Coolie tells me he's a qualified fellow at his other job. Now, why doesn't he go and do it?"

"Ask him." I said, smiling.

"I'll do more than ask him," said Mr. Donner. "If he can't find a job in his own line to suit him in this country, I'll tell him I can give him one over in my country. Now how about that?"

I waited for a few moments, and then smiled again.

"Ask him," I said.

"Time enough," said Mr. Donner. "Claire, don't you have anybody to look out for you?"

"Guardians?"

"People who look out for you. People who know what you're doing, and why you're doing it. People who wonder whether it's the right thing for you to do. People who push you around when you need it, and leave you alone when you don't."

"I shouldn't like anybody to push me around," I told him. "Everybody knows what I'm doing, but since I was about as old as those calves I've run my own life."

"Tell me about your own life," invited Mr. Donner. "I'm kind of interested in your own life."

I laughed.

"It isn't very exciting. I was born in Polden."

"That must have been difficult—being born. Lady Evelyn says that you didn't have any parents."

"Well, for all practical purposes, I didn't. They weren't very young, and my mother died when I was born. And my father died not long afterwards and…well, here I am."

"But you got here too fast," objected Mr. Donner. "You didn't get here all at once."

"Oh, I—"

"Wait a minute. You're a baby, and you don't have any parents. So who looks after you?"

"Oh—various people. Lady Evelyn was one of my guardians, but she was hardly ever in England. The other was my uncle. He and his wife took me in—if that's the expression. Then my aunt died and my uncle accepted the living of Polden—and here I am."

"No, you're not. You're a baby, being looked after by your uncle and aunt. Now, I must get that word right—you call it ah-nt—is that how?"

"Well, yes. An aunt, the way you pronounce it, is a little red or black thing wriggling about on the ground. She wouldn't like that."

"We'll call her your ah-nt. And how did your ah-nt die?"

"Influenza, I think—that dangerous kind they used to have. Cluny says so, anyhow."

"How old were you when you came to Polden?"

"Between eight and nine, I think. Then I went off to boarding school, but I spent my holidays here, mostly. Then when I was older, I used to go and stay with Lady Evelyn."

"And did you go by yourself?"

"No. I went with Stephen."

"And did you go often?"

"Fairly often. Is this really interesting?"

"If you think that I'm—"

"Oh, no, no, no! Good heavens, no! I just thought you'd find it boring, that's all."

"I don't find it boring. I don't find anything boring when it's about nice girls like you. So you and Stephen were going around. He must have been a nice young fellow."

"He was."

"And then you stopped going to school?"

"Yes. I went to Paris to learn dressmaking—just for something to do."

"And what did Steve do?"

"He went up to Oxford. And then I came back and got a job in London and stayed in it until I thought I could be more useful giving Stephen a hand down here—and so here I am... at last."

"And don't you find it kind of slow?"

"No—I don't think so."

"But when you came—when you threw up your job in London, where you had lots of people round you to have a good time with, and came down here—then how about those guardians of yours? Did they think it was a good thing?"

"I don't remember asking them."

Mr. Donner shook his head slowly from side to side.

"Well, if I'd been one of them," he said, "I guess I'd have

had something to say to young Steve for asking you to do it."

"Oh—he didn't ask me! I thought I could be useful to him—and so I am, but I had a hard job persuading him at first."

"How long ago was that?"

"About two years."

"And you're twenty-six—am I right? Twenty-six—and now, after running your life, you're in a village with some fine old people of my age, but with nobody much of your own. Is that where you thought you were running it to? Now"—he held up a hand in the familiar gesture—"you don't have to answer that. But I'm an inquisitive man, Claire. I'm known as the most all-enquiring man between New York and Nevada. If I don't like people, then I don't want to know about them, but I like you a lot."

"Thank you."

"And it seems to me," pursued Mr. Donner, "that you're out of the ordinary pretty, that you've got a figure that would make your fortune in pictures, and a skin like our peaches back home. Now, when I see a girl like that, I like to see her in a place where she can be looked at—looked at and admired by a lot of fellows of her own age. Back in Prophet, the boys would be coming at you so fast, you'd think they were coming out on a fire-call—and maybe they would, at that. But here…"

Mr. Donner stopped, and I knew why. Having come so far, it would be natural to ask what I was doing here. But he knew, by now—and I had known for two years. It was too late, now, for advice. Two years earlier, somebody might have said something, or done something to make me stop and think— but nobody could do anything now, except what Mr. Donner was doing—feel their way and find that it led to a brick wall. But his interest and sympathy, in a world which seemed to have forgotten that I existed, was so sweet that I let it flow over me in the silence, and told myself that if there was much of her father in Coolie Donner, Stephen would have nothing much to worry about.

But I suppose Mr. Donner had got what he wanted: a knowledge of my feelings. He saw more through his glasses than most people imagined. He asked no more questions; he talked with some knowledge about the jobs I was engaged on, and went away when he saw Lady Evelyn going up the hill towards the Lodge.

Coolie called for me the next morning, and my uncle, well wrapped up, followed me out of the house with a selection of scarves guaranteed to keep the chill off my chest. I took one of them, but I had no intention of wearing it; I was, for the first time in Coolie's experience, in town clothes, and she opened her eyes with exaggerated admiration when she saw me.

"My, my," she exclaimed. "Is Miss Maxwell *that* grand?"

"It's nice to be in London clothes—for a change," I said. "Where's your parent?"

"My par-ent's where my par-ent always is; just one step behind Lady Evelyn. You know what, Claire? They're Evelyn-ing and Conrad-ing each other like buddies, and he's asked her to come over to Prophet and stay with us. Lady Evelyn in Prophet! Holy smoke!"

"How would she fit?"

"She'd fit, that's all. I hope she doesn't come, though. Verna'd burst a blood vessel showing her off."

It seemed an unlikely prospect. We drove to the farmhouse to pick up Mr. Donner, and Lady Evelyn waved us off with enough nods and winks to arouse suspicion in the most naive spectator. It seemed odd to drive away without her, but when I glanced down at the speedometer a few minutes later, I forgot everything but my prayers. I understood now why Lady Evelyn found it more exciting to keep her eyes on Coolie's speeds than on the scene that was flying past. I must have had less courage than she had—or more of a driver's nervousness—because I found it better, after a time, to keep my eyes on the scenery and enjoy the soothing motion of the car, which appeared to be cruising at a sober forty.

We got to the outskirts of London, and Coolie and I changed places and we went at a more regulation speed through the busy streets. I got to Kensington and found, without trouble, the address given by Miss Maxwell, but we discovered, when we drew up before it, that it was not the private dwelling we had expected it to be. I was more surprised than the others, because although I had never heard of Miss Maxwell until her name appeared on Christabel's list, nobody had indicated that she was running a business. The name over the doorway, however, stated it clearly:

GERALDINE MAXWELL GOWNS. FURS.

"What d'you know—a dress-shop!" said Coolie. "Pop, hurry and let's get in there."

We got out, and Coolie and her father waited until I ran the car to a car-park further down the street. Then we approached the smart doorway, all wrought iron and plate glass, and pushed it open.

The shop was not large, but it was elegantly appointed. We were greeted by a woman with a stout figure encased— that is the word—in shiny black satin. She floated across the showroom in a gliding movement which Coolie described as coming at us, and wrung plump white hands and showed strong white teeth.

"M'sieur; Mesdames…"

"You do the talking, Pop," commanded Coolie.

"Ah—Amer-i-can!" cooed Black Satin with a visible access of enthusiasm. "Come in, please."

We came in, and I had a closer view of the saleswoman. She was well worth a look; there was an Oriental strain not far back in her ancestry, and it added a touch of the unusual to her familiar smart-business-woman appearance.

"These are the daughters of M'sieur?" she enquired, looking at us with a friendly and not too avid interest.

"They are, and they're not," explained Mr. Donner.

"Ah!" Black Satin glowed into life. "M'sieur wishes to

see some models? *Je vais vous montrer…*"

"No," said Mr. Donner, with great firmness. "*Merci.* Thank you—no. I would like to see—"

"Evening dresses?"

"No, thank you."

"Some *mignonne* nightdresses?" offered the temptress, an octave lower.

"No. Thank you, no. I have come to see—"

"Wait!" She walked to a curtain, moving with surprising grace and swiftness for one so stout, and drew it back with a flourish. "See! The cocktail!"

"Wow!" murmured Coolie reverently.

"Now, Coolie, some other time," remonstrated Mr. Donner. "We have come," he went on to the saleswoman "to see Miss Maxwell."

"Mees Maxwell! Ah! But I am so sorree—Mees Maxwell is engaged. For just a few meenutes—weel you sit down?" We sat down. "While you are waiting, I weel show you one or two things. Oh, no, no, no—you need not buy. The young ladies like to see—no?"

"Yes," said Coolie.

"Now, honey, this isn't the time," protested Mr. Donner. "She has lots of dresses," he informed me—unnecessarily, for I knew, by now, the extent and expensiveness of Coolie's wardrobe. She was not to add to it to-day, however, for a door behind us opened and an elderly, pleasant-faced woman came out, and, with a smile of apology as she passed us, ushered her companion to the door and saw it close behind her.

"And now I'm free," she said, turning to greet us and holding out her hand. "Will you forgive me? I was delayed. Mr. Donner…Miss Donner…and Claire—it must be Claire!" Miss Maxwell pressed my hands warmly. "I knew your mother, and you look like her. I knew I couldn't be mistaken. And tell me, how is Grayleigh?"

Mr. Donner could answer that, and did. Miss Maxwell listened to him with a smile, and then glanced at her watch and spread out her hands in a gesture of gathering us together.

"We are going out to lunch," she said. "You came to talk, and of course, we can't talk here. Fifi"—she turned to the saleswoman, who had long outgrown the name—-"Fifi, I shall be back at three."

"*Bon;* then we shall look at some dresses, no?"

"Yes," said Coolie.

Miss Maxwell left us to put the last touches to her toilet, and Fifi took Mr. Donner aside to explain to him that mesdemoiselles were always mesdemoiselles and could always use an extra dress or two, especially when it came from so kind a gentleman. Coolie looked at me, and murmured her appreciation of Miss Maxwell.

"Business-like," she said. "Maybe we're going to get some place."

I, too, was rather hopeful. I imagined—we all imagined—

Miss Maxwell leading us into a quiet restaurant and across to a table in a distant corner, where we could talk freely, so that I can't say which of us was most taken aback when the taxi stopped in front of some Spanish architecture labelled *Los Burros* and Miss Maxwell, waiting until Mr. Donner had paid the taxi-driver, swept us inside and, after a rapid exchange in Spanish with a head waiter, established us in the noisiest corner of what must have been the most densely populated area in the British Isles.

We sat down—even this was a noisy proceeding, since it was accompanied by apologies in Spanish from the waiter, who had to pull the table out before we could make our way round it. There were Spanish protests from the patrons into whom he had pushed it, warning Spanish cries from bearers of loaded trays on their way past, conversation in all languages all round us, and the buzz and babel of a hundred voices. Coolie and I squeezed ourselves close up to the table, and it was pushed back—to more, and louder, protests and apologies. Mr. Donner and Miss Maxwell seated themselves opposite, and the party was ready to begin.

I accepted an enormous menu—almost the same square yardage as the table at which we sat—and from behind it stole a look at Coolie. She was looking across the table at Miss Maxwell, but that lady was propped up on one elbow, leaning towards Mr. Dormer and shouting – necessarily - into his ear.

"I thought you'd enjoy coming here," she was saying. "All genuine South American—nothing pseudo. And the food is

172

good. I can recommend all the chili things, if your palate can stand them. But we must begin with a drink."

Over a drink, Miss Maxwell brought up the subject which had brought us to Los Burros.

"You want to talk about Jeffry Hansard," she said. "Is what you were telling me about his having left money to that hospital really true, Mr. Donner?"

"Quite true," said Mr. Donner, stretching round a waiter. "Oh yes, quite true. Did you know him well?"

"Yes." Miss Maxwell leaned sideways to allow knives and forks to be placed in position. "I did. I knew him very well, but I didn't know he'd gone off to America. He was always coming and going, you know."

"Yes; I heard that. What sort of a man would you say he was, Miss Maxwell?"

"Sort of man? No, I wouldn't have soup, Claire dear, if I may advise you. The other things are rather heavy, so you should begin with something light. Now—forgive me." Miss Maxwell turned back to Mr. Donner. "Sort of man. Well, very English-looking; full of charm, of course, but not very fond of work, perhaps. Fair hair, grey eyes, a rather misleading, slight stammer—you thought he was shy, and found he wasn't. Clever, naturally, not very fond of sport, but would, I think, have been good at sketching if he'd given his mind to it. Not a good family man, perhaps; not a good man's man either, but good company, on the whole."

173

This recital, beginning with an air of brisk frankness, faltered a little towards the end under Coolie's quiet, unblinking survey. Miss Maxwell looked up after buttering a roll to find the cool gaze still upon her, and I saw a blush darken the discreet rouge on her cheeks. Mr. Donner noticed nothing except the fact that Miss Maxwell had left him, for the moment, free to eat his lunch, and he applied himself thankfully to the business of eating. I ate a little, and thought a lot, but said nothing until Miss Maxwell asked me whether there were many changes in Grayleigh.

"Though it's silly to ask you," she added. "I meant changes since a time before you were born."

I raised my head several times during the course of the meal to find Miss Maxwell's eyes fixed on me with keen speculation, and I didn't have to speculate upon what she was speculating upon: she was wondering how much I knew. And if she was wondering how much I knew, then there must be something to know. My opinion of Coolie's acumen rose greatly.

There was nothing more of any note about Jeffry Hansard. The room grew even more crowded, the noise became shriller and the heat more oppressive. Mr. Donner, hemmed about by waiters, leaning constantly this way and that to allow them passage between our table and the next, looked longingly at the exit and beamed with relief when we all refused coffee. He called for the bill, and there was a pretty scene in which it was brought, at her insistence, to Miss Maxwell, who signed it and led us all out into the welcome coolness of the street.

We took a taxi back to the shop, and there we parted from Miss Maxwell. She seemed to be on the point of saying something more than a conventional farewell to Coolie, but got no help from the latter's polite but far from warm handshake. With a look of regret—or appeal, I don't know which—and with a slight shrug, Miss Maxwell left us and we walked silently back to the car.

I drove all the way back to Grayleigh; Mr. Donner, at the back, yawned several times and then, we supposed, went into a doze. Coolie said little or nothing, and I enjoyed handling the car. I stopped at the Vicarage and got out, and Mr. Donner went inside to have a word with my uncle.

"Well," asked Coolie, "do you believe me now?"

"Yes," I admitted. "But don't you feel that—if there *was* anything—they wouldn't be prepared to drag it out and wave it about in front of strangers?"

"If there was anything about Jeffry Hansard that was... shady," she said, "then his cousin Christabel would have known about it, wouldn't she?"

"I suppose so."

"Then why invite us here? Because she did. She didn't just say that we could come and pick up a few random facts here and there. She said Come, and she meant Come. She said, as plainly as she could say it without actually writing it down, that she knew a lot and that the others knew a lot, too. And they were all going to lay it at Pop's feet."

I said nothing. I was thinking of all that had happened since I had taken the first letter up to Lorna…and Lorna had taken it up to Christabel…and Christabel had brought Mr. Donner and Mr. Donner had brought Coolie, who was sitting here now; who had turned Stephen into a strange and unfamiliar person who looked at me sometimes as though he hadn't seen me…Stephen…

I said nothing. I let them drive away and then I went upstairs and changed into my working clothes and walked down to the farm. I saw Stephen walking over from the farmhouse, and stood still to wait for him, and I noticed a lot of things about him that hadn't struck me before—his thinness, and the look of strain round his mouth.

"Well?" he asked.

"Coolie's quite right; they all know something, and they're all keeping it to themselves."

"I'm glad," said Stephen.

"Miss Maxwell has a shop—it looks a flourishing business."

"I wish to God," said Stephen with a quiet, dreadful sort of bitterness, "I wish to God I had a flourishing business. I wish…Claire."

He stopped.

"Well," I asked, after a few moments.

"Oh—nothing. Nothing. Except that I hate this ruddy farm and everything on it. Sometimes I think that it was a monumental mistake. If it hadn't been for you—and I was a fool to let you come and break up your life and—"

"I like it down here," I said. "That makes it easy for me."

"You don't really like it. If I hadn't got stuck down here, you'd never have given up a decent job and a decent life, and...I should never have let you come down and get caught up in it all."

"You couldn't very well have stopped me."

I looked at him, and suddenly it came to me that I had been thinking a great deal about myself and my feelings, and about Coolie and her effect on Stephen, but I had given comparatively little thought to Stephen himself. And I saw now that he looked drained and haggard, and I forgot everything but the desire to make him happy.

"Stephen," I began.

"Yes?"

"Mr. Donner said something to-day...He said that he could—could offer you a job in your own line over...over there."

"I've no doubt he could. I've no doubt he could offer me dozens of jobs, and all at executive level. It didn't take him long to take my measure as a gentleman of the soil, did it? It wasn't until he...Well, it's brought it home to me."

"You were all right before he came here." The 'he' was safer than a 'she.'

"No, I wasn't, Claire. I was a fool to let you get mixed up

in this."

"You weren't a fool. We talked it all over—if you remember."

"Remember? Good God, Claire, I've spent the past few days remembering every word we uttered. And the more I remember, the more I see myself as some kind of staggeringly selfish…"

He seemed unable to go on, and he looked so white that I went over to him and lifted his arms and put them round me and leaned my head on his shoulder.

"Do something for me," I begged.

"Anything, Claire."

"Stop worrying. Stop going round and round trying to find solutions. Stop thinking about other people. Stop thinking about me."

"About—"

"Just for a little while. You'll do nothing, this way, except hurt yourself. Things have got to straighten themselves out—one way or the other. What I wanted to say to you was this: If Mr. Donner really was serious about that job, then why couldn't you take it?"

"Are you mad? Why—"

"Don't take your arms away yet. I'm nice and settled. What I'm trying to say to you is that taking a job in America is different from taking one here—don't you see that?"

"Yes."

"Do you understand what I'm trying to say?"

"Yes."

"If you want to go, I'll stay here and look after Lady Evelyn. She'll always be happy as long as one of us is with her... You—or me. If you want to go, I'd like you to know that I'd..."

He cradled me in his arms, and we said nothing for a long time. A long, long time. I think we were both saying goodbye to something that had existed between us; something that went back down the years, but that wasn't going forward; that had ended for ever. Leaning against him—quietly, and without any feeling but one of gentle sorrow for something that died there between us, I gathered enough strength for what I was certain, now, was coming.

I looked up at last.

"I made you an offer," I said.

He bent and kissed me gently.

"No," he said.

A small word, and spoken without emphasis, but I knew that it was final.

Chapter Eleven

Nothing can better indicate the state of my mind at that time than the fact of my having gone up to London without first going to the Lodge to warn Lorna that Lady Evelyn was planning to give a party. By the time I had realised what this omission entailed, the invitations had been sent out and it was too late for warnings.

Lady Evelyn had been reared in the grand tradition. When she spoke of having a few friends in for drinks, she meant throwing open both drawing-rooms and engaging extra waiters. Picnics were planned on a Marie Antoinette scale; a dance was not a mere scratched-up affair with seven or eight couples and the radiogram; it was a full-scale ball with an orchestra brought from Town and a champagne supper. With Lorna or Stephen or with me beside her to whittle down her plans to present-day proportions, no harm was ever done, but I had left her with a free hand, and when I remembered this that night, lying in bed and reflecting on the day's events, I could scarcely wait for morning before hurrying up to Lorna with a confession, and abject apologies.

"It doesn't matter," sighed Lorna. "We'll just have to cancel whatever we can."

It wasn't the first time we had sat down to do some can-celling. Lady Evelyn's joy lay solely in the planning; she built up a party, large, well-attended and completely successful, and it took place in her mind as she wrote the invitations. She had given the party for Mr. Donner as she sat happily at the farm-house on the previous day, and she had enjoyed every mo-ment of it. On the real day, she would find her pleasure, not in comparing the plan with the performance, but in chatting to anybody who happened to have taken her invitation seriously enough to come down and attend the function. Thus, Lorna and I were not weighed down by a sense of inflicting disap-pointment upon her.

Lady Evelyn's correspondence was conducted on novel lines. Letter-writing, like knitting and doing her tapestry-work, required two things that were not in her: inactivity and con-centration. Knitting could be left lying about indefinitely; nee-dlework could also be neglected, but friends had a way of de-manding a certain amount of attention. To keep in touch with them there had to be at least occasional communication.

Lady Evelyn had reduced this to what I suppose must be the absolute minimum—both in time and trouble. She kept a great number of postcards in her desk—they varied from beautiful reproductions of world-famous pictures to blurred photographs of Allchester High Street. From time to time, she would seize several of these postcards and in her large, scrawling handwriting dash off five words: lovely to hear from you. It was many years before I realised how fully those words covered the whole range of their writer's requirements. They gave the recipients a lot to think about, and left Lady Evelyn in a very strong position, lovely to hear from you might mean that she had just received a letter and was charmed to have it; on the other hand, the words—to anyone who hadn't written for some time—would convey an affectionate and delicate reproach. In either case, it was their turn.

Her address book was a very large one, and looked, when you first opened it, like a child's exercise book which had been filled and then passed to a younger member of the family to be scribbled upon. Lady Evelyn had long ago filled up all the more usual letters of the alphabet with the names of her friends, and had then overflowed into the X and Z sections, which were not likely, she thought, to be needed. Her travels in Europe had taken her, however, into circles the names of whose members all began with X and Z, and this had created a major difficulty and necessitated a good deal of cross-writing. From time to time, Lady Evelyn opened the book, took a dozen or so postcards and dashed off the usual inscription. She then stopped Roly on his way past the farmhouse and asked him to give them to Mrs. Macmillan at the Post Office and tell her to remember to put the stamps on them before she sent them off. Every now and then, Stephen or I would drop into the Post Office and pay her account.

Her invitations were equally brief; she wrote, simply, the date and the time—nothing else. Nobody, she pointed out with some truth, would expect Monday the seventeenth at a quarter to one, to be anything but an invitation to lunch. Everybody, on receipt of Thursday the twelfth at seven- thirty, would appear dressed for dinner.

It is easy to see what had happened when Lady Evelyn had been left with a free hand. On this occasion, she had exhausted not only her own, but also all Polden's supply of postcards, and they had gone out with "Wednesday the twenty-third at four o'clock" written on them. She didn't, she told us, remember quite how many she had sent; Mrs. Macmillan, hastily applied to for information, gave us the staggering total of one hundred and twenty-two.

"It was to be a joint affair," I explained to the shattered Lorna. "She and Mr. Donner were getting a bit competitive as to who'd give what. He wasn't supposed to know anything about it, but of course, he did."

We didn't know—and never found out—the full list of guests. All we could do in the first dreadful moments of panic was find out the worst that had been planned for us, and try to prevent it. By "we" I mean Lorna and I. This was a family matter, and we were both of one mind in keeping it as much as possible to ourselves. I told Stephen that I was going up to help Lorna to "sort out things"—by which he understood everything perfectly—and I left Coolie to take over my jobs at the farm for the day. It was something I would have liked to avoid, but she would be there, I knew, whether she went to do my work or not.

Lorna and I found out, bit by bit, the greatest pitfalls, and went to work. We wrote first to the Dean of Chellambury, who had been asked, Lady Evelyn said, in case there was any praying to be done at an unveiling. We cancelled the order for one hundred and twenty teas from the Allchester Tea Shoppe; we wrote to the A.A. and told them that they wouldn't he needed to control the traffic. We didn't need to put off the Duchess of Whengram, who had been asked to do the unveiling, as we knew her to be visiting friends in Canada. We told the firm at Allchester that we didn't need the flooring, and cancelled the arrangements for the marquee from London. We telephoned to the *Allchester Chronicle,* the *Allchester Illustrated,* the *Tatler* and the *Sketch* and told them that there would be nothing to report and even less to photograph. We wrote a very tactful letter to the Secretary of the Allchester Folk-Dancing Society and explained that it would be better to hold the exhibition for Mr. Donner at some other time. We rang up the Convent and called off the Maypole Dance and said that we wouldn't be needing the maypole—or the children who were to dance round it. Finally, with my uncle's sanity in mind, I wrote to put off the Allchester Brass Band. We had done it all before, but not, perhaps, to the extent to which we had had to do it that day. This time, Lady Evelyn had really enjoyed herself.

"Oh well…" Lorna gave a weary sigh, "I think we've done all we can, don't you?"

"We'll have to provide some teas of some sort, but Cluny can come up, and we can get some stand-bys from the village.

We ought to be able to manage to cope with anybody who does come, I think."

"It'll be all those foreigners again," prophesied Lorna gloomily.

"It doesn't matter; we've done all we can," I said.

"Yes...What a waste of your day, Claire. You'll have such a lot to make up."

"Not really. Coolie took over for the day. She's pretty good on a farm."

"You mean she's been working there all day, helping Stephen?"

"Yes. There's nothing out of the way in that. She's usually there, helping...one or the other of us."

Lorna made no reply; she was clearing the table on which we had been writing. Her next words seemed casual.

"They won't be here much longer," she said.

"No; I suppose not."

"We'll miss them when they go."

"Yes."

"I can scarcely imagine Evelyn without Mr. Donner."

"Nor can I. But we got on all right before they came here; I suppose we'll get over it."

I may have sounded a little sarcastic; I didn't mean to. Lorna glanced at me and then looked away again.

"Coolie's a nice girl," she said. "She seems to fit in everywhere."

I would have liked to point out that the cuckoo fits in everywhere—when it has pushed something else out of the nest in order to make room for itself. But it was untrue and unjust, and I gathered up the rest of the papers without speaking. I knew that Lorna was seeing, for the first time, a possibility that had never occurred to her before, and I had moments of wry amusement as I wondered whether she would find anybody to talk the matter over with. She could hardly discuss it with me, or with Stephen. Lady Evelyn would not be of much use, and my uncle was, of course, completely out of the picture. Cluny could tell her anything she wanted to know, but she wouldn't ask Cluny. She would have to do what I was doing—turn it over and over and over…and end by waiting, as I was waiting, to see how it was all going to end.

But if the possibility of Stephen and Coolie falling in love had not struck Lorna until then, it would have been brought home to her in the course of the next few days. The situation was rapidly becoming clear to anybody who had eyes. Stephen was never a man who talked very much, but on the other hand he had never gone about—as he was doing now—wrapped in an unending and absorbed silence. He heard what was said to him, but it was some time before he took in its sense, and longer before he answered a question. He looked white and haggard, and he took to going for walks—long, aimless walks—instead of going into meals at the farmhouse.

Coolie was in worse plight. For one thing, she didn't understand Stephen as well as I understood him, and his changes of mood left her lost and bewildered. He was in love with her; so much was plain. He was utterly miserable; so much was even plainer. He looked like a man with a heavy load on his mind, and Coolie—naturally, but quite erroneously —came to believe that I was it. That it was me. That it was I. I could follow her reasoning very easily: she would think that Stephen had made love to me, and that he was now caught, either by loyalty or by something more tangible; he loved her, but he couldn't tell her so.

When she had reached this conclusion, there were only two people who could help her out of her dilemma; I knew Stephen wouldn't, and I knew I couldn't. And now, when I might have been excused for hating her, I found myself looking at her pinched little face and feeling deeply, profoundly sorry for her. Life, which had always unrolled itself like a carpet before her feet as she walked, had now, without warning, brought her to a bleak and stony path. She was going down it alone, and she was getting lost.

But if Stephen had retreated into himself, if Coolie was—for the first time in her life—up against a problem that money couldn't solve, the person who suffered most acutely at this time was Mr. Donner. I suppose I was suffering too, but for me most of the suspense was over. I had nothing to do but open my mind, bit by bit, to let into it something that my heart had already accepted. But for Mr. Donner, it was still all fog and bewilderment. He liked me very much, and he wanted to find out what my feelings were; he liked Stephen very much and could see only too plainly what his feelings were; he liked his daughter most of all, and for her his concern was twofold: he had to make sure of what she wanted, and he had to do what he could to see that she got it. Being Mr. Donner, he didn't want to hurt anybody else in the process, and it would have been of great assistance to him if I had assured him, freely and sincerely, that so far as I was concerned, his daughter could have my heart's blood, and my joyous congratulations thrown in. Denied this pleasant relief, he was thrown back upon guile; he came upon me front and flank and rear and retreated in good order; he tried direct and indirect approaches and found them all securely barred. But he kept trying.

I had a text-book knowledge of the fierceness with which mothers cherish their young: here to my hand was an example of a father who showed an equally keen sense of something that threatened the well-being of his offspring. He reminded me of a fat little page at a wedding who, holding a basket of rose-leaves and strewing them before the bride, comes suddenly upon someone who wants to take the basket away.

There could never have been a man who showed such interest in a farm he didn't own. Mr. Donner was seldom off it; he left Lady Evelyn busy with her plans for the party, and found his way down to wherever I happened to be working. He talked of milk yields, butter-fat content, Jerseys and Guernseys, Friesians and shorthorns. He carried buckets of water and forked loads of straw; he pushed barrows and rolled churns— and in between these laborious tasks, made enquiring thrusts designed to catch me at an unwary moment. I felt very sorry for him; he was fighting for his daughter's happiness, and he was also trying to save me from being hurt—but he was too late and I didn't want to talk about it. Once or twice, I wondered whether Coolie had asked him to probe my feelings, but when I saw his eyes—worried and bewildered—on her face, I knew that Coolie wasn't doing much talking either.

Finally, Mr. Donner waited for me on a depressing evening of mist and drizzle—the first break in the brightness of weeks—and escorted me to the Vicarage, holding over me his golf umbrella, as large as a tent and as gay as a marquee. It is difficult to be evasive with a man who is holding your elbow and seeing that drops don't go down your neck. And I was tired, and it had been a difficult day and we had lost a heifer— all of which Mr. Donner took into consideration. "Girls," he said in a general way, "are funny things."

"Kittle cattle."

"Eh? Yes. Yes, indeed. They're all different, but I'm told it all comes to the same thing."

"Plus ça change…"

"Eh? Yes, you've got something there, too. Now you take my daughter. Wouldn't you say a pretty girl like that would spend her time falling into and out of love?"

I had no opinion to offer, and Mr. Donner went on:

"But no; and her mother was the same. I used to say to her mother, 'Why can't Coolie go after the boys the same way the other girls do?' and her mother would say 'Conrad, it's no use; you've just got to leave her alone; she's just like I was—she'll wait till she sees what she wants, and then she'll go after her man.' "

He paused; not for long, but long enough to allow me to have a clear and sharp picture of Coolie going after her man.

"Now, other girls," went on Mr. Donner, "don't behave that way. They might see a fellow they like—for a time, and then they find they don't like him any more. They tell him it's all washed up, and then they call it all off; no hard feelings, and nobody hurt, and next time, she waits a little longer before she calls it the real thing. You see, you get all kinds. Back home, I've seen good boys—handsome boys—boys with something, and boys with nothing, all trying to get Coolie to give them a break—but after a date or two, she'd find there was nothing to it, and give up. It kind of worried me, but her mother said not to take any notice, because she's the kind of girl that'll go for somebody once—just once— and for always, just as her mother did. When it comes that way, it comes hard."

"Yes, it does," I agreed.

"You don't know much about American girls, I suppose," said Mr. Donner wistfully.

"Oh—one or two facts here and there," I said. "After all, you invented the teen-ager, and they're a much-publicised group. Then you have something called college girls, who put in a lot of time at drug stores, drinking milk shakes and eating hamburgers with the college boys. I think that that part of

American life is something I'd like to establish over here. I think you let your girls begin what you call dating much too early; over here, if sex rears its head in anything under the age of thirteen, we rush it off to a psychiatrist at once. But the life of an English girl between the ages of fifteen and nineteen is—I'm speaking generally—one long yawn. They're all right if they're the student type; in that case, they stay at school swotting away at this and that, and then they go to a university and come down with an honours degree. But the other kind— my kind—who hurl themselves thankfully out of school at sixteen, have a rather arid time until they can call themselves entirely grown up. It's *that* section of English girlhood that could do with a college run on strictly American lines—you work if you want to, but you have a lot of sororities and campuses and handsome college boys on the side. It fills in the time so nicely until you're ready to settle down and marry."

I wasn't filling in time too badly myself; the Vicarage gate was in sight and I still had a lot of breath left. Two more sentences, and I could be through the gate and free—free to pursue, in future, a policy of careful evasion. It's difficult to avoid visitors on a farm, but as a rule they fight shy of coming into the bull's pen.

But I wasn't to get out of it so easily. Mr. Donner didn't open the gate for me when we reached it; he put a hand on it and held it firmly shut. Then he abandoned pretence and looked up at me with open appeal shining behind his spectacles.

He had to look up a long way. I have, for ever, this bird's-eye view of him, his forehead puckered with worry, his mouth pursed in suspense, all his simplicity and kindliness submerged in that open, undisguised, desperately appealing gaze.

"I shouldn't ask you," he said falteringly. "I know I shouldn't ask you. I wouldn't if—if…But I'm a family man and I take a fatherly interest in you. It doesn't seem to me that there's anybody here who looks out for you."

I was tired and I wanted to go away and I wanted to be alone. I looked at him and spoke, at last, frankly.

"Mr. Donner," I said, "don't you think this thing is…between Stephen and Coolie?"

There was a long silence. He stared at me with his thoughts clearly mirrored in his face, and I knew that his first reaction to my words was a tremendous relief at finding himself out in the open at last. Then he dropped his hesitation, his fumbling, and became the straight, direct and simple man that he was.

"If I thought so, Claire," he said, "I'd be a happy man. But I don't think so. I don't feel it's that way at all."

"I don't," I told him gently, "see what you can do."

"She loves him, Claire," he said.

His confidence in me staggered me for a moment. I suppose he felt that the fact was so patent, so plain to read upon his daughter's face, that it was childish to pretend blindness.

"I know," I said.

"This isn't a passing thing," he said. "I know her, you see.

She's…she's in deep. She doesn't sleep at night. She gets up in the morning looking…I wish," he ended on a hopeless note, "I wish her mother had come. I can't handle this."

"That's what I said. You don't have to handle it, Mr. Donner. This sort of thing is just between two people—only two."

"You're wrong, Claire. If there was only that to it, then what would be stopping him from…He's got something on his mind, has Steve. He loves her, and he won't say so. That's why I—I came to you."

"How do you think I can help you?"

"There could be two things on his mind," said Mr. Donner slowly. "The first is—the first could be—money. I—I take it that he gets Lady Evelyn's money when she…"

"All she has," I told him, "will go to Stephen."

"But in the meantime," went on Mr. Donner painfully, "he could feel that he didn't have enough to—to…" There was a long pause. He seemed to be looking everywhere but at me.

"I don't think he feels that," I said. "What was the other thing?"

"The other thing," said Mr. Donner, "would be that he— he—"

He was unable to go on, and I came to his assistance.

"If you're trying to say that he's worrying about me," I said slowly, "then you're wrong."

"How do you—"

"You're quite, quite wrong. There was never anything between us. Nothing. Is that what you wanted to know?"

His eyes were full of misery. "Yes," he said. "Yes, I...I guess so. You were the only one who could tell me that, and I—I—"

"Don't worry," I said. "I'm all right. But that's all I can tell you."

There was nothing else to say. I left him by the gate, looking after me with the misery still in his eyes, but I was hardly thinking about what had just passed between us. I was thinking about Stephen—and about myself. I had only two clear thoughts: one was that if I had handed Stephen over to Coolie on a plate, I couldn't have done it more thoroughly.

The other thing that filled my mind was a feeling that it isn't perhaps necessary, after all, to have a lot of relations. You don't really need them. If you want to be cherished and protected, if you want to have life—harsh life—pushed away from you by a strong hand, if you want affection and care and a devotion that stops at nothing to ensure your happiness, you don't need sisters and cousins and aunts.

All you need is a father like Mr. Donner.

Chapter Twelve

After that, everything seemed to move very quickly.

Coolie came down to the farm immediately after breakfast one morning, and made her way straight to me. "Claire," she said, "will you do something?"

"If I can."

"Will you come out with me this afternoon?"

"What for?"

"I won't say right away. I'll stay here and help you now, to make up for taking you away this afternoon. Then I want you to come to Polden with me."

"All right. I'll come."

She stayed to help me; that is, she stayed with me and watched me. It was not like her, for she could make herself very useful when she wanted to, but on that morning she seemed to follow me about without knowing quite where she was. She was deep in thought, and at last I gave up any attempt at talking, and went on with what I had to do. She came out of her brooding silence at last, and looked at me with a purposeful air. Some instinct made me go towards the tiny ramshackle building we called the ruin. She wanted to talk; if that was the case, the ruin was the place I preferred to talk in.

It had served, originally, as a labourer's cottage, but it was now a virtual ruin. There was a small, dark room downstairs and, up a crazy and somewhat dangerous staircase, there was an upper room in which we kept anything that wouldn't, for the time, fit in anywhere else—sacks of meal, Lady Evelyn's cabin trunks and spare suitcases, old dog baskets, picnic hampers and anything that we wanted to get out of the way. It was also a good place in which to work off steam—there were a lot of things that could be pushed here and there, rearranged, or broken up. The ground floor housed all the wood for the farmhouse fires. Altogether, the ruin was a good place to get warm in in winter, and to keep cool in in summer. But the only reason I had for going into it now to talk to Coolie was that it was dark—too dark for anybody to study expressions. I had learned to dread Coolie's level, unwavering gaze.

I picked up a lampshade that had been brought over for repair, and began to work on it. Coolie watched me, but we both knew what was coming.

"Claire"

"Yes?"

"Oh, nothing much. I was just wondering about…Steve. He isn't happy, is he?"

I said nothing. I was determined to say as little as possible.

"Is he?" asked Coolie again.

"If you mean he doesn't like the farm, then you're right—he never did. I told you to ask him. Why didn't you?"

"I'm tired of asking, that's why." Coolie spoke with a note of hopelessness in her voice. "I'm tired of asking. The only person in this place who hasn't got a muzzle on is Lady Evelyn, and sometimes I wish she had. I'm tired of asking, Claire—I never saw a place like this before. I didn't know there were any places like this. You all live here, you've all lived here so long that you've stopped counting, and nobody knows anything about anybody else. Nobody knew anything about Jeffry Hansard, and now nobody knows…I've never pushed my way in where I'm not meant to go, but what can you do when you want to know something? There are lots of things that I have to find out—I *have* to. Jeffry Hansard is one, but there's something bigger than that. Something more important—to me, I mean."

I said nothing. I was twisting a piece of wire, and enjoying it. Coolie watched me for some time, and then gave a long sigh.

"I wish," she said, "that Pop and I had gone away that first day, when we arrived just after the funeral."

I had often wished it, too. I hoped I didn't show it too plainly now, but with Coolie you never knew.

"Claire," she asked suddenly, "what does a girl do in this country when she likes a man?"

"That's a very general sort of enquiry, isn't it? Can't you bring it from the general to the particular?"

But Coolie didn't. Beyond murmuring Polly Syllabic to herself in a dejected tone, she said no more. I was glad and sorry. Things were only just under the surface, and I was beginning to feel a sense of strain. The sooner they came up, the sooner everything was brought out into the open, the sooner… But perhaps, if nothing came to the surface, she would go away and things would be as they had been before. I didn't think they ever would be, but I had faint, lingering hopes.

Coolie called for me after lunch in a much lighter mood. I thought she looked pale, but as we drove towards Polden a lot of our depression seemed to fall away, and we remembered all the days on which we had driven side by side in the car, and found life pleasant and uncomplicated. Perhaps Coolie's driving had something to do with the improvement in my spirits; with the speedometer needle showing no perceptible movement round the most blind corners, I might have felt that it was as well to enjoy the few moments left to us. I was so busy counting our hairbreadth escapes that for a time I scarcely knew where we were, and then I found that we were past Polden and heading for Allchester.

"Wait a minute," I said, "You've overshot it."

"Relax," said Coolie. "I'm going on a visit, and you're coming with me."

I ran over the possibilities: Mr. Petrie or Miss Ferrier. There could be nobody else she wanted to see.

"Well, where?" I asked.

"We're going to that house that Pop went to with you and

Lady Evelyn. The one with the old lady in it who turned out to be two old ladies."

"Miss Ferrier."

"And since she's two, suppose we call her A and B— unless she's got any other name."

"Names aren't much use to a couple who look so much alike that you don't know which is who. It's always difficult with this pair—you can't refer to them as the twins, because they're not; you can't refer to them as Miss Ferrier and Miss Whoever the other is, because you still wouldn't know which was which. I did hear once that one of them was called something like Coronia, because she was born when somebody was crowned, but one doesn't like to ask which coronation it was."

"Well, whatever they're called, we're going to see them."

"What are you going to say to them when you get there?"

"To start off, I thought I'd tell them that my father said their house was a show place, and that maybe they'd show it to me. He said he drank tea out of cups that would've made Verna's hair curl naturally. He said it was sacrilege to sit on those chairs."

"I don't know about sacrilege. They're hard. I don't think you'll get any information out of Miss Ferrier."

"I don't, either. But I might get one of them—A or B— to admit that they spent that afternoon telling my father exactly nothing."

"But—"

"Nobody," said Coolie, flashing past a scandalised cyclist, "wants to know anything that somebody else doesn't want to tell them. I don't want to hold up anybody and say, 'Talk!'— I want to know why they won't. When I've told Miss Ferrier how I feel, then we'll go up to London and have a talk with that Miss Maxwell—Geraldine. But this time, no burros."

"If you'll bring your speed down a bit," I said, "I'll show you the house they used to live in."

Coolie slowed down, and I pointed.

"There."

"*That* one?"

"No—not that moated-grange affair. That was Geraldine's. At least, it belonged to Geraldine's father. No; the other one was Miss Ferrier's."

Coolie looked at it. It was ugly, like most of the houses in Polden and Allchester, but there was quite a lot of it.

"It's seeing that," I said, "that makes you feel a little cramped when you walk into the house they live in now."

"Claire"—Coolie stopped the car, but left the engine running—"Claire, doesn't it strike you that there's some kind of connection between Jeffry Hansard and...No, I said that wrong. I'll put it another way: Take these people —these Ferriers and this Geraldine. Look at what they used to live in, and look at them now. You say the Ferriers live in a yard-square cottage; Geraldine's running a dress business. Couldn't there be some connection between that and Jeffry Hansard? They were rich; now they're poor. He used to borrow vast sums, and then he showed up in America full of dough. Couldn't it work out some way?"

"I don't think so. For one thing, I've never heard anyone say that the Ferriers lost their money."

"But they—"

"Or that Geraldine did. If you read English social history, you'd know that the rich have had a pretty unsettling time of it in the past—"

"I know, I know. I know all that. They get taxed, and they don't have servants any more."

"And so they have to get out of big, out-of-date houses into smaller ones. You can sell big houses, or turn them into flats, but if you don't feel like struggling to keep them up, the wisest thing is to do what the Ferriers have done—get right out of them and get into something of a more manageable size. Geraldine must have had a certain amount of money to buy a dress business in London."

"Why must she? Somebody could put the money up for her."

"They could. But if you take it from the other angle, nobody knows for certain that Jeffry Hansard had money when he went to America—I mean all the money that he left to the hospital. You're always telling me that anyone with two hands and all his senses can make a fortune over there in no time. Why couldn't Jeffry Hansard?"

"I met him, and you didn't," said Coolie. "I don't remember much about him; he was an old man, and a sick man. But you can tell some things when you look at people, and if he ever earned a dollar in his life—the hard way, I mean— then I'll be surprised. Claire, there's *something*…"

"Well, we won't get at it by wasting petrol and breath in an unprofitable discussion in a Buckinghamshire lane," I said. "Let's do something more practical."

"All right, Polly. Let's go."

We did the last stage of the journey a little more soberly, and turned slowly into the little village street, where Coolie slowed the car to a walking pace and gazed at the two rows of tiny houses. I saw her lips widen in a smile.

"This is it," she said. "England like the picture-books. Now, if Pop had brought me to a place like this instead of to a dump like Polden—I'm sorry! That kind of slipped out."

"It was a fairly accurate description. Go on."

"Well, if he had, I'd have felt I was really in England, that's all. Take a look at those dolls' houses, Claire. This place looks like the builders were doing it for a joke. Which one? Oh, Cherryton—I see."

She drew up outside the cottage and sat, as her father had sat, taking in the quiet beauty of the scene. Seen like this, without Lady Evelyn's instructive comments to break the stillness, the peace was infinitely soothing. Each neat, clipped hedge, each little garden path bordered with gay flowers, leading to a pretty cottage which hid shyly behind a mass of climbing plants, everything had an air of being carefully planned, faultlessly made and lovingly tended, but I thought that it all looked a little too tidy for real life, and I felt glad that I lived and worked in surroundings more suited to my size and energies. If I spent a week-end at Cherryton, I was convinced, the walls would crack as I walked upstairs, and large pieces of thatch would fall off as I sang oratorio in my bath. It wasn't for me—but as a perfect example of England-for-the-tourist, I gave it full marks.

I looked past the village to the beautiful woods in the distance, and remembered that round them and beyond them, the hunting country began—country full of memories of wonderful holidays spent with Stephen when he was twelve and I had been a very fat nine and a half—years, not stones. I seemed to see those long-past days with the Woodway Foxhounds and the Bincherston Buckhounds, and I went out again with Stephen, in my imagination, and saw us—older, taller, growing rapidly—with the harriers in winter and the otter-hounds in summer. I saw myself panting and being left behind...Sandwiches and cider...hair rain-wet or sweat-wet and sticking to my forehead; boots thickly plastered with mud. I don't know how I could ever have been fat; it seemed, as I sat there and stared backwards down the years, that I spent my childhood in strenuous activities which would have pared anybody else down to the proverbial string.

"It's lovely," said Coolie on a deep breath.

Yes…it was lovely…

We got out of the car and walked up Miss Ferrier's little path, and then were met by something we'd never anticipated —a blank. We knocked, at first gently; we waited and knocked less gently; finally, we walked round in the hope that we might find the two old ladies in the garden. But they weren't in the garden and they weren't—as windows tightly closed might have shown us at once—in the house.

It was a setback; Coolie looked like a little boy who had an airgun and could find nowhere to use it. I had to readjust my ideas of the two old ladies, since I had imagined that they lived in the little village without ever leaving it. They didn't look— nobody at Rooktree looked as though they were even remotely concerned with anything so everyday as shopping or going to the bank or going to see friends or relations.

It was no use standing there. We turned and walked away, and Coolie used a word I hadn't heard before, and explained that it was American for "Bother!"

"Perhaps," I said, as we climbed into the car, "we'll find them at Allchester. If they've gone shopping, that's where they'll have to go. But if you don't mind, I'll drive. I don't mind sitting beside you on the open road, but I get cramp in my toes once you get into the built-up areas. Move over."

She moved over, and I drove into Allchester. We patrolled the narrow main street, and the great, green car gave a good deal of pleasure to the little boys pouring out of school. It was of a design which makes the back look very much the same as the front, and whenever Coolie and I got out to look into shops in the hope of finding Miss Ferrier inside, there was heavy betting among the schoolboys as to which was the bow and which the stern.

But there was no sign of Miss Ferrier or her sister. I drove on into Polden and we went through the same routine— looking into all the likely shops—and then we decided to give it up and go back to Grayleigh.

"Maybe," said Coolie, "they saw us coming and shut all the windows and kept out of sight."

"Why would they go to all that trouble? They didn't know you were coming to squeeze information out of them."

"I don't like it when you say it that way, but I guess that that's what it adds up to. But I still think they must have seen us coming, and hightailed it out of the back door."

I dwelt for some time on the thought of Miss Ferrier and her sister hightailing it, and then saw something ahead of me that made me bring the car to a somewhat abrupt stop.

"What now?" enquired Coolie.

"Look ahead," I said.

She looked. Two small, thin figures were marching steadily up the road leading to Grayleigh. Seen from the back, they looked even more absurdly alike than they did when viewed from the front. Coolie studied them with round eyes.

"Gosh, Claire," she said at last. "Where d'you think they're headed for?"

"We'll know in a minute, if we wait. They'll either turn into the—"

"I think," said Coolie, "that we'll make certain of getting them where we want them."

"Where do we want them?"

"Can I take them up to your house and talk to them there? Is your uncle home?"

"I don't…No, he isn't, but he'll be back to tea."

"That doesn't give us much time, but it's better than nothing. Drive up close to them, Claire."

I went forward until the car was beside them, and then brought it to a stop.

"Hello, Miss Ferrier," I said.

"Claire, my dear…"

"This is Miss Donner," I said.

"Ah—Miss Donner. I knew the car, of course. We were just going up to the Lodge to see your father."

"We'd just driven over to Rooktree to see you," said Coolie. "Please—won't you get in?"

We got out and helped them into the back of the car, and they both sat bolt upright—no mean feat on those deep springs—and smiled at us.

"If you don't mind," said Coolie, "we'll go to the Vicarage. I wanted to talk to you somewhere where we could be alone."

They showed no surprise, and raised no objection. Coolie and I climbed in and we drove to the door of the Vicarage.

My uncle was out; there was a good fire in the drawing room and we went in and I settled the two old ladies in comfortable chairs. One of them seemed to like the window seat, but her feet didn't reach the floor, and as I couldn't bear to see them dangling, I moved her—I had to prevent myself from picking her up and carrying her—to a chair by the fire. Once we were settled, Coolie wasted no time.

"How do I know," she asked "which of you is which?"

"People always say Miss Ferrier, and it does for both, you know—but we're not twins. I am the elder—my name is Coronia, and my sister's name is Rose. Nobody—except our parents—could ever tell us apart, but when we were small, I was made to keep my handkerchief in my pocket, and my sister's was pinned to her pinafore with a little safety pin, and so people could see which of us was which. It worked very well, but sometimes we changed over and my sister pinned my handkerchief on to my pinafore. Nobody knew the difference."

Coolie glanced at me, and I knew that she was calling my attention to this early tendency towards deceit.

"I am sorry," the soft voice went on "that we weren't at home when you called. We wanted to see your father about this." She opened her neat little handbag and took out a letter, and I saw to my surprise the large, straggling handwriting of Lady Evelyn. "We got a postcard from Lady Evelyn, and also a few lines in which she explained that the object of the party was to…she mentioned a memorial to Mr. Hansard."

"Oh, it's only a small thing," said Coolie. "It's being put

up on the front of the house."

"But Lady Evelyn seems to say that there's going to be quite a—a ceremony, and that a great number of people are…"

"Oh, no," smiled Coolie. "It's really just a farewell party for my father."

She regretted the words the moment they were out, for it was clear that they produced in both Coronia and Rose an instant feeling of relief. Tension eased out of them visibly; the anxiety that had been plainly written on their faces slowly disappeared and was succeeded by an air of placid composure.

"Lady Evelyn didn't make it very clear," said Coronia.

"No. It sounded as though…We rather felt, you know, that it was some sort of public function," said Rose.

Coolie fought off her conviction—which was my conviction too—that the interview was over, and made another attempt at bringing the conversation on to a business-like footing.

"What did you want to see my father about?" she asked.

"Oh, that was all," said Rose. "We hadn't realised it was a farewell party. It sounds as if it will be a very jolly affair."

"Very jolly indeed," said her sister. "Claire, how beautiful the garden is looking."

Coolie looked at her helplessly, and I felt sorry for her. Something in the wording of the letter had alarmed them; they had found that Lady Evelyn had given an exaggerated account of the ceremony that was to take place, and their anxiety was laid to rest.

"Look, Miss Ferrier," said Coolie, with a note of firmness in her voice, "I'd like to—"

She got no further. The door had opened to admit my uncle, and the warmth with which the old ladies greeted him would have puzzled a more observant man. He was holding a parcel in one hand, and when the stir of greetings had died down, he undid the wrappings with a loving hand and showed us a flat cardboard box in which reposed four gramophone records.

"Now, which ones are these?" asked Rose.

They were religious works by Haydn, he told her, and asked whether she knew them. She was not sure, and so he hummed a few bars of each. Rose said that she didn't know those, but hummed a few bars of something else and asked my uncle if he knew that. She found, to her delight, that my uncle had the record, and soon he was leading the sisters into the study and the door had closed on the trio.

"Nice work," commented Coolie. "Mittens, cameo brooches, lace collars and crooked characters."

"Oh, not quite—"

"—crooked. No, just kind of shady. Maybe it would have been better to let them go to the Lodge—maybe they would have said something to Lorna, and then we could have got it out of her."

"I think it would have come to the same thing."

"But we could have worked on Lorna more than you could on those two old pieces of egg-shell. Listen to that! Organ music! Can you beat that, Claire? Your old stained-glass saint of an uncle, and those two wispy characters, all sitting in there with their hands folded and their eyes rolled up to heaven, listening to holy music, and all the time they know, and they know that we know, that they've slipped out from under us— for the second time. That letter of Lady Evelyn's frightened them. They thought there was going to be a jamboree, with everybody yelling their head off for Hansard, and they didn't want that. But when I let out that there wasn't going to be any band, and no fireworks, they felt better about it. But I'm not finished yet. You know what I'm going to do?"

"No."

"I'm going to get hold of that other one, and this time we're going to get something."

"Miss Maxwell, do you mean?"

"Geraldine. And this time, no donkeys. And if there are any donkeys, then—"

"Are you going up to London?"

"I'm going and you're going. That is, if you'll come. Will you, Claire?"

"Yes, I will," I said.

Chapter Thirteen

Coolie found it difficult to decide when and how to see Geraldine Maxwell. She refused to consider telephoning or writing for an appointment; surprise, she said, was everything. The idea of driving up to the shop during working hours was the obvious procedure, but she felt that a procession of customers, to say nothing of the presence of Fifi, would make it easy for Geraldine to avoid anything in the nature of a private talk.

The question was answered the next day by Geraldine herself. I walked out of one of the farm buildings to see a neat grey car standing in the yard; stepping out of it, in a neat grey outfit, was Geraldine. I stopped and looked at her, but I could find nothing to say beyond a somewhat inadequate "Hello."

She looked at me across the yard and mapped out a dry course across the intervening space; following it with dainty footsteps, she came to a stop beside me and looked round her with a critical gaze.

"I don't think I'd care for this," she said. "Wet pavements are as near to rough living as I care to get."

In spite of her sardonic manner, I saw that she had lost some of the poise that had characterised her when we had met her in London. She glanced at me for a moment before speaking again.

"You looked surprised to see me," she said.

"Well, just for the moment, I—"

"I was surprised to see you looking surprised," said Geraldine. "You ought to have expected me. I'm quite sure our little American friend does."

"As a matter of fact, she was—"

"—going out to look for me," finished Geraldine. She gave a brief, impatient sigh. "Well, my dear, now that I'm here, I'd really like to get it over and done with. I came to find you first because I want you to help me."

"Of course—if I can."

"What I want you to do, if you will," she went on, "is to find somewhere where I can talk to Miss America alone. If you'll put me there and then go and fetch her, I'll be very grateful. But—I don't want to seem rude—I don't want her father, or Lady Evelyn, or Lorna Wells or any of the other local residents. Not to-day. Not now. All I've come for is to see Miss Donner and have a little talk with her. Can you arrange it—quietly?"

"I'll try. I'm afraid the Lodge is no use—Mr. Donner's there and so is Lorna. But so," I added on a more hopeful note, "is Lady Evelyn, which means that you could use the farmhouse. There's a daily maid, but she won't be in the way."

"Will Lady Evelyn mind?"

"No; I'm quite certain she won't. In any case, she—"

"—won't know anything about it until I'm on my way back to Town. Well, Claire, lead the way. I do wish I'd brought my stilts with me."

I took her across to the farmhouse and, with a word of explanation to the maid, settled Geraldine in the drawingroom. She took a cigarette case and lighter out of her bag and lit a cigarette with deft, impatient movements. Then she leaned back in her low chair and looked up at me appraisingly.

"You're very much like your mother—I suppose you know?"

"I'm told I am. It's difficult to tell from photographs."

"She was smaller than you are, I think, but not—if you can abide compliments—so good-looking. She—"

We were interrupted by Stephen, who put his head in at the door and spoke before noticing the presence of Geraldine.

"Car outside," he said hurriedly. "Find out who, and if visitors, throw out pronto. I—Oh, I beg your pardon!"

"Nobody is going to throw me out," said Geraldine calmly. "I'm here on legitimate business, and I have the advantage of having taken the position by surprise. I also have the advantage—do come in, it's so difficult to talk to a disembodied head—of knowing who you are, while you have no knowledge of who I am, and probably, also, have no desire to acquire the

213

knowledge."

"My word!" said Stephen. "I can't come in—I'm sorry. I've got dirty boots on."

"Naturally, after having negotiated that quagmire out there," said Geraldine. "I was going to suggest to Claire that some kind of overhead way might be built for visitors, but I see that you have other ideas for callers. How is your grandmother?"

"She was very well twenty minutes ago," said Stephen. "I think you must be Miss Maxwell."

"Really? Why do you think so? You were three years old when we last met."

"My grandmother remembers you. She says—"

He stopped, and Geraldine gave a pleasant laugh in which Stephen and I found ourselves joining.

"I know what she says," said Geraldine, "and you were tactful to stop. She says—or used to say—that there was only one tongue in the district more acid than mine, and that was Christabel Hansard's. She used to go from one to the other of us, advising us, begging us to give soft, sweet answers, at any rate, to young gentlemen when they hovered—if they hovered—round us. Sharp-tongued young ladies, she pointed out, would never, never catch a husband. And time proved her right, you see. I was just telling Claire that she's even prettier than her mother was."

"Well, don't lay it on too thick," warned Stephen. "The

girl's got a job to do, and we don't want her head turned. Are you waiting for my grandmother?"

"I am not. I came in here—I trespassed, but I hope she won't mind—to have a private talk."

"Oh. Pardon *me*," said Stephen, retreating.

"Big and handsome," commented Geraldine as the door closed. "Does he own the farm?"

"No. He rents it."

"And what do you do? Give him a hand now and then?"

"Oh, no. I came down here to—to run it with him. It's not very large, but it's too large for one. The two of us can manage it pretty well, with a bit of extra help at the busiest times."

"How long have you been doing this?" asked Geraldine.

"Me? Oh, about two years. Look, I think I'll go and telephone to the Lodge and ask Coolie to come down and talk to you."

"Coolie... Yes, that was the name. I couldn't remember it. It's a pity, isn't it? She would have made such a pretty Barbara or Susan or Felicity. Yes, Claire—would you telephone?"

I didn't telephone. I went outside with the intention of getting into the car and driving up to the Lodge to fetch Coolie, but when I got to the shed which went by the name of garage, I looked across to the stables and saw that she was already on the farm. She was standing beside Stephen and they were watching a new—and very beautiful—foal. To be more correct, Coolie was watching the foal and Stephen was watching Coolie. They were standing close together, and her hand was resting in his with an ease and naturalness that told the most casual observer how often it found its way there. They were not talking; there was no need for them to talk. They were together, and they loved one another.

I didn't have to call to them; Stephen came to himself with a jerk, glanced at his watch and went away to make up for lost time. Coolie's eyes followed him and then she turned and walked towards me slowly, her eyes on the ground. She looked up and saw me, and our eyes met and both of us saw a great deal.

"I came to fetch you," I said. "Miss Maxwell has come."

I had to repeat the name before Coolie took it in; her mind was a long way away. Then I saw her give herself a shake, and she looked at me with her attention fully given to what I was saying.

"Geraldine! You mean she's here?"

"Yes. She's at the farmhouse. You'd better go on up. Lady Evelyn's not in at the moment, but she might come back before Geraldine wants her to."

"Well, come on," said Coolie. "Let's go."

"No—you go alone. I think it's best. This is nothing to do with me."

Coolie faced me squarely.

"You've got to come," she said. "Gosh, Claire, someone's got to be on my side! If Steve knew that Geraldine was in

216

there, he'd throw her out. He thinks I shouldn't ever have started all this."

"I know. But he came into the room and saw her. He didn't ask what she'd come for, but I suppose he can guess. Didn't he say anything to you just now?"

"He said he supposed I'd come to write the last chapter. But I didn't know he meant Geraldine."

"Well, she's in there."

"Then you'll have to come in with me, Claire. You're the only one who's with me in this."

I could have found a great deal to object to in this statement, but Coolie gave me no time. She took my arm in a firm grip, and we walked up to the farmhouse. Geraldine said nothing when we went into the room, but she leaned forward and pressed out her cigarette and seemed to be preparing for a difficult interview.

"Well"—she smiled up at Coolie—"I've been watching the door of the shop, waiting for you to come bursting through it. But you didn't come."

"Why did you think I would?" asked Coolie.

"Your face said so, plainly, when we had lunch together. It had a dire threat written all over it. I haven't been able to sleep soundly since."

"I'm glad," said Coolie, "that you find it funny."

I found myself admiring her very much. Geraldine was leaning back in her chair, looking up at her with an expression that was more than a little hostile. She looked formidable, and Coolie might have been forgiven for losing a little of her courage, but she stood in the middle of the drawing-room and faced Geraldine with her usual ease and lack of self-consciousness.

"My dear," said Geraldine, and her voice sounded tired and a good deal less hard. "My dear, I don't find it in the least funny. I wouldn't have left my work and driven down here to see you merely for amusement. I would have come down earlier, but I was certain, somehow, that you'd come up."

"I was coming," said Coolie. "I wanted to come. I was just wondering how to fix it so's I could see you alone. People act kind of strange whenever you ask them to tell you anything about Jeffry Hansard."

"Yes," said Geraldine. "I suppose they do."

"I was coming to see you," said Coolie, "because it seemed to me that you might be someone who'd be able to see things my way. I went to see those two old ladies—"

"The Ferriers?"

"Yes. They weren't there, but Claire and I came back and found them on their way to see my father. So we picked them up and kind of kidnapped them and took them to the Vicarage."

"Why were they—"

"—going to see my father? We never found out, for sure. They came to say something, but they didn't get it out. They'd had an invitation—"

Geraldine had opened her handbag, and she took out of it a replica of the letter that Miss Ferrier had shown us the day before.

"—from Lady Evelyn," she said, ending Coolie's sentence for her. "I had one, too. She sent me one of her famous postcards, but she also did something which made me feel that the occasion must be a very special one: she wrote eight lines to explain that a memorial was going up—or had gone up, and was to be shown to the world. A memorial to Jeffry Hansard."

"Lady Evelyn planned it all on rather a grand scale, but it isn't really going to be anything big," I explained. "In fact, Lorna and I are hoping that very few people will come."

"And you told the Ferriers that, and so laid their fears to rest," said Geraldine slowly. "And they went away without telling you anything that they hadn't told you before. Is that it?"

"That's how it went," said Coolie. "Ask Claire."

Geraldine didn't ask me. She took out another cigarette, and I saw that the hardness had gone from her expression, and that she was looking white and tired. Coolie took a step forward and stood looking down at her, and then began to speak quietly.

"Miss Maxwell," she said, "I'd like to explain something. I guess it looks to you like I'm trying to find out about things that aren't any of my business. Well, that isn't so. My father is my business. I'm not interested in Mr. Hansard; I only met him a couple of times, and I didn't talk to him much. I don't know anything about him, and if Pop wasn't in this, I wouldn't want to know. But when Mr. Hansard died and left all his money to the hospital, the folks asked my father if he'd bring back a few facts from England about who and what this Hansard was before he went over to America. They were grateful to him, and they thought it was right to try and find out something about him to tell to people over there. So my father says he'll do that, and he comes over and starts going round and seeing people over here and asking them questions, and what happens? Nobody tells him anything."

"My dear—" began Geraldine.

"One minute, please. I've got to say this, so's you'll see that I'm not just pushing in. I'm nearly through, and when I am, maybe you'll understand how I feel. You see…Pop's a honey, but he's easy to fool. He's got—now—all the money anybody wants, but he made it—he and Verna, my mother, made it themselves, working from the bottom up. When Verna met him, Pop was a skinny little boy working on his father's farm and knocking up kids' toys in his spare time. Verna went to stay there, and she thought the toys had something—and so they have; they're…But I guess that's away off the point. Verna said why didn't he sell some of them, and he said he didn't figure he could make anything out of them, and so Verna said she'd take some away with her when she went back home, and see if she could find anybody who'd give her real money for them. And that's what she did. Then she went back for some more, and waited while Pop put them together, and while he was doing that, they fell in love and got married, so when Verna went back East, she was selling something she felt she owned. Pretty soon she had Pop off the farm and into a workshop, and then he was surprised to find himself in business. Then Verna said they'd have to have a name, and Pop said they'd call the toys Papoose toys, and so they did. Now there are Papoose toys from one end of the States to the other. Pop still makes the original models, and Verna says he does it because he never stopped being a kid himself, and so he knows what other kids like. He never did anything but that side of it; it was Verna who always had to do the business end, because every time Pop gets to a business end, it kind of softens up and falls apart, and instead of Pop selling something to somebody, he comes back home with something that somebody's sold him. That's what I want to explain—that if there isn't somebody to watch out for him, he's easy to fool. So when he starts out with his notebook and takes down what everybody tells him about Mr. Hansard, he doesn't see he isn't getting anything; he thinks he's doing fine. He writes it all down, and he's happy because he thinks he's getting facts— but he isn't getting facts. Nobody, up to now, has told him anything that amounts to anything, and that's what I'm worried about. They think a lot of my father in Prophet, but if he goes back there with a notebook full of nothing, they'll know he's been fooled. He's going to put up a tablet to a man that nobody'll say anything about—a man who may have been anything or done anything. If he was that kind of man, then nobody ought to let a nice guy like Pop put a memorial up and make a fool of himself—and of everybody back there in Prophet. It wouldn't be right and it wouldn't be fair. I don't want to know anything that people don't want to tell me, but I want to be sure that nobody's fooling my father. That's all."

There was silence. Geraldine groped in her bag, produced her cigarette case and held it out to each of us in turn. Coolie and I shook our heads, and Coolie held a light and Geraldine lit her cigarette, glanced up at Coolie and gave her an odd little smile.

"Nobody ever thought of fooling your father," she said.

"I'm glad," said Coolie.

"But the reason I had to come and see you again—and the reason that brought the Ferriers over yesterday—was…this invitation of Lady Evelyn's. You see, in the first place—when you first came over here—we were merely asked to meet you and your father and tell him a few facts about Jeffry Hansard's early life, which we did. They weren't, as you saw, important facts, but we didn't think it would matter very much if we kept to rather superficial details. It wasn't until I got this letter that I—that it seemed to me that there was going to be a sort of public meeting with flags and brass bands and a general glorification of a man who—"

She stopped, and I put in a word of explanation.

"Lady Evelyn…"

"Yes, I know," said Geraldine. "But there *is* going to be some form of memorial?"

"Yes," said Coolie. "It isn't large, and there isn't going to be any floor show. It's just a—a token of gratitude, that's all. But before it's put up, and before my father's responsible for having it put up, I'd like to find out whether it ought to be going up at all. If you'll just answer one question, that's all I need to know. This Mr. Hansard—was he a good man or a bad man?"

Geraldine hesitated.

"That's rather…arbitrary," she said.

"Maybe; but let's stick to the wording," said Coolie. "Is this—was this Hansard a good man or a no-good man?"

"I think," said Geraldine slowly, "that he'd go very easily into the no-good class."

"I see. Then in *that* case," said Coolie decisively, "no tablet."

"But that," said Geraldine, "is something that we've got to discuss."

"Why?" enquired Coolie. "There's nothing to discuss. If that's the reason that people have been holding out and saying nothing—and I kind of guessed it must be—then he doesn't have to have any plaques put up to him."

"Perhaps," said Geraldine gently, "you can decide that when you've learned a little more."

"I don't want to know anything you don't want me to know," said Coolie.

"You've got to know now, my dear," said Geraldine. "The

matter will then rest with you, and my conscience won't give any more trouble. You see, I hadn't any objection to your father's going back with only half a story, but I couldn't stand by and let him put up—with a flourish of trumpets—a memorial to a man who doesn't deserve one, in the very place in which he did so much harm. I felt that I had to come and see you and…But I'll tell you, as briefly as I can, all the facts.

"Jeffry Hansard wasn't really a villain—at first. He was merely a young man with expensive tastes and not enough money to indulge them. He lived with his Aunt Emily at the Lodge, where you're living now, and Christabel lived there too; in fact, they were brought up together. Emily thought it fair that she should leave her money to Christabel and the house to Jeffry; both of them knew of this arrangement, and both of them had agreed to it. But I suppose, as Jeffry's debts mounted, he began to look round and wonder how he could get money. He borrowed from one or two people, but that couldn't go on indefinitely. So I think he made up his mind to try and persuade his aunt to leave him at any rate part of her money. He settled down at the Lodge—instead of going to and fro and only staying for brief periods—and began the business of charming his aunt.

"Christabel must have seen what was going on, but she had nothing to fight him with. He was using charm and tact and graceful persuasion, and she…poor Christabel, she hadn't any weapons to use against those. She had her sharp eyes and her sharp tongue; she could see what was happening and she could warn her aunt against him, but what chance has an angry, jealous woman against a smooth-tongued, handsome and attractive man? He could get anything out of Emily that he wanted, and when she died he found that he'd got just what he wanted—her money. Christabel got the house, which she had always hated. But that easy success showed Jeffry Hansard, for the first time, I think, what power he had with women. Any woman—young or old. Any woman, that is, who had what he wanted most…money.

"At first, I think, he really felt that he could use the money better than Christabel. And he may have been right. She wasn't a…likeable character. I think he may have meant to see that she was not left without money. But that, and other good intentions, got thrown overboard later. He was too busy following up the success he'd had with Emily. And, of course, he had unique opportunities. He was a partner in an old-established and trusted firm of solicitors; he was a native of the district, and he was well known to us all. We'd known him—some of us—for years. And he was tall and handsome and more charming than he had ever dreamed—until old Emily fell so easily under his spell— and then, I think, and only then, he began to realise that there was enough money round him—if he could get hold of it—to make him a very rich man.

"There were rumours, of course, about the time that Emily died. Christabel had plenty to say; but everybody felt that she was half-crazed with jealousy, and that it wouldn't do to believe all she said about her cousin. And it wouldn't have mattered much, anyway, because by that time he was on the point of getting what he had planned for—money. Not Emily's money; he'd got that. My money, and the Ferriers' money.

"I must tell you that I didn't wait to be swindled. I begged for it. If my father had lived, Jeffry wouldn't have got his hands on a penny; my father made bis money painfully, and he meant to keep it. But he was dead, and I was lonely and ignorant and ready to do anything for any delightful young man who took an interest in me. He didn't make love to me —he was too clever for that, and I was at any rate intelligent enough to be on the look-out for that kind of fortune-hunter. Jeffry knew just what I needed, and gave it to me: a sort of friendly companionship, an apparently genuine pleasure in my company, a way of making me feel that he found something fresh and amusing and alive about me. And while he was making me feel that, he was busy swindling me, and it served me right. He robbed me, but I deserved it for being taken in."

She paused for a few moments, but there was more to come, and we waited for it.

"That," she said at last, "is what I didn't care to tell your father. It's easy enough to expose a man's villainy, but it's hard, in doing so, to have to drag out such a sorry picture of oneself and hold it up for the inspection of strangers. You can see why I wasn't anxious to bring up the past. And that's the reason the Ferriers wanted it left alone, too. I can't speak for Mr. Petrie. He must have felt the disgrace keenly— in fact, it's made him into a sick, embittered old man. But, apart from his partner's villainy, I know no reason why he couldn't be frank, except that if he did speak, there was a danger that your father would guess the whole truth and realise that we—the Ferriers and myself—were involved. I'm grateful to him for not saying anything. Do you mind if I have another cigarette?"

Coolie held a light for her, and Geraldine looked up at her through a little haze of smoke.

"Thanks," she said. "And now I'm going to say something else. Jeffry Hansard robbed me, and he robbed the Ferriers, but we bear him no grudge. I myself have nothing but gratitude for what he did. He drove me out into the world, left me enough money to set myself up in business, and turned me from a lost, bored woman into a busy and a happy one. He did even more for the Ferriers: he turned them out of a house which had long ceased to be theirs. They were a timid, mousey pair, very rich, and quite unable to deal with all their parasitic relations. Their home was used as a free hotel by every relative—close or distant—that they possessed. Some of them even used to hire horses in the hunting season and leave the bills to be paid by the sisters. Jeffry Hansard at least rescued them from that. They've been happier in their little toy house than they ever were in the old days—and of course, nobody can fatten themselves on them any more. So you see, it's all over and done with, and nobody wants to drag it out again. Jeffry Hansard went to America with all our money, and it's nice to think of its being used to build new hospital wings."

"One thing I'd like to ask" I began hesitatingly.

"Well?" said Geraldine.

"I thought that things like that—embezzlement and so on—caused a lot of scandal. Yet nobody in Polden or Allchester seems to remember anything at all about—"

"There was no scandal of any kind," said Geraldine. "A woman who allows a plausible man to swindle her out of practically all she owns doesn't like it shouted from the house-tops. There could be no question of criminal proceedings, because the criminal had vanished. All I wanted— certainly all that the Ferriers wanted—was to be allowed to readjust ourselves as quietly as possible and put the whole wretched business behind us."

"We've caused you," said Coolie slowly, "a lot of trouble."

"There hasn't been any trouble yet," said Geraldine, "but there will be unless you take some advice."

"Well?" asked Coolie.

"Don't tell your father what I've just told you."

Coolie stared at her, astounded.

"B-but—to let him put up—"

"Listen to me," said Geraldine. "I came down here because I liked the look of you. You looked full of sense and intelligence, and—young as you are—I decided that I'd put myself in your hands. I told myself that the honest thing to do was to explain to you, before that memorial affair was put up, what kind of a man Jeffry Hansard was. That's obviously what the Ferriers told themselves, too, after getting Lady Evelyn's letter. But they found that there wasn't, after all, going to be a fanfare, and so they went away without saying anything. If there was to be no publicity, you see, then there was no danger of anybody outside Polden—who might have known who and what Jeffry Hansard was— coming along and telling what they knew to your father. But I've told you the facts because I felt that I owed…Well, anyhow, I've told them to you. But now that you know them, I think you should let the matter rest. The tablet is going up, not to the Jeffry Hansard who robbed us of our money, but to the Jeffry Hansard who gave it to your hospital. So let it go up. To refuse to let your father go on with this now, would mean explanations to the whole of Grayleigh and Polden, and a dreadful general curiosity about matters that are best forgotten. Your father is satisfied; my conscience is at rest, because I've told you all I know. The thing is finished; the money did some good. The hospital has got it, and it was Jeffry Hansard who gave it. Let him have his memorial."

Coolie was staring at us with a thoughtful frown on her face. She seemed to be searching her memory, and presently she spoke to Geraldine with a smile beginning to show in her eyes.

"You know," she said slowly, "Lorna said something like that one day, when we talked about Jeffry Hansard. She meant what you did just now, when you said that he'd done some good. Only Lorna said it another way."

"Well, what did she say it was?" enquired Geraldine.

"She called it an Act of Contrition," said Coolie.

229

We took Geraldine out to her car and saw her off. Stephen joined us as we stood in the yard saying goodbye.

"Secret mission accomplished?" he asked.

"Yes, thank you," said Geraldine. "I'm going to drive up to the Lodge just to look in on Lorna and your grandmother, but I shan't stay long. I've got to get back to Town."

Stephen looked across her into the eyes of Coolie, who was standing on the other side of the car.

"Does the plaque go up," he asked slowly, "or doesn't it?"

Coolie's face showed a brief surprise, and then she answered him simply.

"It goes up," she said.

"I see," said Stephen expressionlessly, and turned back to Geraldine. "Half a moment," he said. "I'll open the gate for you."

He walked across to do it, and Coolie followed him to help him. Geraldine's eyes rested on them and then turned to fix themselves on me in a long, speculative look.

"Claire," she said.

"Well?"

Her eyes were on Stephen and Coolie as she answered.

"Would you allow me—as an old friend of your mother— to give you some advice?"

Our eyes met, and I smiled.

"You're very kind," I said, "but I'm afraid you're too late."

"That's what I thought," said Geraldine, and was gone.

Chapter Fourteen

I had to go into Allchester that evening, and I was rather late in going home again, so I drove with a speed that almost equalled Coolie's. I was on the road between Polden and Grayleigh when I saw a figure ahead of me, and slowed down. I thought I recognised the familiar black coat, and I was right. When I came up to him, I saw that it was Mr. Petrie, and he was in a state which alarmed me very much.

He was moving slowly and—it seemed to me—with difficulty. His head was down, and he seemed to be walking as though he scarcely knew where he was going. I leaned out and spoke to him, but when I saw how white and ill he looked, I got out and went over to stand by his side.

"Mr. Petrie," I said, "can't I drive you anywhere?"

He peered at me through dim, watery eyes, and seemed to have difficulty in deciding who I was.

"Lift?" he said at last, in a thick, breathless voice. "No, no—nearly there. Going up to the…going to see…going to the Lodge."

"Then I'll take you there. Do get in and I'll run you up

there—please!"

But Mr. Petrie seemed to have lost the thread of my remarks, and was gazing round him as though wondering where he was. He looked so unsteady that without further words I put my hand on his arm and guided him into the seat beside mine. I started the car, but saw that he was leaning back with his eyes closed, looking so much like someone in a coma...or dead... that I abandoned the idea of taking him up to the Lodge, and made straight for the Vicarage. Cluny had his faults, but he could deal competently with a situation like this.

I got to the house and, leaving Mr. Petrie where he was, ran indoors and opened the door of the kitchen. Cluny looked up, wiping his hands on his apron.

"Cluny, do come," I said. "I've got Mr. Petrie out there in the car, and I think he's ill."

"What's he doing here?" enquired Cluny, following me out through the hall.

"I found him on the road, walking up to the Lodge. He mumbled something about Miss Wells, but he's not talking very clearly."

"Walkin', was he, the ole fule?"

"Yes. He—"

"He'd walk all the way from Allchester, and no' be able to say where he was going," said Cluny. "The man's no' fit to be left to wander. Come on and let's see, noo."

We helped Mr. Petrie out of the car. Leaving Cluny to

help him indoors, I went into the drawing-room, and when the old man came in, weak and trembling, clinging to Cluny's arm, I had a stiff drink ready for him. Cluny settled him in a comfortable chair and put cushions at his back.

"There, noo," he said. "Rest ye awhile."

Mr. Petrie appeared to be only too glad to rest. He sat, saying nothing, gazing at the fire, and presently Cluny took up the drink and steadied the glass as Mr. Petrie drank the first few sips.

"There," he said. "That'll do ye more gude than runnin' round the place on a pair of legs that won't hold ye up properly. Noo, drink it up, drink it up, and Miss Claire'll gie ye some more."

We watched in silence as Mr. Petrie recovered himself a little, and saw some colour returning to his cheeks. After a while, he looked up at Cluny and nodded once or twice.

"Better," he said. "Yes, better. Thank you. I must go up and see Miss Wells."

Cluny put some coal on the fire, poked it vigorously, and went to the door.

"Jest let him rest," he told me, before going out. "Keep him there until he's stronger. He'd be better at home an' in his bed, the old…"

The door closed, fortunately, on the last word, and I sat on a chair and waited quietly for Mr. Petrie to recover fully. He put down his empty glass and passed a hand over his sparse white hair.

"I'm sorry to give you this trouble," he began. "I—"

"Oh, please don't! I've just been—"

"—wondering why you didn't ring me up and ask me to come over and fetch you."

"I would have—"

"No, no," said Mr. Petrie. "I've given you trouble enough. And I hadn't time to…I've been away and I only got home an hour ago, and when I went in, I—I found this…"

He stopped and fumbled in his pocket, but I didn't have to be told what he was searching for, and felt no surprise when Lady Evelyn's sprawling handwriting came into view once more. I thought that those three letters must be the first she had written for many years, but they had certainly produced some extraordinary results.

"Do you know anything of this?" asked Mr. Petrie.

"I—well, I know that the—"

"It can't go on," he broke in abruptly.

I looked at him, but said nothing. He was not in a state in which one could argue with him.

"It can't go on," he repeated, his voice thickening—this time, I thought, with rage. "It's a monstrous farce, and I won't have it. I won't blame anybody—except Lorna. Lorna should have known. Lady Evelyn…I won't blame her; I won't say anything. But Lorna…Good God! To let this thing take place in her house—in Christabel's old house, in the house that—

that—"

"Mr. Petrie, please, couldn't you leave this for a minute or two and just rest? Look, I've got an idea. If—"

"This affair," he went on, unheeding, "is to take place in front of a crowd of...Look! It says so." He held the letter up in front of me and shook it angrily. "It's—it's monstrous! I don't want to sit here and rest. If you'll do me the kindness of taking me up to the Lodge, I'll—"

"You didn't hear me out. If you want to see Lorna, let me go up and drive her down here to see you. You probably won't see her alone up there—and now that you're sitting down, and warm, and resting, I can leave you and go and fetch her."

He looked uncertain for a moment, but the wisdom of the plan was plain, and he nodded his head.

"Yes. I—yes, that would be best, if you would be so kind. But your uncle—"

"My uncle's down at the Church, and won't be back for another hour. I'll go and get Lorna and you can talk to her here."

I went outside, but before I could shut the front door behind me, I heard voices, and looked up to see two figures approaching. One was Lorna's; beside her, looking inordinately smug, strode Cluny.

"Ye were goin' to fetch Miss Lorna, I'm thinkin'," he said.

"You know I was."

"I knew more than that; I knew y'd have to go. It was

235

stickin' oot. You couldna expect yon old…gentleman to go dancin' all over the place. An' so I fetched her doon."

"Thank you."

"Och, there's no need for thanks! I'm no needin' thanks, and I'm no wantin' the credit. Go on in wi' ye, noo."

I took Lorna into the drawing-room, feeling that Mr. Petrie would think that we had been jet-propelled—but he was past doing any calculations involving time and distance. Lorna hurried over to him and took his hand and patted it, but Mr. Petrie snatched it away angrily and used it, instead, to flap Lady Evelyn's letter at her.

"You knew of this!" he said accusingly. "Good God, Lorna, you must be out of your mind!"

"George—I know how you feel, but I had no idea that Evelyn was…The thing was out of my hands. Wasn't it, Claire? Oh Claire, don't go! You must come here and explain. Come back, please, Claire."

I came back, but not very willingly. A little while ago I would have been interested in seeing the end of the trail of events leading from Mr. Donner's arrival in Polden, but I was tired and depressed, and I felt that I could guess, now, the thing that had been eluding me for so long. The sight of Mr. Petrie, the emotion he showed at the thought of the memorial, his determination to prevent its being put up—all this cleared the fog from something I had been looking for, unconsciously, for some time.

I brought Lorna a low chair and put it near Mr. Petrie's, and then I sat on one of the fender stools. Lorna began to speak gently to the old man beside her.

"Nobody realised what Evelyn was doing, George," she said. "We all thought it was to be a little thing—a farewell to Mr. Donner and his daughter."

"That isn't the point, and you know it," said Mr. Petrie. "There was nothing—there was never anything said to me, at any time, about this…this fantastic proposal…this plaque."

"Dear George, we—"

"You knew that it was to be put up?"

"There was no possible………."

"You knew that it was to be put up?"

"Yes," said Lorna. "I knew."

"You knew—and you allowed it. Knowing what you knew, you said that they could actually place a—a tablet, a—Good God! a memorial to that…"

Lorna put a firm hand on his, and leaned forward and spoke slowly and gently.

"From the first—from the very first, George, I struggled to have things left as they were. Months ago, when the idea was first broached, when Christabel had a letter—Claire brought the letter up. Do you remember, Claire?"

Months ago…It seemed years ago, or even some other dim and forgotten existence. It was even difficult to arrange the pieces as they had been before: Christabel in the big, ugly bedroom; Lorna downstairs; Lady Evelyn happy and busy with her own concerns, as she had been before Mr. Donner came and as she would doubtless be when Mr. Donner went away again. Stephen at the farm—with me. Two of us...only two of us...

"Yes," I said. "I remember."

"I took the letter up to Christabel," went on Lorna, "and I tried to—"

"You could have stopped it right at the beginning," said Mr. Petrie. "You could have kept those people away."

"I don't think you understand, George. I did my best. I was dealing with a woman who had worked herself up into a—it was almost a frenzy. I felt certain that if she wrote and told Mr. Donner to come, if she got involved in a correspondence which would take her back, more and more, to things that were better forgotten, then...it would kill her. But to oppose the scheme steadily, as I did, was almost equally dangerous. She gave in, finally, and agreed to write and say that she wasn't up to meeting anybody—but she wrote, I'm sorry to say, quite another kind of letter. When I discovered what had been going on, it was too late to do anything."

"You didn't have to send them to see me, or to see the Ferriers, or send them all the way up to London to see Miss Maxwell. You could have spared us that. You could have put that list of Christabel's into the fire."

"That would have done no good," said Lorna. "She had sent the names to Mr. Donner. But I wouldn't have destroyed the list when Christabel was dead…"

"She was dead, but she had lied to you and deceived you—you, the person who'd spent years of your life nursing her and looking after her. She lied to you, and died lying to you. How do you think that makes you feel bound to go on with the mischief she began?"

"She was dead…"

"Of course she was dead. You were right when you said that the thing would kill her. It did kill her. She wasn't strong enough to contain all that hatred and plan all that revenge."

"George, you mustn't speak of Christabel—"

"Listen to me, Lorna. Christabel only had one motive—to get her revenge on him. That's all. I knew her, and I know just how she was planning to do it. She wanted to get the Donners here to spread the news of Hansard's generosity; she wanted to get his name into people's mouths once more. She would have allowed the plaque to be put up with the fullest ceremony— and then she meant, with everybody there to hear her, to tell the truth about him. She would have dragged those poor little Ferriers in to tell their story; she would have had Geraldine Maxwell's history paraded before everyone. And she would have told the story of my…"

"George—"

I saw tears in Lorna's eyes, but Mr. Petrie went on, unheeding:

"That was her plan. She was a wicked and a vindictive

woman. She was like him; they were two of a kind. There was no apparent harm in them—until a spark fell and lighted up all the latent rottenness in them. In his case, the spark was greed; in hers, it was her determination to get her own back on him after all these years."

"He robbed her."

"He didn't. Emily robbed her. Emily had the money to leave, and Emily made the will leaving it to Christabel. Emily altered the will and left Christabel without a penny. He worked on old Emily, of course; but if Emily had had a shred of character, she wouldn't have allowed herself to be led into so gross an injustice. I did what I could—and I talked to him, too. He knew well what I thought of him. Sometimes I think it was because I made it so plain that he…that he…"

"George, what is the use of bringing all this up now?"

"I was content to let things be as they were," said Mr. Petrie bitterly. "That man came to see me—that American—and brought his daughter. I said nothing. I imagined that he would accept the few facts I gave him, and then go away and leave us all in peace. Never for one moment did I dream that there was to be a…And then I got Evelyn's letter, and I came over at once to see you. I won't be the only one, you'll find. Do you think that the Ferriers, and Miss Maxwell, are going to stand quietly by and let—"

"Yes," I said.

He had some trouble locating the sound. He'd forgotten that I was there, sitting in the shadow in the darkening room.

240

He glared at me out of pale, angry eyes and I hurried on.

"They know," I said. "You see, they thought—just as you did—that Mr. Donner would go away after meeting them and talking to them. I was with Mr. Donner when he went to Cherryton, and I was with him, and his daughter, when they went to see Miss Maxwell. And like you, they didn't tell Mr. Donner much, but he was satisfied. But his daughter wasn't."

"What's it got to do with her?" demanded Mr. Petrie.

"She"—I chose my words carefully; he was over-excited, and it would be wise to cool him down—"she noticed that you were very evasive when they called to see you. Her father noticed nothing, but she did. She said that you were deliberately keeping back information."

I saw his mind switch to the interview that had taken place and felt that a dangerous moment had gone by. His colour, which had been deepening alarmingly during his speech to Lorna, became more normal, and when he spoke again, it was in something approaching his usual hesitating voice.

"Are you telling me that neither Miss Maxwell nor the Ferriers are going to say anything to stop this—"

"Nothing," I said. "Miss Maxwell told Miss Donner a good deal about Mr. Hansard and his connection with her and with the Ferriers, and then she advised her to let things go on just as they'd been planned."

"But he's still in complete ignorance, according to your story."

241

"Yes; but it's unpleasant to feel that people are being se-
cretive when you don't know the reason. Miss Donner felt that
her father was being—in a sense—trifled with. But now she
understands. She doesn't—"

I stopped. It was impossible to tell him that Coolie Donner cared nothing for Jeffry Hansard; that, apart from his connection with her father, he was nothing but a dim figure from
the past—old, uninteresting. It was true, but it was not possible to put it into words.

"And so," said Mr. Petrie, "I'm expected to stand by and
watch this farce."

"I honestly think it would be better," I said.

He looked at me; I don't know what there had been in my
voice, but as he looked, a change came over his face and an
expression came into it that I couldn't bear to look at. All the
life drained out of his eyes and they looked old, and tired, and
bitter. I think that what I hadn't said was written somewhere
on me. Sitting there in the twilight, with the firelight on me, I
must have brought home to him the two aspects of the case—
the old and the new. I had been speaking for Coolie Donner,
but I represented the new, fresh life that cared nothing at all for
any of those old, forgotten things belonging to Mr. Petrie and
his tragedy. I turned away and stared into the fire, but I knew
that nothing more would be said. Time had swept away Emily
and Christabel and Jeffry Hansard; Lady Alison was gone, and
Mr. Petrie looked as though it would not be long before he
joined her. It was over; nobody cared to bring it back.

We sat in silence in the almost-dark room, and the fire glowed steadily. At last there was a stir and a sigh, and Mr. Petrie rose to his feet. Lorna and I rose with him, and I went to the door.

"I'll take you home," I said.

"No," said Mr. Petrie. "I've given you trouble enough. If you'd let Cluny drive me back—"

I wouldn't have let Cluny drive me, but Mr. Petrie had been driven by him on one or two occasions, and knew what he was letting himself in for. I went into the kitchen and found Cluny deep in preparations for dinner.

"I'll take over, Cluny," I said. "Mr. Petrie wants you to drive him home."

"I'll gie him another drink first," said Cluny. "Watch yon greens, noo—we dinna want them mushed."

Lorna and I walked out and stood by the car, and presently Cluny brought Mr. Petrie out and we watched them drive away. The headlights threw broad bands of light on first one side of the road and then the other, and I wasn't surprised, when we went back to the drawing-room, to find two glasses on the table instead of one. It would be a lively journey, but it might do Mr. Petrie good; certainly it would take his mind from matters that were long since dead, and turn his attention to the business of being—and remaining, if possible—alive.

When Lorna left, I walked to the gate with her.

"Thanks for coming," I said.

"Poor, poor old man…"

"Lorna," I asked suddenly.

"Well?"

"Don't answer if you don't want to. Anyhow, I think I know the answer already, and I think—I don't know why, but I'm almost sure—that Stephen has guessed it, too. Tell me— why was it so much worse for—"

"For Mr. Petrie?"

"Yes. They all lost money, after all—the Ferriers, Miss Maxwell—"

"Yes. But you see, Mr. Petrie lost his wife, too."

"You mean—"

"Jeffry Hansard didn't do irreparable damage to anyone else. But Alison Petrie…Alison loved him."

And then the last piece fell into place, and I knew something that I had known—unconsciously—for some time past.

Chapter Fifteen

It dawned on us, at last, that Mr. Donner and Coolie were going away. No day was fixed; no time had been mentioned, but we all realised that their visit was almost over. Small things happened to remind us or to shock us or grieve us depending upon how each of us regarded the prospect of their departure. Stephen said nothing. Coolie said nothing. Lady Evelyn said a good deal, and seemed to dread their going so much that for the first time, the approaching party appeared in the light of a blessing. It took her mind off the awful fact of Mr. Donner's departure, and provided us with a topic which we could present to her mind whenever she became gloomy.

Lorna would miss them, but she was already fully occupied with plans for the future. The nuns had bought the house; Lorna was going to and fro to complete the details of the sale, and from time to time, one or two of the nuns came over to look round the house and to measure windows and floors.

My uncle, who had accepted Mr. Donner and Coolie as calmly as he accepted new shoots in spring, would view their departure with the mild regret with which he saw the leaves falling in autumn; it was a pity, but it had to be.

Cluny was puzzled, and said so.

"I thot he would have got it settled by now," he said. "Has he no' said anythin' to her?"

"I don't know. Do you have to discuss people's affairs?"

"Ye were aye ready to discuss Mr. Stephen's affairs before noo. Maybe she'll no' tak' him."

"Well, it's no use talking to me about it."

"Maybe she'll no' be wantin' to live in this country. She'll be wantin' to go back where she came fra'—and I'm no' blamin' her."

"Well, if you've got that all worked out, could I have some more coffee?"

"Aye; I'll fetch it. That's what it'll be; she'll no' settle here."

This conclusion appeared to satisfy him, but he would have liked to have been assured of its accuracy. Nobody, however, had any ideas of how things were between Stephen and Coolie. They were in love; their looks declared it, but their actions seemed to deny it. They smiled at one another, and talked with an appearance of ease. But she was packing, and Mr. Donner was writing to steamship companies, and the nuns were to have the house as soon as the deeds were signed. It seemed probable that Lady Evelyn's party would prove to be the last function which Mr. Donner and Coolie would attend, and so we looked forward to it—each of us— with varying emotions.

The day came, and the sun shone, but Lorna's feelings scarcely matched the brightness of the weather. She was faced, at last, with the worry and the confusion that attended all Lady Evelyn's parties; nobody had any idea of how many people would come, or what kind of people they would be. They varied from old friends from a more gracious past to new ones picked up anywhere on her travels.

We made what preparations we could; we put a large trestle table on the lawn and loaded onto it urns and kettles and sandwiches and cakes, plates and cups and saucers. We dressed ourselves up and assembled at four o'clock to await who knew what. As a last precaution, we rang up the three taxi services at Allchester and asked them to meet the buses arriving from London at four o'clock and five o'clock. After that, said Lorna, they could walk.

The people from Polden were the first to arrive, and the first thing that became apparent was that nobody was in the least interested in the plaque that had been put up to the memory of Jeffry Hansard. It was there, skilfully put up, neat, unobtrusive, quietly blending into the wall on which it had been placed. It was there to be admired by anybody who could spare the time to look at it, but Lady Evelyn's postcards had said nothing about a plaque; only her supplementary letters to Miss Maxwell, Mr. Petrie and the Ferriers had contained any reference to it. And so the guests arrived and, without concerning themselves about Jeffry Hansard, divided at once into three separate groups: those who came to see Lady Evelyn, those who wanted to see Mr. Donner, and those who wanted tea.

I had gone up early to help Lorna, and Coolie stayed with us, doing what she could and helping to carry cakes to the guests. Stephen was to come up later; unwillingly, but at the express wish of Lady Evelyn, who promised to let him get away as soon as possible after he had put in an appearance.

I found the first part of the party dull, but I was content to wait until the bus had time to reach Allchester. If any of Lady Evelyn's more colourful friends were coming, they would be on that.

They were. The first taxi brought up three people I had often seen before—an Italian husband and wife and their teen-age son.

"Luigi!" cried Lady Evelyn, stretching out her arms and embracing husband and wife at one clasp. "Teresa! My darlings! Come along and meet a charming American friend of mine—Mr. Donner. And you too, Beppino. Do you know, Beppino, the last time I saw you, you were *piccolo,* and now you're *alto.* Dear me, isn't it lovely to speak Italian again! Claire dear, take Beppino and show him where the food is, will you?"

I showed him, but I was sorry for it later; I had forgotten what Beppino could put away. I had to leave him in order to go and see what the next taxi-loads brought, and found that the new arrivals were an Austrian family of four—mother and three daughters; the Countess of Pleutsch, who had got caught up with two very seedy-looking gentlemen speaking Spanish; Professor le Brun, who said that he had been on the point of returning to Paris when Lady Evelyn's summons had reached him; and a pretty girl who appeared to speak no known language, and who was addressed by Lady Evelyn as Zouche. Zouche clung to me with a sort of desperation, resisting all my attempts to lead her into the company and leave her there, but I finally discovered that— like Beppino—she found the attractions of the tea-table strong enough to keep her there for the rest of the afternoon.

I don't know how many of us enjoyed ourselves. For Polden, it was an afternoon well spent in watching what they would afterwards describe as antics. For the foreigners, there was pleasure enough in seeing Lady Evelyn again and recalling the view from the house above Como, or speculating upon what had eventually become of the terrible couple in the ground-floor apartment in Paris. Mr. Donner was in his element; his private worries were, for the moment, laid aside; he was talking to a number of interesting strangers, and I was glad to see the beaming, happy smile on his face once more.

Lorna and I worked like horses, and Coolie almost as hard. We had urns to fill, kettles to heat, new batches of sandwiches to cut and extra drinks to provide for those who didn't like tea. Cluny did the heavy work, stopping only once to engage in a wordless and inconclusive argument with Beppino on the subject of how many sandwiches it was good for a boy to eat.

There was an interesting moment when a car drew up and four nuns appeared among us. This was an unheralded visit; a business call, but I gave them tea, and Lorna took them inside for a consultation and Coolie and I were left, with Cluny, to cope with the work. Lady Evelyn had no idea that there was any work to be done. I don't know where she thought that the tea and drinks and sandwiches were coming from, but if she had dreamed that their preparation had given anyone any trouble, she would have been deeply and genuinely shocked.

"Mixed lot," said Coolie, surveying them with a smile.

"They always are. I used to find it very instructive when I went to stay with her. I learned several words in several languages."

"These people who arrive in taxis," asked Coolie. "Do they pay for them themselves?"

"Some do, and some don't. Some think that as there's no suitable public transport in Polden, we ought to have the privilege of paying for them."

"My father didn't want Lady Evelyn to have any of this to pay for, but she—she kind of talked him down."

"Don't worry about that."

"But…this was to be a joint thing; they were both in it."

"Don't worry," I said again. "She's having a wonderful time."

"Who's this coming now?" asked Coolie.

I looked up to see my uncle coming on to the lawn, leading a tall, dignified-looking clergyman.

"I've never seen him before," I said.

We learned, in a few moments, that his name was Mr.

Elliot. He had arrived in Allchester that morning, and was to preach there on the following Sunday, and to appeal for funds for a mission. He had called on my uncle and found him setting out to go to the Lodge, and so had accompanied him.

It sounded a very simple explanation for his presence, but I was to learn that Fate had sent him on a more deadly errand. As I looked up at the gentle, pleasant face of Mr. Elliot, as we exchanged some comments on the scene and I handed him a cup of tea, I was mercifully unaware that he was soon to give the last twist to the knife that had been plunged into my heart. It was the only time I was to see him, but I remember his mildness, and his apology for the trouble he was giving me...

By six o'clock, I had had enough of the party, and when I saw Stephen coming, I decided that I would go and finish off a few odd jobs on the farm. I went into the house to try to find Lorna, but she had taken her visitors out by the other door, and was walking with them to their car.

Coolie had followed me, and we stayed in the empty drawing-room for a few moments, glad of a rest. We spoke very little, and we were both startled when the door opened and Stephen came in.

"Tired?" he asked us both impartially.

"I'm tired," I said. "I'm going down to finish off a few things, and then I'm going home."

"Well, the party's breaking up," said Stephen. "They're all going home, thank God. I'll probably come down and join you later."

"All right," I said.

"Oh—and Claire—"

"Yes?"

"All those cheques that Granny's been handing out in the village—you might collect them and give them back to me, will you?"

"I will," I promised.

There was a small sound from Coolie, and I turned to find her looking at me with eyes wide with astonishment. Then her gaze was turned on Stephen.

"But she c-can't…"

"Yes, she can," said Stephen.

He was standing with one arm on the mantelpiece, his eyes on her, his expression inscrutable. Coolie managed a puzzled little smile.

"I guess I don't understand," she said. "Why do you have to get them back?"

"Because I'd like to have them back," said Stephen.

I took a step forward—with some idea, I suppose, of getting between them, and paused as I heard Coolie's voice.

"This thing—this party—was a two-way one," she said, and her voice was cold. "My father didn't want anybody to spend any money on it if he could have helped it, but Lady Evelyn—"

"I know," said Stephen. "She's like that. Open-hearted. Open-handed."

She faced him, and there was no mistaking the challenge in her tone.

"If your grandmother wants to spend her money," she said, "then she can spend it, I guess."

"You guess wrong," said Stephen, and his voice was as cold as hers. Then he took a step forward and spoke appealingly. "Look, Coolie, why don't you let me run my grandmother's affairs?"

"You're welcome to," said Coolie. "But this is my father's affair, too. They were to go shares. If she wants to go shares, then why shouldn't she?"

Stephen's voice was no longer appealing; it had an edge on it that I had seldom heard.

"Let's say," he said, "that I like her to keep her money."

"You don't have any right to do that!"

"No?"

"No; you don't. Why don't you go to my father and tell him to pay it all himself? He'd like to. He wants to. He always wanted to—but Lady Evelyn wouldn't let him. So you go tell him you won't let her. I'd like to hear you telling him."

"Coolie—" I began.

"Keep out of this, Claire," said Stephen.

"No," said Coolie. "I'll keep out."

She turned and walked out of the room, and I was left to look at Stephen's white, sick face.

"Stephen, I..."

253

"Don't say anything," he said. "Please, Claire."

I turned and left him, and went down to the Vicarage and changed into working clothes. Then I went down to the farm and worked until it began to grow dark. It was time to go home, but I didn't go home. I went up to the little upper room of the ruin and pushed a box against the window and sat down on it and put my head on the window-sill and…cried. Howled. I went on for a long time. I don't know that it made me feel any better, but it made me feel tired in a different way. After a time, I didn't even tell myself what I was crying about; I just went on crying. Then I sat in the dusk and waited to get myself put together again. The place was still and quiet, and I felt that—at last—I had made myself face facts. The fact that I'd never kindled in Stephen's eyes the light that shone in them whenever he looked at Coolie. The fact that when she went away, a part of him would go, too.

It wasn't only myself that I was crying for. I felt sorry for Stephen in a dull, impotent way. He had had to accept something, just as I had accepted something just now, and he was only just beginning to realise what that acceptance meant. I knew what he was feeling, but I didn't see what I could do for him—I'd already done all I could. I was weeping for him as well as for myself—but it didn't do either of us much good.

When I realised this, I thought about getting up and going home—but I waited a few moments longer. I didn't want to go back and face Cluny with my eyes in the state I knew they must be in.

But it would have been better to have gone. Only—once again—I had no warning of what was coming. If I'd known what was good for me, I would have got up and gone out of the room and hurried home as fast as possible. I would have been saved from a good deal...but I didn't go. I sat there— too long, for when I had finally made up my mind to go, it was too late—Stephen was coming into the yard.

Now I had good reasons for staying where I was. To go down and meet him with a face blotched and tear-stained was bad enough, but I had been sitting on a dusty box and my clothes were dirty and my hands, with tears and dust, looked as though I'd been scooping up mud. I heard his footsteps as he walked about, and guessed he was looking for me, but I kept very quiet, even when I heard his voice.

"Claire! Claire, where are you?"

"Up in the top room, crying for you." I didn't say it. I made no answer, and was relieved to hear him come into the room below, where the keys of the farmhouse were hanging, and take them off the hook. Then we both heard the sound of light, swift footsteps, and we both knew whose they were.

"Steve! Steve!"

"I'm in here, Coolie."

She came to the doorway, and there was an odd pause.

"Steve—"

"I'm just going," he said. "I'll walk up with you."

"No, Steve—don't go. I—I'm sorry about what I said up

there—about the money. I—oh Steve, darling, please listen! I love you so, Steve!"

I had got to my feet and I suppose I was on my way down, but that sentence halted me. I think Stephen must have been as paralysed as I was, because there was no sound for some minutes, and then he seemed to recover himself.

"Coolie," he said gently, "you're going home. Come on."

"In a minute. I came down…I saw you coming to the farm and I…I…" She stopped. "Where's Claire?"

"Gone. And you're going, too. Come on."

I gave a gasp of relief, but it wasn't over—and I was trapped. Not for anything in the world would I have gone down there and faced them, looking as I did. Short of walking down and describing my feelings in detail, I couldn't have told them more plainly what was the matter with me. Stephen had one woman on his hands; I was going to stay where I was. I closed my eyes and prayed—but I can't remember what I prayed for. Deafness, I suppose; I'd heard enough, and I didn't want to hear any more.

"Steve." Coolie's voice was steadier, and I knew that she was holding herself under control. "Steve, I'm sorry I said it that way. But I've got to talk to you!"

"This isn't the time or the place," said Stephen.

"I don't see you alone any more. You won't do any of the things we used to do. I never see you unless there are other people——and it never used to be that way. What's happened,

Steve?"

"Nothing's happened, Coolie. I was off the job too much. A farm doesn't run itself."

"You haven't been on the farm—you've been off by yourself. Steve—you're not happy, are you?"

He seemed to consider.

"No," he said at last. "I'm not."

"I'm not happy, either. Do you wish I'd—I'd never come here?"

"No," said Stephen. "No, I don't wish that."

"Then what's happened? When I first came, you...we liked each other. Then I loved you and you...I thought you loved me."

"Coolie, my dear, I—"

"Don't say anything for a minute, Steve, please. Just listen. You're twenty-eight, and I'm going on twenty-three. We're grown up. We know our own minds. I think that we could be happy together. I've liked you ever since the first day I saw you; now I love you. It's usual for a girl to wait to be told...but there isn't much time, and until a few days ago, I was so sure...I'm still sure. I wouldn't make that kind of mistake. A little while ago, you loved me. Since then....since then you've...you've acted kind of strange. All right; if you don't feel the same way as you did, just say so. I won't die of it; girls don't, I guess. But I've got to be *sure*—sure of just one thing. The other things won't be important, and we'll come to them later—some other time. All I want now— for the first and the last time, Steve, because I won't bother you again: Do you love me?"

Cool, clear, reasoned; more than that, burningly sincere and desperately, desperately appealing.

"Do you, Steve?"

He gave a sound somewhere between a sigh and a moan.

"God knows I do," he said quietly.

"Oh, my darling—"

"But you're wrong," he went on in a quiet, level voice. "You're wrong about the other things."

"The other things," said Coolie, "aren't important."

"The other things," said Stephen, "are much, much more important...And now I'm going to take you home..."

I found myself, a long time later, still sitting on the box with my head against the window-sill. But I wasn't crying any more.

Chapter Sixteen

I walked home in the dark, and when I got to the Vicarage, I found, to my infinite relief, that neither my uncle nor Cluny had yet returned from the Lodge. I went upstairs and undressed and turned on the bath water and lay, presently, in the warm water, letting it lap quietly round me in the still and calm of the house.

There was nobody about when I went downstairs, and the fire in the drawing-room had gone out. I relit it and then went upstairs to put on a coat, for the room was chilly. When I was on my way downstairs again, I heard the front door opening, and saw my uncle come in, followed by Cluny.

Something—I don't know what—made me pause before speaking. I think it was the expression on Cluny's face. He looked white and ill, and he was looking towards the open door of the drawing-room with an expression in which apprehension showed clearly.

"—but I'm quite sure," my uncle was saying insistently. "Indeed, Cluny, I'm sure. I saw Mr. Stephen tear it up and then give Miss Coolie the pieces and—"

"Hush, noo, hush!" said Cluny. "Give me your coat."

"But I—oh, there you are, Claire."

"What happened, Uncle?"

"It wasna anything," said Cluny. "Ye needna keep your uncle standin' in the cold hall."

"It was the cheque," said my uncle in a worried voice.

"Do you want to go upsettin' yersel', noo?" asked Cluny.

I led the way into the drawing-room, but to my surprise, Cluny followed us in and busied himself with some obviously unnecessary tasks in the room.

"What happened, Uncle?"

"It was very odd, Claire. They—"

"Now, would ye like me to get ye a drink to warm ye up?" asked Cluny with unusual solicitude.

"No, thank you," said my uncle. "I think I'll go into the study."

"That's right," said Cluny with obvious relief. "In ye go."

"What happened, Uncle?"

"It was the cheque, you see. Mr. Donner—"

"Can ye no' tell her after dinner?" asked Cluny.

"She'd like to hear it now, I think, Cluny. You see, Claire, Mr. Donner learned that Mr. Elliot was here to appeal for funds, and he very kindly wrote a—a very generous cheque. When Lady Evelyn heard about it, she, of course, insisted upon writing an equally generous one—but Mr. Elliot had gone. She wrote it, however, and gave it to Coolie and asked her to take

it with her next time she drove into Allchester, and give it to
Mr. Elliot. Then she left the Lodge, and Mr. Donner and I
went with her. But Lady Evelyn wanted to send a message to
Stephen, who had come back to the Lodge with Coolie—and
as I knew they were in the drawing-room, I said that I would
go back and tell Stephen what his grandmother wanted. I got
to the door of the drawing-room, but I...I didn't care to go in.
I heard Stephen ask Coolie to give him the cheque, and she
refused and...it's rather..."

"I'm asking ye," begged Cluny, "to—"

"What happened, Uncle?"

"She refused to give it to him, and he...he leaned over
and took it out of her hand and he...I'm afraid he tore it into
little pieces and—and then put the pieces back into her hand. I
didn't care to—to face them, and so I went away without deliv-
ering Lady Evelyn's message. It's all a misunderstanding, of
course, but I do feel that someone..." My uncle stopped, looking a little bewildered. When he said that he was going to his
study, nobody did anything to prevent him. I heard the study
door close, and then I found myself in the hall, going towards
the front door. But Cluny was there first, and he put out a hand
and caught my arm in a firm grasp.

"Let me go!" I said.

"I'll let ye go in a minute," said Cluny. "Listen to me."

"Let me pass!"

"He's gone. He followed us oot o' the Lodge, but he did-

261

na' speak to any o' us. He went in through the farm, and up to the farmhoose. The ithers didna see him, but I waited— and I watched for him, and he came oot wi' a sma' suitcase in his hand, walking as though the De'il was comin' after him. He's gone. He'll walk into Polden, an' then he'll get a taxi and it'll tak' him into Allchester, an' he'll get one of yon main-line buses, and he'll be away an' he'll no' come back until she's gone. It's the truth I'm tellin' ye."

I believed him, but I pulled my arm from his grasp and opened the front door and then found Cluny's horny hand on my arm once more.

"Let me go…How dare you!" I said between my teeth.

"Hear me first," begged Cluny. "If it was goin' to be, then it wadna hae turned oot like this. Let him go, and let her go, too. She's got money and palaces and dozens o' men she can get to dance after her. Let her go back to them, and let ye keep what's your own."

"Take your hand off me!"

"Miss Claire, I'm askin' ye…"

I tore my arm free and ran out of the house, out of the gate and into the road. I was off it again in a moment, taking the steep short cut up to the Lodge, slipping at every step, catching my coat on sharp thorns and tearing it away again. I had run up this slope a hundred times, but I had never run like this, in the dark, in the clothes and shoes that I had on now. I had to stop, every now and then, to fight for breath —but it wasn't the steepness of the slope that made me stop—it was the force with which I was having to drive myself. I came down on my knees and got up with my coat and dress caked in mud, and stumbled on, every instinct in me fighting to turn me back... or even to slow me down. Delay was sufficient. If I didn't get up to the Lodge before Stephen reached Polden, he would be gone, nobody knew where— and he would not return until Coolie was far away. If I delayed, she would go back where she belonged and leave Stephen where he belonged; the stir of her coming would die down; life would go on and he would forget her, in time. I had only to wait—and then it would be too late...And yet something stronger than myself was driving me up the slope with even greater speed than before.

I don't know why I went. I was convinced, as I ran—and I'm still certain—that if Stephen had never seen Coolie, he would have married me and found me a loving and faithful and entirely satisfactory wife. Even if he had loved her, and lost her, I think that he would, in time, have come to love me. Childhood associations, happy memories throughout the years, our long friendship and affection and comradeship—all these were strong ties between us, and they would have drawn us together. But feeling this, I still fought on up the hill, because I saw the choice that lay open to me, and knew that I had already made my decision. It had been, from the beginning, an open competition between Coolie Donner and myself, and it was going to remain an open one; there would be no handicaps.

I got to the house and saw the big green car standing outside. I went up the stairs and ran down the corridor and opened the door of Coolie's room without knocking.

She was lying face downward on the big bed, with her head resting on her arms, and she was crying. I came to a halt in the doorway and she looked up and I saw, clutched in one fist, the torn remnants of a cheque. I came into the room and shut the door behind me, and she got to her feet and faced me.

If I looked terrible—and I must have done, with my hair wild, my coat torn and my face smudged—she didn't look much better herself. Her eyes were swollen with crying, and her cheeks were white and tear-streaked.

"Why did you come?" she asked.

"To say something. And I've got to say it in a hurry."

"If it's about the cheque," said Coolie "then I won't—"

"—listen. Yes, you will," I said.

I stepped forward and took her hand and removed from it the scraps of paper.

"This was the cheque that Lady Evelyn gave you to give to Mr. Elliot, wasn't it?" I said.

A little sob came from Coolie.

"He—he tore it up," she said. "He took it out of my hand and he tore it up…"

"Why did you think he did it?" I asked.

She was silent. I suppose you can't put things like that into words; if you try to, you hear how monstrous they sound. I could understand Coolie's hesitation.

"I don't know why he did it," she said at last. "I don't know. For the first minute, I thought he...I thought he was thinking of himself. It wasn't his money; it was hers—but I thought that he was thinking that one day it would be...it would be his." Her voice rose a little. "I only thought that for a minute," she cried, "and I don't think so any more. Only—I don't understand. I don't. I don't! He could have told me, Claire, if there was a reason. He could have told me! He could have explained—"

"No, he couldn't," I said. "He would have done, if you hadn't shown him that you thought...what you did think. But with that showing in your eyes, I can see why he didn't explain."

"But he can't do that!" Coolie said fiercely. "He can't stop Lady Evelyn from spending her own money. He—"

"Lady Evelyn," I said, "can't spend her own money, because she hasn't got any money to spend."

I could see that Coolie hadn't taken it in. I gave her a little time, and then I said it again.

"Lady Evelyn," I said, "hasn't one penny of her own in the world."

"B-but" gasped Coolie, "she—"

"She gives large cheques—vast sums—in the way in which she used to give them when she had them to give. But she hasn't got any money now—do you understand? She hasn't got any money. She hasn't got a sou—a cent—a brass farthing.

She's penniless."

Coolie stared at me without speaking, and I waited for a few moments.

"All right," she said quietly at last. "Tell me."

"You would have been told before—you and your father— but it isn't the kind of thing…You see, people here have to know, but you were different. There was no need for you— for either you or your father to know, because there wasn't the smallest likelihood of her ever giving you a cheque. Why should she? And the decision to tell you, or not to tell you, was Stephen's."

"And he—"

"He refused to let me. But I think he made it too hard for you. You couldn't guess…"

"Then the cheques are—"

"They're quite worthless. But—as long as she only distributes them locally—they're also quite harmless. Everybody in Grayleigh and Polden knows this, and so when she gives them a cheque, they thank her and…leave it at that. When she wants a new cheque book, Stephen gets her one. If ever a stray cheque slips out beyond the circle of people who… understand, the Bank recognises them and does nothing. But banks can make mistakes, and so it's better not to let any cheques run the risk of being sent back to Lady Evelyn."

"You mean she—she—"

"She hasn't any idea that she isn't as rich as she was years ago. And she isn't going to know. But I came here to tell you because—because I think that somebody ought to tell you."

Coolie walked to the window and stood staring out, and I followed her and stood beside her.

"Have you heard of Lady Alison Petrie?" I asked.

"Yes. She was Lady Evelyn's sister."

"Yes. Both the sisters had a good deal of money. Mr. Petrie was a solicitor, and his firm handled all the funds. Lady Evelyn went abroad with her husband, and the interest was paid to her regularly. When Lady Alison died, Mr. Petrie went across to see Lady Evelyn—but he didn't go to break the news to her; he had other news to break. The money was gone; there hadn't been any for years, but as long as Lady Alison was alive, George Petrie had gone on paying the interest as usual to Lady Evelyn. It had crippled him—I think it crippled him mentally as well as financially—but it was the only way to avoid exposure—not for himself, but for Lady Alison."

"You mean she—"

"Lady Alison fell in love. She—"

There was no need for me to finish. I heard a gasp from Coolie.

"Jeffry Hansard!"

"Yes. Until you and your father came, Stephen didn't know who the man was. He knew most of the facts, but he was never told who...Perhaps they thought that Jeffry Hansard would turn up again one day—or that Stephen would meet him somewhere, some time. I don't know; but he was never told, and it wasn't until lately that he guessed—"

"But if Lady Evelyn knew," said Coolie. "If she was told by Mr. Petrie—"

"Two years ago, she and her husband were in a car accident abroad, and her husband, Mr. Brunswick, sent for Stephen; the doctors had told him that he would never recover, and there was something that he had to tell Stephen before he died. You see…the accident had done Lady Evelyn very little bodily harm, but it had wiped out of her memory all the facts about her sister's—about her fortune. The doctors said that if her memory didn't return naturally, it was better…safer …that it shouldn't return at all. So when his grandfather died, Stephen brought Lady Evelyn home, and from the first the cheques became a difficulty. Abroad, she'd got used to living on the interest; here at home, it seemed to her sensible to spend vast sums if they were for good causes. So she couldn't be persuaded not to write cheques. Stephen had a good job in London, but he couldn't go to work and leave her at home in the flat, because she'd made up her mind to make up to him for all the years she'd been abroad and unable to help him. She arranged little surprises—new furniture and new carpets were some of the surprises. I saw something of what was happening, but I didn't guess what it meant. Then at last Stephen had to face a choice—of staying where he was, in his job—or of leaving it to look after his grandmother. There are places, of course, where you can put old ladies whose memories aren't as good as they have been. But if you do that, they begin to wonder and then they begin to…understand. Stephen loves his grandmother, and he regards her as a sort of—of trust. So he brought her down here and rented the farm, because it was the only place he could think of where he could work at something and keep her with him. She could write cheques here; everybody understood. She could be free and happy and feel that she was doing some good in the world. She could be with Stephen; she could be in a place she remembered from her earliest days. So they came here—and I followed them and gave up my job in London. And before I did that, Stephen told me the truth. Everybody else knew that the money had gone, but only a trusted few knew how and where it went. Even Stephen didn't know the whole truth until lately."

"Claire—"

"Wait a minute. I haven't finished, and there isn't much time. I made an offer to Stephen some time ago. I told him that if he wanted to go to America and take that job your father keeps offering him, I'd stay here and keep on the farm and look after Lady Evelyn. He refused, but the offer still stands."

She stared at me, and then took an impulsive step forward.

"Claire," she said, "I—I want to tell you I went to Steve and—"

"I know," I said. "I heard you. I was trapped upstairs and I heard what you said. And I heard what he said. How— after hearing that you could let yourself believe what you did, even for a single moment, is something that I'll never understand, but if I were a man and a girl had shown me—even for a second—that she thought that about me, when she knew I loved her, then I'd do just what Stephen has done. I'd pack a bag and I'd walk into Polden and catch the first taxi that passed me, and drive to the first bus that left Allchester for foreign parts, and I'd..."

She wasn't there. She hadn't been there for some time, but I'd wound myself up and found it hard to stop, and so I went on until my breath ran out—and then I could hear the crash of the front door and the low, rushing sound of the car as it shot out of the gate. And then I turned round slowly and stared out of the window and watched the lights of the car until they went out of sight, and the road, and the countryside and my heart were all left in darkness...

Chapter Seventeen

Before me, as I write, lies a postcard depicting the main street of Prophet, Arizona. On the back of it, in Lady Evelyn's handwriting, is scrawled: *lovely to hear from you.*

She hears from me often, and the news that I don't get from her comes to me from other sources. Mr. Donner sends me frequent letters; Coolie writes long but not very detailed letters; Stephen's letters have no details at all—but it is from Verna that I get long, regular letters that tell me everything that goes on over there. Sometimes she writes and sometimes she types, but the letters arrive, without fail, every week. It was from Verna that I learned of the return to Prophet; she told me how glad she was to have Conrad back; she told me how Stephen and Coolie were looking; she described, in vivid detail, the effect that Lady Evelyn had had on the natives. She has still got the string-bag, the umbrella and the handbag; I have got the two dogs.

Stephen and Coolie are very happy. They have been married for four months, and live in a house three miles from Prophet. Stephen drives into his work in Prophet every morning in a car which looks very much like the big green one I came to know so well.

Lady Evelyn lives in a cottage—she has named it Brunswick Lodge—in the grounds of Mr. Donner's house, and is looked after by a woman who comes in every day. She is an Italian and is called Francesca—Lady Evelyn would like that.

She never signs cheques for vast sums, because she wasn't allowed to take vast sums into America. Never extravagant in her personal expenditure, she manages very well on an allowance from Stephen and the extra money she earns as a baby-sitter. I don't like to think what goes on when she baby-sits, but there haven't been any sensational reports— probably because none of the babies can talk yet.

The object of Verna's steady correspondence is less to keep me in touch with them all than to keep—as she calls it— plugging away at me to go over and join them. If her statements are to be believed, there are good farms in Arizona falling into ruin because of my refusal to go over there and work on them. There are firms in Prophet advertising desperately for English girls to work for them. There are dress shops crying out for models with the right measurements and English accents. There is even a spare bedroom in each of three houses full of people who love me.

Lorna's house, now well equipped and well furnished, is run by nuns with the help of Lay Sisters—Lorna is one. The house is now called The Resting Place, which I think sounds very depressing. In it are a number of elderly men and women of moderate means who, though in good health, are not strong enough to cater for their own needs. Lorna is trying to persuade Mr. Petrie to give up his own house and his succession of hopelessly inadequate servants, and come and be well looked after at The Resting Place—but Mr. Petrie steadfastly refuses, and, I feel, will go on refusing. If he ever managed to overcome his hatred of the house which had so close a connection with Jeffry Hansard, I think the sight of the plaque confronting him whenever he entered the front door would be sufficient to keep him away.

I didn't go back to London. I'm in Scotland, where I belong. Cluny has been up twice and will, I think, be up again soon. He says that he feels he ought to stay in Scotland; he has neglected his wife for too long. But my uncle is an insurmountable obstacle to his coming up to me—though Cluny regards it as a purely temporary one, for he feels that my uncle should retire, and where, asks Cluny, could he better retire to than yon hoose of rest where Mr. Petrie in his stubbornness refuses to go? Miss Lorna, he points out, would keep a special eye on the Reverend. He keeps his own eye resolutely turned from the three main reasons why my uncle is not likely to make application for admittance: his position as a Church of England clergyman, his indisposition to retire, and the attitude of other guests towards the unceasing playing of his gramophone records.

The farm at Grayleigh has also been taken over by the nuns, who call it the Home Farm. There is a hint in Lorna's letters that the Resting Place is proving so successful a venture that if my uncle ever showed any signs of wanting to sell the Vicarage and go back to the real Vicarage at Polden, he would find a ready market for the house.

Verna's last letter was full of her intended visit to England —and Scotland. She is coming alone, but she hints that she will not be returning alone. But I think she will.

The person I see most of, nowadays, is Geraldine. Her help, in the days that immediately followed Coolie's engagement to Stephen, is something that I can never think of without wonder. I haven't much recollection of the details, but Geraldine was always there, it seems to me, right in the middle of everything. She was—and is, whenever she comes up to see me—wonderful. She says that she would suggest my going into partnership with her, but is prevented from doing so by the conviction that I won't always be as free as I am now. She would like me to marry, and I have no objection to marrying. All I'm waiting for is the right man. He must be as tall as Stephen, and as broad; he must be as young and as strong. He must be as solid and as amusing, as patient and as moody. He must have the same cool, grey eyes, the same huge, clumsy, gentle hands…

I think I shall wait a long, long time.

THE END

The Frenchman and the Lady

by

Elizabeth Cadell

Mrs. Belchamber had managed, without much effort, to keep herself to herself all the way from Paris. By employing her usual deterrents—a gaze of piercing dislike, a twitching of the nostrils as if scenting unpleasantness and, in extreme cases—as when the stout Frenchman had attempted to enter the carriage at Perrier—drawing back her head and looking like a cobra about to strike, she had secured seclusion. And space. Her suitcases were on the rack, but her coat, her travelling rug, her books and papers were disposed upon the three vacant corner seats, while her crochet bag, her flask and her travelling handbag of expensive make, occupied the middle ones. She was very comfortable. If the French had only known how to build trains that made less noise; if the French children in the adjacent carriages were less in evidence, and if the deplorable public sanitation of the French was brought into line with English standards, she would have gone as far as to say that she was enjoying her journey.

She looked at her watch, saw that it was five o'clock, and decided to pour herself out a cup of tea at the next station, when the excessive swaying peculiar to French trains would cease and she would not be forced to waste any of the excellent tea she had made herself before leaving Switzerland. She put out a bony, be-ringed hand and took up her crochet bag, into which she had slipped some of her favourite biscuits.

The train slowed and then stopped and she lifted the *pince-nez* hung round her neck and placed them on her nose in order to read the name of the station: Les Hautiers-sur- Mouelle. Pretentious, to say the least, she reflected, for a place which was no more than a third-rate market town. It was a pity she had not been able to go by the boat train; it would have flashed by all these drab little stations and given them no more notice than they deserved.

Some tea. She hoped that the flask, which was unfortunately of Swiss make, would have kept the tea reasonably hot. Her English flask had outlasted innumerable foreign ones, but had unfortunately been broken just before she left Montreux. She was about to unscrew the top of the Swiss substitute when she paused, noting with displeasure that a large group of people had gathered at the door of the carriage with the obvious intention of entering.

This, she felt, was gross impertinence. They could see plainly, if they only looked, that she was an elderly English-woman travelling alone and just about to take her tea. To be thrust upon, to be invaded—for this had the appearance of an invasion—was intolerable. Mrs. Belchamber put the biscuits back in the crochet bag and prepared her first line of defence—

the stony stare.

This had no effect. A stout Frenchman with a red beaming face gave her a rapturous smile and threw open the door, letting in a shaft of the pleasant spring sunshine.

"*Voila!*" he exclaimed to the chattering, gesticulating companions crowding behind him. "*Mais voila!* An empty carriage with nothing but an English lady and plenty of room. But see!"

"But see!" exclaimed an excited woman, pushing him aside and giving the glaring Mrs. Belchamber a friendly bow; "—but see, here is plenty of room for everybody."

"But see!" shouted two more Frenchmen, poking their heads inside. "Here they will be comfortable."

Mrs. Belchamber understood French imperfectly; in her forty years residence on the Continent she had found that English did perfectly well; but she did not need to hear the dreadful truth; her eyes told her that some, if not all, of these entire strangers proposed to foist themselves upon her. She made a last protest by seizing the door of the carriage and banging it firmly, leaving the intruders outside, but two more stout men threw it open again and, with an excited burst of speech and charming smiles, ushered in two small boys in French sailor hats, a smaller girl in a modified version of the same headgear, three suitcases, a small tin box, a large toy boat, a cardboard box smelling of cheese and apples, several overcoats and, finally, a larger suitcase. Mrs. Belchamber's effects were treated with reverence, and the two men, who had now been joined

277

by two women, begged that she would not disturb herself. If she would but allow this to go in this place—so!—and that in that place, and the other—so!—in the other, then all would be comfortably disposed. All would arrange itself; all would march......

Mrs. Belchamber sat in her corner, her bony frame rigid and withdrawn. She saw the last piece of luggage stowed neatly, and realised that the two women, in chorus with the crowd outside, were bestowing vociferous farewells on the three children. To her bewilderment, the two stout men also appeared to be taking their departure, and a wave of horror swept over her; the three sailor hats were travelling alone.

She looked the three over; yes, they had an unmistakeable air of having travelled, a calmness and self-possession which showed them capable of undertaking journeys unaccompanied. No doubt, thought Mrs. Belchamber, shuddering, they would eat cheese and apples for the next hour, sail the toy boat up and down the corridor, shatter her peace as completely as they had shattered her privacy and be collected, at the next Hautiers-sur-Mouelle, by as noisy a band of friends and relations. They would take their possessions and go, and she would be left with the memory of the cheese and apple.

The train doors began to close, the farewells grew louder; the guard came up, and with the complete lack of attention to duty which Mrs. Belchamber had noticed in French officials, joined the party for a brief exchange of views, plans, family history and mutual compliments. Finally, he raised a small horn to his lips and seemed about to blow upon it the rude noise which served as a signal, when the group parted and a tall young man, with a brief, pleasant nod of farewell that embraced every member of the party, stepped into the train, shut the door firmly and, without incommoding Mrs. Belchamber in any way, arranged the three children at the window in the best position for making their final salutes. The trumpet blew, the train moved, the children waved and the cries of the farewell committee died away in the distance.

Mrs. Belchamber found, with deep relief, that the newcomers were silent. She had not heard one word from the children; they had smiled, their eyes had twinkled, but, beyond a murmur or two of farewell, they had said nothing. She studied the three of them as they took their seats, and decided that their mother might just as well have saved herself trouble and had one child instead of three, for—apart from their size and the fact that the girl's hair was somewhat longer than the boys'—she could not detect the smallest difference in them. There was the elder boy—he might have been ten, with a brown skin, brown hair and large brown eyes. There was the younger one; about nine, brown skin, brown hair and large brown eyes. The little girl, she thought, would be about seven; brown skin, brown hair and large brown eyes. They looked typically French, and so did those ridiculous hats, but it was pleasant—if surprising—to find that French children could behave with English calm.

Mrs. Belchamber's eyes went to the young man, and

she experienced a distinct feeling of shock. She had already gained an impression of height unusual in a Frenchman, and now she could see why; he was not a Frenchman. He was as unmistakeably English as the children were French. He had it written all over him—Mrs. Belchamber read it with pride and pleasure—all the hallmarks, all the solid, the reassuring signs. Eton and Oxford. A splendid product of a splendid race. Nobody—except, perhaps the Norwegians—would have the effrontery to claim to be able to produce a finer physical type. The first—Mrs. Belchamber bit into a biscuit and brushed away contemporary history with the crumbs—the first in the world.

She looked the young man over with unabashed scrutiny and wondered what he was doing with three French children. Tutor, probably. But they were too young—and he didn't somehow, look like a tutor, though he was obviously in charge of them. It was a piquant combination—the tall young Englishman and the three self-possessed little French children. It would be interesting to know...but of course it wouldn't do to ask. It wouldn't be the thing. It wouldn't be the thing at all.

"Friends of yours?" she enquired of the young man.

Christopher Heron paused in the act of sorting tickets and rested a pair of cool grey eyes upon the stranger. He sensed rather than saw a rich old lady—one got the impression of plain but good clothes, good luggage, general wellbeing. He mistrusted the look of her; she had a disagreeable expression and a long thin nose with a sharp point which he did not care

280

to have thrust into his affairs. He placed her as one of a type which considers its own good breeding sufficient cover for a display of bad manners.

He answered her laconically, and went back to his sorting.

"Relations," he said.

Mrs. Belchamber flushed with anger, and the three children looked at her with calm interest. She glared back at them, but her curiosity was stronger than her anger. If information was withheld in one quarter, she could get it elsewhere. She looked at the elder boy, assembled her French and addressed him.

"*Quel est—er—votre nom?*" she enquired.

He took his time in replying—it was plain, thought Mrs. Belchamber angrily, that he didn't know his own language.

The answer came, at last, in halting but correct English.

"My name is Robert," he said. He pronounced it with the English ending, and went on to introductions. He indicated first the younger boy, and then girl. "This is my brother, Paul, and this is my sister, Josette."

Mrs. Belchamber stared at him.

"You speak English very well," she informed him.

He gave her a short, un-English bow.

"Thank you," he said.

"I, too, speak English very well," said Paul.

"*Moi aussi,*" said Josette.

"That," explained Robert, "is because we are English."

281

"That is true. I am English," corroborated Paul.

"*Moi aussi,*" said Josette.

There was a pause. Three pairs of brown eyes were fixed upon Mrs. Belchamber, but she was a little bewildered by this accommodating response; information was not always so easy to extract. Out of the corner of her eye, she saw the Englishman stirring restlessly, and hastened on with her questions before he could divert the children's attention.

"Where are you going?" she enquired. "To England?"

"Yes," said Robert.

"To England," said Paul. "I have been before."

"*Moi aussi,*" said Josette.

Christopher leaned back and closed his eyes. To England. He thought with relief of the journey's end— though it was not to be quite the end. It was a pity to be taking the three of them to a London flat, especially in April, but it was all the home he had at the moment and it would have to do until he found a more suitable one. Perhaps it would have been wiser, when he heard of the fire, to have postponed coming over to fetch the three of them, but the arrangements for transferring them permanently to England had been long and elaborate, and he had felt it best to stick to the plan.

⊙≫

End of preview.

To continue reading, look for the book entitled:

"The Frenchman and the Lady" by Elizabeth Cadell.

About the Author

Elizabeth Vandyke was born in British India at the beginning of the 20th century. She married a young Scotsman and became Elizabeth Cadell, remaining in India until the illness and death of her much-loved husband found her in England, with a son and a daughter to bring up, at the beginning of World War 2. At the end of the war she published her first book, a light-hearted depiction of the family life she loved. Humour and optimism conquered sorrow and widowhood, and the many books she wrote won her a wide public, besides enabling her to educate her children (her son joined the British Navy and became an Admiral), and allowing her to travel, which she loved. Spain, France and Portugal provide a background to many of her books, although England and India were not forgotten. She finally settled in Portugal, where her married daughter still lives, and died when well into her 80s, much missed by her 7 grandchildren, who had all benefitted from her humour, wisdom and gentle teaching. British India is now only a memory, and the quiet English village life that Elizabeth Cadell wrote about has changed a great deal, but her vivid characters, their love affairs and the tears and laughter they provoke, still attract many readers, young and not-so-young, in this twenty-first century. Reprinting these books will please her fans and it is hoped will win her new ones.

Also by Elizabeth Cadell

My Dear Aunt Flora
Fishy, Said the Admiral
River Lodge
Family Gathering
Iris in Winter
Sun in the Morning
The Greenwood Shady
The Frenchman & the Lady
Men & Angels
Journey's Eve
Spring Green
The Gentlemen Go By
The Cuckoo in Spring
Money to Burn
The Lark Shall Sing
Consider The Lilies
The Blue Sky of Spring
Bridal Array
Shadow on the Water
Sugar Candy Cottage
The Green Empress
Alice Where Art Thou?
The Yellow Brick Road
Six Impossible Things
Honey For Tea
The Language of the Heart
Mixed Marriage

Letter to My Love
Death Among Friends
Be My Guest
Canary Yellow
The Fox From His Lair
The Corner Shop
The Stratton Story
The Golden Collar
The Past Tense of Love
The Friendly Air
Home for the Wedding
The Haymaker
Deck With Flowers
The Fledgling
Game in Diamonds
Parson's House
Round Dozen
Return Match
The Marrying Kind
Any Two Can Play
A Lion in the Way
Remains to be Seen
The Waiting Game
The Empty Nest
Out of the Rain
Death and Miss Dane

Afterword

Note: Elizabeth Cadell is a British author who wrote her books using the traditional British spelling. Therefore because these books are being published worldwide, the heirs have agreed to keep her books exactly as she wrote them and not change the spelling.

Printed in Great Britain
by Amazon